DEDICATION

For all their support and encouragement and for just being them, I dedicate this book to my family. Michelle, my wife, Matt & Rosie, my son and daughter-in-law and Stacy my daughter.

Also, to Lesley my sister and to Hazel, my mum.

Plague of Hypnosis

M.P. WINSON

Plague of Hypnosis

First published in 2017
M.P. Winson

ISBN 978-1548976750

Madness

Sergeant Sally Reid was a cockney girl by birth, of medium build, fit and agile for a forty-year-old woman who was content with her image in most respects, she just wasn't tall enough, she frequently told herself. She was blonde diversifying from time to time into brunette or redhead, but for now she was content with keeping to her natural. Her usual specialty within the Chillborough Police Force, was to act undercover where normal enquiries were insufficient. However, she had been disappointed more than once, having only being promoted from detective Constable to Detective Sergeant, she was still stranded in the sewerage pit of life with nowhere to go. Her recent annual appraisal was very much a crap sandwich, which only flagged up the fact that her heart wasn't in the job, that her attitude was apathetic and attendance spasmodic. In reply she criticised her seniors for not supplying the support that she required, for giving up on her largely and for side-lining her, sending her on bogus errands, investigating lost children that were in fact next door playing hide and seek, or on reports of shoppers being terrorised by war veterans dog fighting in Tesco's with their half-filled trollies. She had inherited these duties after recent failures in certain cases that were in her opinion, quite baffling. In fact, if she wanted clarification that this was the case, she had to look no further when on this summery Monday afternoon, she was called to attend the Clearwater Hospital for the mentally insane. This was based mid-way between the rural town of the same name and the Chillborough metropolis where she also had a small flat. But for why she was called there she didn't know!

She was stopped in her car at a two colour barrier, by a tubby and uniformed security officer, whose credibility was shot due to the stretched shirt he was wearing that gaped between the buttons down his front. Therefore, there was no check and the barrier was quick to open for her to drive under and park, in the very organised car park. It seemed to her from this vantage point, that 'secure hospital' was just another phrase for 'maximum security prison'. The razor wire topped fencing, spotlights and checkered barriers seemed to go on and on into the distance, never once appearing inadequate or misjudging of the capabilities of the inmates. She had encountered many a crook and had witnessed many comic book villains in many outrageous acts of criminality, but few she thought that would have ended up here.

She locked her car, having taken a file from the boot before checking in at reception and being shown beyond several iron doors, each opened with an almost medieval key, into Mr. Byford's dark wooden clad office. He was the prison warden or chief physician, she wasn't sure which, who met her with a punishing handshake. Perhaps it was the norm for staff to appear masculine and 'hard', she thought to herself, or perhaps they genuinely were toughened up by the job. Tea and one perfunctory digestive biscuit was all that she was offered before Mr. Byford's conversation turned to more serious matters. "Sergeant Reid, I thank you for being so prompt in visiting the hospital, I did explain to your Superintendent Daniels just how urgent this is." He was trying to appear calm, but he couldn't hide the fact that he was perspiring quite readily, compounded by his three-piece woollen suit and choking ribbed tie, clothes purchased by his wife from her 'Hip Husbands' magazine, delivered twice monthly.

"It's my pleasure Mr. Byford, however, as yet no one 'as

told me why I'm 'ere," Sally said letting her east end cockney accent slip like an eel from the Thames.

"The Superintendent was asked not to tell you anything until we were sure of the circumstances," he replied trying to settle himself before taking a breath. "The fact is one of our inmates is missing, which sounds straightforward you might think but believe me it's not. This inmate has only been here a week, having been arrested in France and repatriated almost immediately. The authorities there were more than keen to have no more involvement, which is why the consequences of this escape could be quite serious."

"A he or a she?"

"He. Well I say he, but he looks female from the back with his long hair, which frankly is only just longer than the beard he has at the front and what with the fact that he wears long white robes, the permission for which I might add did not come from me, well, he's a veritable hippy!" Sally recoiled at hearing this, her suspicions rising before her like some sort of late night zombie.

"And what exactly is his name?" she asked.

"Well, we don't really know as he refuses to give it, prefers to be called..."

"Teacher, 'e prefers to be called Teacher doesn't 'e, not Mr. Teacher or anythin' else, just Teacher."

"Oh, my God," said the warden, "you obviously know who we are talking about. That's presumably why the Superintendent said he would send you, being his expert."

"Expert! Not out of bloody choice," she said as the gravity of the subject matter dawned on her. "You say he is missing?"

"Well yes, or maybe no," the warden said very much in keeping with the confusion that Sally knew Teacher was capable of instilling. "Truth is we can't find him, we've turned the place upside down, had teams of security guards combing the wards, basements, outbuildings and everything. But there's no trace of him exiting the grounds, no hole in the fencing or tell-tale fabric on the razor wire, he hasn't activated any of the alarms or disturbed any of the dogs, he just seems to have disappeared into thin air!"

"Have you had any issues with him since he arrived?"

"Yes, we've found him on two occasions half way down the exit corridor, past three security doors, being accompanied by one of my orderlies who for some reason seemed to be delighted to unlock each one as they went."

"And 'ow was 'e stopped?"

"He couldn't get past the last door, controlled by an SBI," he explained.

"A security biometric identity lock?"

"Yes, more commonly known as an eye scanner."

"And what did yer orderlies say after the event?" Sally asked predicting the answer in her head.

"They couldn't remember anything, it was like a pencil rubber had been dragged across a page of drawings, leaving nothing behind," he explained.

As soon as Sally had all the facts safely recorded in her file, she thanked the warden and asked if she could examine the security facilities, especially at exits or where there were junctions with exits, whilst he continued the search from within. Her step was brisk as she left the building eager to get away from the paranoia of the warden's conversation that was still ringing in her ears. Even her eyes were trying to deceive her as she circled the massive building in a clockwise direction, suggestive of a round-the-world yacht race, with the hint of a distant sail on the horizon that may well be Teacher in his white robes. She pulled her police radio from her top pocket as soon as she was far enough away from other people so as not to panic them. "Five zero this is Five two," she said anxious to alert the station as soon as possible. "I can confirm that Clearwater 'ospital 'as lost a patient, but more importantly that 'is name is 'Teacher' of Briars Brook fame," she said eluding to the last time she was involved in an operation to catch him – but with no success.

"Roger Five two," came the anonymous reply. "Six zero is here and has heard your report, he's putting out an APB now, over."

"Roger, out," Sally said as she resumed her circuit. Finally, having covered the world over, she reached the car park and her car, electing to go for some lunch before continuing. She fumbled to get the keys from her pockets overloaded with tissue remnants and stray polo mints, with a shaking hand that proved she was either frightened at the prospect of another encounter with her nemesis, or very possibly excited by it.

Always a conscientious driver, knowing what a speeding fine could mean to her career, Sally found the short journey to the McDonalds on the edge of town more challenging on this morning than any other. She was cursing and swearing at the law-abiding drivers and sightseers as the country-side slowly evaporated and the sprawl of the urban town of Chillborough crept up on her. How she wished now she had taken one of the unmarked Subaru's that morning and had the blues and two's blaring and the exhaust growling as she would scream past all other cars and be back at the station within minutes. But things were about to get worse, the traffic was building obdurately and the traffic lights were kicking in and out like table-top footballers at a disco. This was causing the stop-start driving Sally so detested. The sleeping colleagues beneath the car were causing her to bump and bang up and down every few yards, throwing her head forward and back as the car's sump grated on the tarmac below. Then without warning, the boot lid was jolted open obscuring her rear view. She clearly hadn't closed it properly at the hospital. "Damn it!" she cursed, tempted to keep going but knowing that she couldn't if she wanted to overtake the dawdlers. So, she checked her wing mirror and sprung out of the car to slam the lid shut as quickly as she could.

It was then that she got the fright of her life as in leaning across the back corner of the car, something stopped her closing the lid, something from within the boot itself, so she rounded the rear of the car to see what this was. Suddenly, Teacher, a man that looked about sixty years of age, with flyaway hair and beard, dressed in the white robes he insisted upon wearing, jumped out on her, knocking her flat to the ground. He would have given her no more than a contemptuous glance as he believed her to be no more than a method of escape, but he suddenly stopped, staring at her intently down his long nose, until something clicked in the depths of his memory...

"PC Sally Reid!" he said with an understanding nod of his head. Then with a deliberate look in his eyes, he stepped over her, his robes whipping her about the face as he stared down into her eyes. "May the psychics of the universe come upon you with all the sharks from the oceans and snakes from the land, whether you are behind me or being stalked by the curse from my hands, whether you are under my gaze or that of your God." He paused looking to finish his curse upon her when the number seven bus behind him started parping its horn, causing him to finish quicker than he intended. "You will now be struck down to re-join the bowels of the Earth from where you came!"

After what appeared to be a blinding flash of light, Sally finally recovered her vision to find Teacher had gone. For a man of his age, he was off like a whippet at the races hurtling down the road dodging round the stationary traffic with no thought other than to get away from the bitch, who had on two previous occasions come closer to detaining him indefinitely, than anyone else. For Sally's part, she wasn't going to let this opportunity slip by; he had dented her pride, suppressed her career progression and had her on her back, figuratively speaking, many times. Her intention was therefore to spring to her feet to chase after him, but she suddenly found that she couldn't get up. She was still lying on her back finding that sitting, rolling to one side or the other, was impossible. It was almost as if she had been fixed there with an extraordinary-sized blob of super glue.

She was panicking now; Teacher was getting away and there was seemingly nothing she could do about it, until stepping down from his bus came the driver who had intended to come to the rescue and punch Teacher right on the end of his pointy nose. He was a gentleman who thought there to be no excuse for assaulting a lady and being as big as he was for someone in a sit-down job, he was used to confrontation with school-aged pranksters. He was more than ready for Teacher.

"Quick, quick 'elp me up," Sally shouted, "'e's getting away." It was the driver's intention as a knight of old, to look after her ladyship and restore her to grace before requesting that he be allowed to act as her bodyguard and chase the villain off with her handkerchief tucked under the epaulet on his shoulder. He reached down and with a grandiose sweep of his chunky arm, he offered the still struggling Sally, his hand which she took quickly, being pulled upright in one fell swoop.

"Ta for that, you're a real lifesaver," Sally said somewhat embarrassed. Then without stopping, she shot off out of the blocks on Teacher's tail, leaving the poor driver looking somewhat abandoned and confused.

"No worries love," he said, "just another day in the life of a bus driver. Just a pity that there's never a bloody copper around when you want one!" Unfortunately, his day was just about to get worse as he realised that Sally had left her car in the middle of the road blocking him in.

Now upright and making tracks, Sally could see Teacher's long white hair and trailing robes flapping around in the air behind him, flagging his position above the traffic as he ran in and out of it, swinging his hips from left to right to avoid protruding car wing mirrors. Strangely, he refrained from taking to the pavement or cutting through the park, as Sally thought he might, and remained in the road. She at least jumped out of the gutter onto the pavement and whilst shouting a warning to the shoppers and sightseers, sprinted past the window dressings and 'For Sale' signs, until she began to make ground on him. It was only then that she realised what he was on with, as he caught up with the earlier bus further down the road and threw himself onto the open-door platform at its rear as it started to move off. He then stood leaning out of the door-way with one leg wrapped around the chromium hand rail, laughing incessantly at Sally whose step, in seeing this, had slowed to a shuffle. "Always the defeated, PC Reid," he shouted over the accelerating engine and honking of car horns, which had her feeling so deflated that her concentration had all but ebbed away. As the crowds increased and her focus was lost, it became impossible to avoid crashing into people whilst also jumping up every few seconds, craning her neck, to keep an eye on the target. She could have been forgiven had she given up at this point but then, as she wiped the perspiration from her face, she suddenly noticed the bus indicating to pull into its next stop.

"Oh ho, you never thought of that, did ya," Sally cheered as she re-applied the gas.

"By the laws of everything sacred," Teacher shouted as he realised that the bus was taking longer to pass the shops and stores as it was turning into a lay by, "if this were a sacred Friday I would no doubt, have bones in my fish," he cursed. Looking across the sea of traffic with a hand over his eyes, he was hoping that Sally had given up, but his turn of bad luck was escalating as he spotted her leaping over some pavement railings like a practiced hurdler, with eyes focused on the finish line. Responding without thinking clearly, he ran the length of the bus from the door at its rear to the cab at the front. "Get going, get going," he demanded of the driver who was sat with his iPad, like the computer nerd that he really was. Realising his escape plan was now flawed, Teacher scrabbled around the catalogue of excuses he had in his head and added, "my intended is waiting at the church and I'm going to be late for the service."

"Late?" said the opinionated driver. "Listen here mate, before you marry a person, you should do your homework. Make 'em use a computer with a slow Internet service to find out who they really are, if they have any patience and therefore, if they'll wait for you in times of trouble. Seems to me you haven't worked this one out yet, so I suggest you get a taxi!"

Sally was closing fast now as Teacher was running around in a panic, from one end of the bus to the other and back again, like a schoolboy needing a pee. He knew now that he had used up his advantage and could wait no longer. So, in a decisive moment he threw himself out of the rear door just as Sally came within fingertips of him, crashing into the back of the bus with a clatter from the telescopic metal baton she had in her hand. As he escaped, he seemed at first to be taking a totally random direction, first into the traffic, onto the central reservation and then back again, running along the curb stones with all the skill of an urban free-running-athlete. This only proved to him that he needed to get away from the road, perhaps under the cover of the shoppers as they browsed their way through store after store. Then suddenly, as he reached the pavement, a new plan came to him and he swung about crashing through the double doors of the town's indoor market, pulling over a metal mesh litter bin as he did so, which spewed Coca Cola and beer tins behind him like hand grenades. Sally took this change of plan more as an opportunity than a problem and got on her radio again calling breathlessly for backup as she resumed the chase.

The entire layout of stalls in the indoor market was a permanent one, each of them being octagonal in shape and fitted alongside the next. This resulted as the planners had hoped, in a maze of retailing that a shopper could and frequently did, get lost in. Being out of the country for so long and not being a local himself, Teacher hadn't realised this and soon found himself within the maze not knowing how to get out again. Sally however, was used to shopping there, not that she didn't find it infuriating, but she did know how to find 'Elvis's un-used wardrobe', an innovative clothes stall and 'Dot's Hot Hardware' (for the meaner cleaner). She was also aware of the fact that there were only two ways in and out. So, assuming that Teacher wouldn't leave by the same door he entered, she charged around the outside of the stalls, past the coffee shops and cafés that hugged the outer walls, bumping into people and upsetting the white plastic chairs and tables, until she could see the southern exit. It was now that the mental pressure intensified as the fast-paced chase switched to one of stealth and ambush, for which extra help would be imperative and so she called again on her radio. "Five zero,

Five two, where's my bleedin' support?"

"On its way Five two, you are priority," was the reply.

"Roger Five zero, location now Chillborough market, over."

"Roger Five zero," came the calm acknowledgement, the desk staff having heard it all before.

"What's up, chuck?" said the fishmonger from his fascinating stall, decorated with a huge fisherman's net containing plastic prawns and crabs, suspended above slabs of haddock, cod and coli, all set out upon the corner just before the exit.

"Hiya Freddy," Sally said still breathing like a coal miner. "I'm chasing someone who has taken to hiding in the middle of the market; he's wearing white robes and sandals, if he's still here, that is."

"White robes and sandals?" Freddy was aghast. "Oh, he's still here," he said as there was a frenzied clatter from somewhere in the middle of the stalls and some rounded fruit cannoned out from one of the aisles. It was Sally's turn now to run up, down and back again whilst trying to cover the exit, which single-handed was proving near on impossible. Finally, as she was just beginning to lose the will to live, two beat coppers arrived, responding to her calling, helmets in hand. "He's somewhere in the middle, white hair and white robes," Sally said, relieved to see them both.

"White robes?" one of them asked, unbelieving.

"Yes, yes, be quick," she said directing them with hand signals to go around to the entrance and comb their way through to the exit where she would be waiting. So, without delay they nodded and set out with batons drawn.

Of the three aisles that emerged at the exit, one was directly opposite and the other two at a dogleg. It was important, Sally thought, that Teacher could see a way out which would prevent him from turning on himself and disappearing back into the maze of stalls. Therefore, she positioned herself with her back to the third aisle facing the one directly opposite the exit, just as a further commotion erupted from the middle of the market.

The backup officers were now working their way towards her aided by helpful shouts from the community of stall holders, who had realised what was happening. Teacher was now zig-zagging around the stalls changing direction in a snap, which in fact only helped the two officers as the rubber from his sandals squeaked on the red composite floor. He was also carrying out some spoiling tactics as he demolished stands and displays, leaving the debris across the aisles as did Rommel on the beaches of Dunkirk. Row by row now, the officers advanced as the squeaking Teacher sprinted from pillar to post looking for the way out. He hadn't realised that Sally was in fact in front of him until he caught sight of her at the end of the hall, so he zig-zagged at a right angle to obscure his approach to the exit.

She was ready for him now, doing her best to bring on the two officers by shouting over the noise of the market. "Good stuff, keep coming, keep coming, we've got him now." Almost in confirmation, from out of the third aisle there came another wave of rolling fruit displaced from the greengrocer's stall. Sally turned and braced herself to tackle Teacher whom she expected to follow on behind. She could only imagine that he would be travelling at considerable speed, especially if he had been panicked and was making an all-or-nothing bid for freedom. Yet another wave of rolling fruit now shot out of the far aisle, so Sally, reacting quickly, jumped into the space beyond to intercept him. This was fatal as she then slipped on the opened skin of a stray banana and swivelled on the spot, losing her balance, unusual for her especially twice in a day. She then found herself on her back once again. She made a move to stand and chase with a grit that she called on in such circumstances, but couldn't as the super glue that had her pinned to the road earlier, now grabbed her again. She could hear Teacher approaching, cursing and swearing whilst his sandals were still squeaking and the two officers raced up behind him. But she could do nothing about it as in a flash of white, having tricked Sally with what was a fruity diversion, he ran out of the middle aisle directly opposite the exit. She was done, caught on her back with no impetus to restart the chase.

How many times, Sally asked herself, had Teacher escaped her by a whisker of his long white beard? How many times had he been banged to rights only to disappear in front of her; how many times had she had the opportunity to get him off the streets and flunked it? But she hadn't counted on the community spirit that the indoor market was renowned for; they were a team, a part of the greater good and they had the bit between their teeth. As Teacher bolted for the doors, whilst the two chasing officers now struggled to find their own way out of the maze, Dot from the hardware stall was chasing after him with an angry sweeping brush and the man from the grocery stall was throwing his displaced stock after the two of them. Then as quick as flying fish, Freddy the fishmonger and his slight apprentice appeared like jacks from a box and pulled their plastic fishing net, prawns and all, down over Teacher's head. He was then landed as one would a game fish in high seas, left flapping and gasping for air, squirming about on the market floor.

"Got ya," Sally yelled in triumph.

NO HOLDS' BARRED

Sally had worked tirelessly as a police officer in Chillborough and been attached to Madely Common and Briars Brook authorities in an undercover capacity, on cases involving Teacher. However, she never envisaged that she would see him again, let alone arrest him or have the opportunity to see him convicted. And so, by this following bright Tuesday morning, Teacher had been processed at the Chillborough Police station and imprisoned in one of the cold and bare cells.

Superintendent Daniels sat pompously at his desk with Sally in his office. "Right then," he said as he gave a brief cough. "We will be charging Mr. Teacher with offenses contained within the Fraud Act 2006." He coughed again to disguise the irritating nasal drip that he had come to live with since contracting pneumonia one ruined Christmas.

"Paddy Mut is 'is real name," Sally said.

"How do you know that?"

"The Sergeant from Briars Brook did a check on him."

"Really? Make sure then that he's been finger-printed as a part of his booking in."

"Well there we are then, that's why you have been entitled my expert. Seems to me this kind of thing is best left to the women so us men can focus on the real crime," he said brushing back the two grey tram lines of hair left on either side of his bald head.

"Expert, so I 'eard," she said remembering what the hospital warden had said.

Daniels gave another cough as he was about to go on, when his office door opened more or less in sync with the required 'knock knock'.

"Guid mornin. Och sorry, sir, a dina realise ye 'ad Sally in wi' ye," said Jock McCall, the busy desk sergeant with a pile of mail under his arm.

"Well, you do now," said Daniels, "so clear off until we're done, and get me a coffee."

"Aye sir, sorry sir," he said giving Sally a mischievous wink as he disappeared back through the door.

"Where were we, young lady?"

"Fraud 2006," she replied.

"Oh yes," he said poised to continue as Jock opened the door again.

"Dous Sally want a wee coffee too?"

"What, couldn't you have asked last time you barged in?"

"Yes, please," Sally replied, as Jock disappeared again.

"For God's sake. Can we get on my love, please."

"Wait a minute, 'young lady' I can cope with, but I'm not your 'love'," Sally said finally.

"Yes yes, that's fine, my dear. Now then, the Fraud Act 2006 – parts six and seven."

"Dou ye want sugar and milk wi' yer coffee?" Jock asked as he popped open the door once again, this time without knocking at all.

"Get out! You Scottish pillock... get out!" Daniels yelled as he threw his computer mouse at the closing door, which merely travelled the length of its cable then jerked to a stop before it fell to the floor. "I'm losing the will to live this morning!" he said, coughing again as he turned back to Sally with a contempt he seemed to show to all the female PCs, which had the blood boiling down her spine.

"The Fraud Act 2006, part six states that a person is guilty of an offence if he has in his possession any article for use during any fraudulent act. On conviction, we can get him sent to prison for five years. However, if we can get him on part seven where a person is guilty of an offence if he makes, adapts, supplies or offers to supply any article during or in connection with fraud, then we can do him for ten years and probably fine him for the money he buggered off with in the first place!"

Sally knew all she needed to know, as it was the charge that the Briars Brook Police had intended to use during her involvement with the 'My Mind' case. Talking of which, she pulled a file out from her oversized leather bag and laid it on the desk filching through the pages until she came to a list of witnesses.

"You asked me for these in connection wi' the 'My Mind' case in Briars Brook," she said. "There were six people involved in Teacher's cognitive therapy course in 'is shop called 'My Mind', if you include me."

"No, for reasons of entrapment I can't, so we will be relying on the other five."

"Ok. That leaves Mrs. Brenda Scope, young Billy Doncaster, Mr. and Mrs. Abrah and Arisha Kundi and finally Mr. Simon Jenson," Sally replied seemingly upset at that point as she shed a small tear.

"What's the matter?" Daniels questioned, his throat grumbling.

"Oh nothing, trying times that's all."

"Ok then, get them checked out and then get them here to give a statement to verify any they might have given before. Then do an ID parade with each of them to identify Teacher."

"All of them?"

"Yes."

"Wha' if Brenda and Billy come up trumps, then we wun't need the others, would we?"

"I want statements from all of them," the Super said adamantly, punctuating his speech with a quick sniffle.

Teacher had been sat in his cell in nothing but a pair of grey underpants and his long white beard covering his modesty, whilst his robes were being searched and washed as a courtesy. He had been sat in the lotus position since the previous evening, meditating, which occasionally would result in him dropping off to sleep with loud snoring, until he finally toppled forward smacking his Pinocchio nose on the cell floor. By the afternoon, there were notices and signs fixed on the prison door and in the corridor outside, warning everyone to avoid looking into Teacher's eyes, given the accusations and records of his ability to hypnotise people. The only conversation he had had was complaining about the handcuffs he was wearing, which he said were too tight, but Jock had insisted they would give and slacken off once they had been worn in. This must have been the inescapable truth as they were now sat in front of Teacher, one side stacked neatly upon the other, despite everyone's insistence that they had not unlocked them or taken them off.

Sally had spent a nice evening the night before at her flat, on her own with nothing but a bottle of wine and the past weeks' recordings of Coronation Street. Unfortunately, after relaxing in a nice warm bath before bed, she found that she still couldn't sit up once she had laid down horizontally. Fortunately, Teacher's curse hadn't prevented her from rolling onto all fours and climbing up the shower hose before she contracted hypothermia and drown. And so, with a purpose, she had arrived to work dressed neat and tidy and yet powerfully, in a blue office suit. After speaking with the Super, she went to see Teacher, just in case the whole thing the day before had been a dream or an illusion concocted by him.

"Is there anything you want?" Sally asked through the letterbox opening within Teacher's cell door.

"Apart from the obvious, Sally?" Teacher said calmly without opening his meditating eyes.

"Well, obviously!" she replied contemptuously.

"I think the Psychics of the Universe can best represent me now," he said as Sally shivered remembering his words as he stood over her at the roadside the day previous.

"You best prepare them then, as you will be interviewed

today as soon as the victims of your escapade at Briars Brook arrive."

"Oh, Arisha and Abrar, Billy and Brenda, it will be nice to see them again. And of course, your darling Simon, we can't forget him, can we."

* * *

Jose Doncaster was at home that morning and heard the phone ringing in the hall, at an hour where she would normally ignore it. But for some reason, on this occasion she answered.

"3674, Jose speaking," she said in a practiced manner.

"Jose, it's Sally Reid 'ere, from the Chillborough Police, you might remember a couple of boozey nights we had together a couple o' years ago, when I was investigating Teacher and his cronies from the 'My Mind' shop?"

"Oh Sally," she sounded pleased at first to hear from an old friend but then changed her tone as she said, "that's right, turned out you were a copper, creeping around behind everyone's back, pretending to be everyone's friend. My Billy trusted you, he was never the same again after that night when you attempted to arrest Teacher."

"He would have killed everyone had I not broken the electrical circuit 'e 'ad us all wired to."

"Everyone was ok until you did," she said, "besides, you still didn't catch him then did you?"

"No I didn't, but I do 'ave 'im now, in custody, 'ere at Chillborough nick. So, it's your Billy that I need to speak to Jose, as 'e was a part of the therapy course and witnessed everything." Sally spoke quickly to finish what she was saying before being cut up again by Jose's barbed rantings.

"Well, you can't," she said, furious at being asked. "That night damaged him, even more than the depression and suicide attempts that he was attending the therapy course for in the first place. He left almost immediately afterwards and I haven't seen him since!"

"What, where did 'e go?"

"Half way around the world, to take part in the Festival of Telepathy, for Christ's sake."

"Yes, but where, we need to speak to 'im."

"Well, how the bloody hell would I know, they don't send written invitations or emails, these telepathics just perceive these things; it's not called the Facebook Festival or the Twitter Games you know."

"Well 'ow can I find out?" Sally asked pathetically.

"Try the lotus position and singing Teacher's Mantra, or better still ask him!" she said as she slammed the phone down hard, giving Sally every reason to be sure that Billy wouldn't be a part of the prosecution and that she would have to do without him.

After taking near on an hour to recompose herself after being verbally battered by someone Sally thought to be a friend, she lifted the receiver again and dialled Brenda Scope, another participant and possible victim of Teacher's therapy course.

"Hello, is that Brenda, Brenda Scope?" she said as the call was answered.

"That's right my love, and what can I do for you?"

"This is the Police Mrs. Scope. We're calling you today as we 'ave a Mr. Mut at the police station today, alias 'Teacher'. He 'ad a shop on the Briars Brook 'igh street a couple of years back, where you attended his cognitive therapy course."

"Ooh yes, that's right, my love. Run by Mr. Teacher. A lovely man, a bit hairy but with a heart of gold. Very clever, told us all about hypnotism, not that I needed his help with that as I am already very good at it. I had Mr. Griffiths here only yesterday for an afternoon of hypnotics, sherry and tiffin, if you know what I mean. I do hope Mr. Teacher is all right; I wouldn't want anything to happen to him, such a caring man, just a shame he had to leave when he..."

Sally cut her off mid-sentence. "Thank you, yes, thank you Mrs. Scope," she said trying to get a word in edge-ways.

"Ooh that's all right my dear, it's a lonely life as an old-age pensioner, I was saying this to Betty at Bingo last night, just how difficult..."

"Yes, thank you, Brenda, I understand, 'e's fine, there's nothing for you to worry about. Yes, yes."

"I don't do the hypnotism thing anymore my dear. Taken up singing in the rock choir! I didn't realise just how good some of them old songs are, didn't pay much attention to all the oilers in my day!"

"Greasers," Sally said correcting her.

"Paranoid, Smoke on the Water and what about God Save the Queen, the fascist regime. Ooh they don't make 'em like that anymore!"

"No, they don't Mrs. Scope."

"You don't know my love, you'll never understand until you're my age! The only thing that's good about it is that there's no bloody peer pressure," she said breaking out in a cackle characterised by the Witches of Eastwick.

"Thank you Brenda, yes thank you, goodbye, goodbye," Sally said as she finally managed to put the phone down. "Don't think I'll bother with her either, I'd never have enough paper to record her statement."

Shortly after, a sniffling Superintendent Daniels peeked around the door to the operations room, wiping his nose across the back of his hand. "How are you getting on?"

"Not brilliantly," Sally replied, a bit fed up.

"I see," he said looking over her shoulder at the shrinking list. "Still got three more to go at?"

"Yes, I'll try Arisha and Abrah Kundi next."

"What about this Simon Jenson fellow?"

"I'm leaving 'im till last," she replied as another misbehaving tear welled up in the corner of her eye, this time noted by the Superintendent.

In the meantime, despite his meditative exploits, Teacher was becoming bored and was looking for a way out of the situation he now found himself in. As his lunch arrived neatly contained within several cellophane packages on a plastic tray, he assessed the susceptibility of poor Sergeant McCall who had been tasked to deliver it. Despite the warnings plastered all over the walls, the Sergeant came a little too close and in mid conversation he found himself looking into a pair of faraway eyes. Like a barn owl, Teacher's hypnotic gaze grabbed Jock's attention and held it tightly whilst he talked slowly and calmly to him, causing him to nod his head in compliance at relevant key points. In silence, Jock then scrabbled together the uneaten lunch putting it back on the tray and disappeared, returning directly with Teacher's newly washed and ironed robes and his Jesus sandals. As the prisoner continued to talk to him, Jock then took a large circular key ring from his belt and opened the cell door. He stood then reverently to one side as Teacher, now dressed, glided across the floor and into the corridor outside.

Within the corridor there was a plethora of cameras hugging the ceiling, all pointing in different directions, but clearly no one was monitoring them as Teacher and Jock locked the cell door behind them and boldly made their way towards the exit. Through intermediate corridor door number one they passed, whilst Teacher waited patiently like a guide dog for the blind, until Jock closed and locked the door behind them placing the key ring back on his utility belt. There were only two more doors now, intermediate corridor door number two and the last large windowed, red door which gave access to the rest of the station. Again, with a few directions all given quietly so not to allow anyone to ask who it was that Jock might be talking to, they approached the second intermediate door.

"Hey!" said a man peering through the letterbox opening in his cell door. "What you doing, where you going, whose he?"

"I am being released, my friend," Teacher said matter-of-factly.

"No, you're not! The rules is that you afto 'ave two officers to escort you," the frequently arrested man insisted as Teacher stooped to make eye contact with him, his eyes flaring as he did so.

"You're not really interested in where I am being taken," he said.

"I'm not really interested in where you're going," the man replied.

"You don't want to come along and would rather stay here."

"Besides which, I would rather stay here," the man said with his eyes still locked into Teacher's.

"You're going to say goodbye now."

"I'm going to say goodbye now."

"Well?"

"Goodbye," the man said, closing the letterbox quietly behind him.

Sally was on the phone again with her feet on the desk and coffee in hand. She had to find someone from the Briars Brook escapade to testify against Teacher, or they may very well be left high and dry, having to justify the reasons for his arrest and probably his very dubious imprisonment at the mental hospital.

"'ello, is that Mr. Kundi?" she asked as the phone was answered.

"Yes, for vat can I do for you?" said an Indian man in reply.

"Ah, that must be Abrah, it's Sally Reid here, from Briars Brook."

"Oh, the lady from the polus?" he said remembering.

"That's right Abrah, 'ow nice to talk with you, how is Arisha?"

"She is velly well, no thanks to Teacher, but I had to take her to the hasptaal you know after the business with the electricity on the last night of the therapy course."

"Oh dear, is she all right now?"

"The daaktar said it greatly upset her and for a little while she had a worsening of her bally epilepsy, the velly damn thing we went to Teacher with in the first place!"

"Well, some good news for you then. He is 'ere, Teacher is 'ere, in custody. We just need you and your wife to come to the station, complete a statement o' witness and take part in an ID parade. You may even get back some of the money you lost to 'im."

"Oh well then, that is velly good news afsar, we will come down directly."

Teacher and Jock were now at intermediate door number

two. Neither of them seemed phased or in any kind of panic, maintaining a charade equivalent to a normal collection of prisoner for release, apart from there only being one officer. Once again, standing patiently, Teacher had Jock un-hook his jangling bunch of keys from his belt, identify the correct one and unlock the door. They went through and closed it with a clang as the iron bars reverberated against the frame. Jock then locked it as Teacher focused himself on the red solid windowed door, that sat between prison and freedom.

Striding forward sensing his imminent release, Teacher was slightly confused as Jock merely approached the window and stood quietly, leaving the keys still sat upon his utility belt. So, he lifted them, handing them to Jock whilst lifting his eyebrows as a prompt, but he still stood as if all the power from his robotic batteries had drained away.

"Open the door," Teacher said maintaining as much of the quiet approach as he could. But still Jock stood motionless.

"Open the door," Teacher hissed through clenched teeth, very nearly succumbing to an increase in temper. Suddenly a face appeared at the door's window, waving a second bunch of keys.

"Nice try Teacher, but this door must be opened from out here," said the Superintendent who had been watching on the internal close circuit television after realising how long it was taking for lunch to be delivered.

Sally had intended to leave the next phone call till last. Simon was, as far as she was concerned, a witness to a crime first and a friend second. She had maintained her professional integrity with him throughout her involvement in the 'My Mind' case and had been sure to keep her distance, always with one mind on what would happen if he was called to give evidence. But of course, Teacher had evaded arrest and gotten away and since she had sworn never to have anything to do with any future case relating to him, she thought there to be no reason to remain distant to the clear advances Simon had been making. As she relaxed her aching defences, they met every night as their romance blossomed and they got closer and closer, until finally on one lustful night, they went to bed together. It was passionate and everything that Sally wanted of a relationship, becoming a regular thing to go to bed in the afternoon and sleep over until the following morning. But this was where Simon's nocturnal epilepsy raised its ugly head after Teacher had failed in his promise to cure it cognitively. Sally found she couldn't cope with the violence in the night and the mood swings during the day, not to mention his incessant preoccupation with his condition. So, without facing up to telling him, she left the relationship one afternoon with no more than a suitcase and a tear in her eye.

Back in the operations room, Sally was once again on the phone. "Is that Simon Jenson?" she asked as someone answered.

"Hello you," Simon acknowledged without any more explanation, which didn't help as she couldn't determine his mood, this being the first time they had spoken since separating. "Have you decided to come back to Briars Brook?"

"No," she said still trying to be civil.

"So you're not coming back to me?"

"No, but that's not your fault," she said.

"No, that's more Teacher's fault than anyone, but it's still partly down to you!" he said.

"Please don't, I'm calling on business, not socially." Sally drew the box of tissues on her desk closer to her.

"Do you know how difficult it is to go to bed at night, go to the bed that you shared with me? Do you know how I have to face up to the auras every night, the electrical disturbances and the fear?"

"I think I do."

"No, you don't, or you wouldn't have left me."

"I had no choice. I need a partner who is a true partner, someone who puts me before his illness, who accepts my help. I didn't know from one day to the next whether you were going to love me, or bite my head off."

"But the mood swings were always a part of it and still are to this day."

"Then I sing the praises of those that accept that and stay with their partner…they are special, special, people." She caught another tear, but knew underneath that she wasn't one of those people. "My call is more to do with the first person you mentioned."

"Teacher?"

"Yes, believe it or not, he's here in custody, but we need the evidence now to put him away."

"My evidence?"

"Yes, we'll need a statement and you might be required to attend an identity parade." She could feel the tone of the conversation easing and moving on now, at least.

"If there's anything I can do for you, just ask," he said as his lighter mood flattered her, "Besides, I'd love to come face to face with that bastard once again." he said, his mood predictably slipping without warning, proving her point.

"You don't have to flatten him!"

"Would I?" he said obliquely.

"Yes, you bloody well would," she snapped back which did at least have them tittering slightly.

"What time?" he asked.

"If I said three, would you make it for half past?" He laughed again lightening things a little more for Sally, hopefully making it a little easier to face him when he arrived.

"Fine, I look forward to seeing you then," he sighed, knowing that any chance of a reconciliation would be difficult at least.

As Teacher was reinstated in his cell, he was no longer controlled, calm and calculating, he had even kicked a PC's backside as he went in ahead of him as the replacement jailor, to do a cursory search. "It won't be long Mr. Teacher, before you are back in the mental hospital if you carry on behaving like this."

"You think so?" Teacher asked, trying to antagonize him and re-position himself to make eye-to-eye contact.

"Think so, I know so," the PC exclaimed as he turned the key in the cell door without looking back, and repositioned, more prominently, the sign warning people not to look into Teacher's eyes. "And as for you…" he said to the highly-embarrassed Jock, watching from a safe distance.

Sally's desk-com reverberated. "There's a Mr. and Mrs. Kundi at the front desk," came a call, to which she responded immediately, by skipping into the reception area.

"Oh, am I glad to see you," Sally said throwing her arms around the couple which was greatly reciprocated by both, as if sharing a challenge in the face of adversity.

"We are so much pleased to see you too Ofsaar Sally," said Arisha with a smile from one side of her nodding head to the other.

"Especially if the polus can get back some of my money, if you please," said her husband.

"Oh Abrah! Money isn't bally everything you know!" Arisha was keen to point out, although truthfully her husband hadn't told her exactly how much they were talking about.

"Come through," Sally said guiding them into one of the vacant interview rooms, "Drink: coffee, tea?"

"Just water please," said Abrah on behalf of his wife.

"Milk, I'll have the milk!" she corrected him. One thing that Teacher did do cognitively was to give Abrah's wife the ability to talk for herself.

"Ve just want this bally madman sent back to vere he came from!" he concluded in frustration.

After nearly an hour, Abrah had completed a statement of witness, recording the many times when Teacher had convinced him of the value and need for the vast array of 'old ancient artefacts' that he had purchased at ridiculous prices, from the 'My Mind' shop. It further covered the final night of the cognitive therapy course where Teacher had coupled Abrah and Arisha, to a van de Graf generator and threatened to electrocute them unless they gifted their entire estate and all worldly possessions to 'his cause'.

Sally came finally to the last obligatory statement. "Let me read this for you Abrah, before you sign it, 'This statement consisting of three pages, each to be signed by you, will be true to the best of your knowledge and belief?..."

"Of course," said Abrah, interrupting Sally before she had finished.

"And that you make it knowing that if it is tendered in evidence..."

"And so it bally well should," came the interruption once more.

"Tendered in evidence, you will be liable to prosecution if you have wilfully stated in it anything..."

"Quite right!"

"Anything which you know to be false or..."

"I do not tell the lies," said an insistent Abrah.

"Husband!! Will you bally well shut up, Sally is trying to finish your statement, sorry Sally," said a very assertive Arisha which totally surprised everyone, given her usual timid, mouse-like appearance and squeaky voice.

"False or not to be true," Sally finally said, being as irritated as a twitching eye, straightening the crumpled edges of the paper statement, where she had gripped it so tightly in frustration.

Very soon it was Arisha's turn. The lady with a partial mental problem that had her losing consciousness momentarily, almost like a daydream. She had been the reason Abrah had signed up for Teacher's therapy course, but it actually inflamed her problem despite, to be fair, the breaking of her timid-ness. However, this latter development had not contributed to the acceptable domination of a Muslim wife, or justified the monetary cost that Abrah had incurred.

"Is that all Sally?" Arisha said as she too completed the final statement and signed the foot of the page, as her jittery hand returned to plague her.

"Are you all right?" Sally asked seeing this.

"Just nervous," she said, but Sally suspected something more.

"Well, we still have the ID parade to do yet, will you be ok with that?"

"Bring it on Ofsar Sally, let my wife have sight of the bally man; he deserves to be incarcerated for a velly long time," Abrah said vehemently. Sally looked to Arisha, who now was seemingly regressing back into her world of timidity.

"I am ready husband, I am ready Sally," she said, apparently confident, but a little more quietly than before.

After every white-haired man with a beard or not had been rounded up sheep-like from across Chillborough and every white sheet or fleck of white material had been cobbled together, six very similarly robed men were paid thirty pounds each, to stand for less than two minutes in the identity parade. The validity of the statements of witness could only be verified should Abrah and Arisha correctly pick Teacher out from the ID parade. But for many other reasons, it wasn't going to be easy for them to face him again. And so, after a short wait as he was escorted from his cell by two officers both in mirrored sunglasses, he was brought to the ID corridor. Superintendent Daniels and Jock had arrived to monitor proceedings and ensure that everything was carried out to the letter. This was a big moment for Sally too, who stood like a town centre statue, trying to appear unmoved and merely going through the motions. Underneath her tough exterior she was just waiting to punch the air, just as soon the job was done and yell at the Superintendent, 'I told you so'! She wanted to prove a point, to justify herself to the powers that be and ironically, to herself as well.

As Teacher arrived, he was invited to take his part in the line-up, wherever he wished, and so, cleverly he thought, he went right to the end, whereupon he had a giant number seven fixed to his chest with a couple of bright safety pins. As Arisha entered the corridor, those in the line-up were told to maintain their silence and look straight ahead, whereupon she began walking down its length with an officer on her arm, examining each subject in turn. The first two were not tall enough, she could easily visualise the level at which Teacher appeared to her before now, the third was too dark and the fourth too old and wrinkled. The fifth had no beard where all the others had, but she paused as she got to number six, as she thought there to be something familiar about this man. After two minutes of looking him up and down, the officer on her arm whispered in her ear and advised her to look at all seven before making a choice, so she moved to the subject at the end of the row. It was when she got here that the atmosphere in the room seemed to change, like a dark cloud had just scudded across the sun, causing her to shiver. This man she knew. He continued to look straight ahead at this point as instructed whilst she looked him over from head to toe and back again, when she then stepped forward and placed her right hand on his left shoulder. Suddenly, he looked down along the bridge of his long nose through his white fringe and locked his eyes with hers. She shook momentarily, remembering the last time this happened, when electricity was coursing through her veins and she couldn't release the hands of the others in the circle about her, including her husband, all of them being under Teacher's control. She let go of his shoulder and stood shell-shocked as Teacher looked calmly ahead once again. But the damage was done. "No," she cried. "No!"

Abrah had been waiting in another room whilst his wife had faced up to the identity parade, so that he could not be accused of compromising the process. However, it was to here that Arisha was brought before he would take his turn, whereupon as soon as she saw him she burst into fits of tears and threw herself into the security of his arms. "What is this my wife, why are you so upset, did you see Teacher, did the bally man touch you?" he asked, his face now being pale and devoid of the energy he had when he arrived.

"Yes, but looked at me he did, in the way he did before. He is going to kill me, my husband, kill me!" She burst into tears once more as Sally temporarily suspended the ID parade.

"You said, 'No' when you were in the ID parade, what did you mean…that he wasn't there?" the Superintendent asked.

"Yes," she whimpered, "but he is there, he is there."

"You need to say which one my dear, which number of the seven?"

"No! I cannot. I will not and I withdraw my statement, Mr

Daniels." Arisha cried again as the Super put his beaten head in his hands and blew his nose on an oversized handkerchief.

"Abrah still has to complete his parade Sir," Sally said offering a lifeline.

"Of course," the Super said prompting his response.

"Oh, but vait, I am velly sorry Supreetendant, but you cannot ask me to go against my wife's vishes. It would not be proper, not be the Muslim thing to do."

"But we are getting desperate here, Abrah," the Super said.

"I am velly sorry Sir, sorry Sally, Arisha is more important than him, more import'ent than the money and more import'ent than your proseecution!"

"But what about all the people 'e may go on to extort an' 'urt?" Sally asked despairingly.

"I am velly sorry," said an embarrassed Abrah, "but the way that I see this Sally, is that this is your problem, not ours."

Teacher was very well aware now that he had been in custody without charge for nearly twenty-two hours and that should the police not progress the case within the statutory twenty-four hours, they would be obliged to release him. This was being reflected within the urgent meeting in the Superintendent's office.

"Well, it seems to me that we underestimated Mr. Teacher. He's either very clever or very stupid, knowing that we are becoming more and more desperate to see him locked up," said the Super.

"Och, never have we had such a bri brain, in custody," said Jock.

"The question is, what are we going to do about it?" The Super looked directly at Sally.

"Well, I was 'oping it wouldn't come to this, but there is still Simon, Simon Jenson I mean. He took a big part in the operation at Briars Brook and is just as determined as we to see Teacher behind bars, permanently."

"Aye, still hope there, then," Jock said nodding his head. But the Super was not so pragmatic; he had a different agenda for discussion, as he had suspected there to be a problem.

Picking up the intercom, he pressed the comms button and asked if a PC Susan Jetson could join them. As this fresh-faced twenty-five year old constable entered the room, Jock acknowledged her, "Hey Jet!"

"Hiya Jock," she said with the biggest of smiles painted across her face, until she saw the Super sitting waiting for the informality to end. "Oops, sorry Sir," she said standing up straight.

"Do you have to humour them as you do Jock?"

"Who Syr," Jock replied.

"Women constables, of course." Both Jet and Sally looked at each other, each expecting the other to stand up for their rights as women, but neither did. "How much involvement did this Simon have in the Briars Brook case?" the Super asked searchingly.

"Well, I declared me true position to him, as being an undercover cop, after some time when I realised 'ow much 'elp 'e could be, being a local an' all," she declared, sparingly, suspicious of this line of questions.

"So, he knew you were working for the police?"

"Yes."

"And you were careful not to let your personal feelings get the better of you?"

"For the duration of the case, yes." Sally was on a back foot, now knowing why she was being ganged up on.

"For the duration of the case, what does that mean? Did you at any point have some sort of relationship with this bloke? Think carefully Sally because I have already seen you getting upset when his name has been mentioned."

"Everything was over by then; Teacher escaped and I made a decision not to get involved undercover again, there was no continuation of the case…"

"No continuation! What do you call this?" the Super said as Jock looked down at his feet, like a guilty puppy, knowing he could no longer support Sally as Jet pulled her chair alongside to provide the female support she believed she had been summoned for.

"Was it a serious relationship?"

"Possibly."

"Sexual?"

"I don't fink that's any of your business," Sally said feeling tears welling up inside her not for the first time that day, as she shrugged herself from Jet's sympathising cuddle.

"Was it bleeding sexual?" the Super shouted as she fell quiet. "Answer the question!"

"Yes. For about two weeks, then it ended, I ended it."

"You stupid, stupid girl; that's our last witness and you have just eliminated him from our enquiries. There's no way I can suggest to the CPS that he will be unbiased, not now."

"But there's no one else, Sir." Sally looked perplexed over the tears that were now running down her cheeks, unchecked by any of the handkerchiefs that Jet was offering her.

"Then we have to let him go! You have to let him go – it was your actions that dictated the way of things," the Super said making his point, having to contemplate already how he was going to tell the Chief Superintendent and Commander.

"But, but…" Sally appealed.

"It was a request Sally, so you could sort it out in your own good time, but as you're not listening, I'll spell it out. He will not be giving evidence and that's final!" The Super had finally lost his temper, writing a note to his secretary to inform Simon that he would no longer be required. He clearly couldn't trust Sally to do it.

"Would anyone like a bri cup o' tea or coffee pr'aps?" Jock asked looking to clear away the fog of battle.

"Don't start that again, Jock!" the Super said as Sally shook her head, knowing that her ambitions within the police force may very well have just taken another nose dive.

A HAWK AT THE NECK OF THE WOODS

The little traders' market in the country town of Clearwater consisted of only eight stalls. They were set out opposite each other, leaving a wide corridor in-between for the public to funnel through. The majority were traditional with multi coloured canopies blowing gently in the breeze, but there were also three caravans, one at either end and one on the left in the middle. The market used to be a much bigger thing and mightily successful until the local shopkeepers complained that it was ruining their trade. The council agreed, therefore, to close those stalls mimicking existing shops, leaving only those that were different, not regarded as competitors. This was the plan, but Joe Public seeing all the closures assumed that the town was suffering from a downturn in its economy and voted with its feet, to do their shopping in Chillborough despite the ten-mile drive.

Fortunately, the community of stallholders were of one mind, to make a stand, fight for themselves and provide the public with a good level of service at all times. This Wednesday morning, was to be much as any other. On stall number one was Guido Belafonte, a short Italian man, dark in complexion with swept-back black hair to match, an expert in making and selling, from his Gypsy decorated refrigerated caravan, the most tongue tingling Tuscan Ice creams. He was stood talking to Betty, from stall number eight opposite him. No one knew her surname, but she had been a part of the market since dinosaurs roamed the earth, selling everything and anything to do with looking after a pet. There was dog food, cat food, meats and treats, fish food, bird seed and crates of rubber bones, all leaving very little of the table beneath on show. These two near on O.A.Ps started their day similarly at five to nine every morning, discussing changes to the market, empty stalls, possible improvements and how to get the better of the shops on the high street. They had adopted the title of 'de management', but everyone seemed to be as happy with the arrangement as sleeping pigs in sunshine.

"There isa de rumour that plot e numero seven 'as a new trader," Guido said folding his arms and looking across the precinct at the empty stall, which whilst it remained so, was, he believed, to be a blot on the market's credibility.

"That'll be right chuck, it'll be nice to be a complete market again. I fancy it be a nice young man selling men's underwear and the like, whilst doing a bit of modelling on the side," she said with a cheeky grin.

"Waita de moment, we 'ave a da Lucy's Fruity Undies already, right 'ere," he replied.

"Yes, of course me dear, but they only look after knickers, G strings and kinky bras. I need a well-engineered job to stop these buggers from travelling any further south," she said tweaking her more than ample bosom.

Hearing this, Guido stepped to the front of his van and took in a deep breath, then in the most glorious operatic tones he sang, "Save your love my darling save your love..." whereupon greatly rehearsed, Betty, being his evening partner at the Clearwater operatic society, like the second in a pair of doves sat next to each other on a telephone line, replied in similar dulcet tones. "For summer days with the sun and the moon above," she sang as Guido took over again.

"With tutti fruity, rum and raisin, vanilla and strawberry, made in heaven."

"Come and try his ice cream, just for me," Betty concluded, as the two of them began clapping and giggling uncontrollably.

Sandra looked up as she opened another box of Mars bars for the front of her stall, 'Sue and Sandra's Sweeties'. "Oh God, there they go again!"

"Oh, I quite like it," said Susan. "In fact I reckon I could join in, we could become a trio."

"Try giving Guido some free sprinkles for his ice cream and he might let you," Sandra said, as she continued to re-stock.

"I was just thinking that," said Susan, being Sandra's identical twin, their telepathic talents complementing each other like lemon and lime.

"I know," she said in return, flicking her blonde fringe to the right, being the only difference between the two blue-eyed girls.

"What time is it?" Sandra asked expectantly.

"As if you didn't know," was Susan's reply as they both put their hands over their ears.

At exactly 9 am, many of the other stallholders checked their watches and prepared themselves as there came a whirring and clicking of gears as the top of the hour arrived. Then down to the precise second, the bells, beeps, chimes and rings of every watch, clock and timepiece, erupted from out of stall number five, 'Ferrer's Clocks and Watches'. Mr Sebastian Ferrer, a ten-year legal immigrant from Switzerland, stood rubbing his hands together, so pleased that his goods were working well and already advertising themselves to the early morning customers. As the last chime echoed across the market he stepped out to the front of his stall, "And a very goot morning to Clearwater," he shouted across the pavement with his arms wide, welcoming customers and the comments of his colleagues, all under the umbrella of his German accent. "Come along zen Johnny, ve is vanting our bratwurst and early morning coffee, shnell shnell!" he smiled as Johnny of 'Johnny's Mobile Café and Burger Bar', at plot number four, arrived late yet again. To open on time, he began hurtling from white plastic table to white plastic table throwing salt, vinegar and sauces upon each, with all the finesse of a formula one racing car cornering on an oil spill.

"You mind your bleedin' manners," he yelled back at Sebastian. "You could always give us an 'and you know."

"Help, nein, nein! I don't do ze greasy café, sticky sauce and such, only on a good jagerschnitzel."

"Bloody kraut," Johnny fired back mistaking Sebastian's accent for nothing more than echoes of the fatherland, which was exactly the reason why Sebastian persisted on winding him up, that and the fact that Johnny was far more entertaining when ruffled.

As cash floats were emptied into tills, receipts prepared and final tweaks made to the goods on the stalls, the market was declared open. Not that much happened that early, not until the number seven bus packed with the day's shoppers groaned into the station at least, by which time Guido and Betty being the self-appointed market managers, would take objection to any of the stallholders setting up late. So, they were a little perplexed when a white, old and battered, Ford Escort van, rattled its way onto the precinct nearly ten minutes late and parked at plot number seven, without so much as a by your leave. Two men got out, without any intention to rush the job, dressed in jeans and T-shirts emblazoned with the logo of a pirate's chest and the words 'The Treasure Trove'. They looked rough sorts, thought Betty, who couldn't have known that one was a part time sewerage worker and the other an ex oil rig diver, both in need of the extra cash. So, she stayed behind her tower of discount dog food with one hand on a rubber bone ready to defend herself.

The lateness of the newbies, rough or not, wasn't going to deter Guido, who at risk of allowing his Tutti Frutti to melt, it still being sat on the side pleading for a place in the freezer, stormed across the precinct to confront them. "Eh, watta you doin', tis after the nine o'clock you know," he said, looking quite angry.

"A, up," said one of the men as a warning to his mate.

"What's occurring Bach?" Owen Quick replied, a fifty-year-old Welshman whose double chin was the only thing that gave his age away. His rugby shoulders and ripped frame were kept on display to deter troublemakers and so he was employed wherever muscle was needed. This meant of course that he had been detained at Her Majesty's pleasure many times, some not so briefly.

"You know what, I reckon there's trouble heading our way," said the other man, Joe Watt, the sewerage worker.

"Trouble, you is right, bastardi, you isa latea setting upa your stall, no?" Guido was not to be put off merely by the six foot, nineteen stone Owen who turned to greet him with a serious lack of a smiling face.

"Whatever your problem is boyo, I suggest you calm it down, keep it to yourself. To tell you the truth, if you need to complain, then complain to the boss, tis 'im you need to talk to. We 'ere is just doin' what he says, isn't it." He looked directly at the Italian whilst standing up as straight as a telegraph pole, which seemed to be regarded by most as a postscript for, 'unless you want to make something of it'?

"Then I be a seeing 'im as soon as 'e arrives," Guido said still masterfully, more to impress Betty than anything else, but stepping back strategically all the same, if only to attend to his melting ice creams.

"Right then Bach, we best get on with it before Teacher gets here," said Owen always wary of getting on the wrong side of his boss.

Out of the back of Teacher's van there then came a procession of bulging cardboard boxes, some were clearly lightweight and some not, some taking both men to lift them, especially when they had no handles. No one around the market knew exactly what it was that the new stallholders would be selling, which meant no one had checked to see if anything similar was being sold in the shops. World War II between stalls in the market and shops on the high street had only just subsided and no one wanted World War III. There was some relief as the first large box was opened as if straight from Tutankhamun's tomb, revealing a huge ornamental candle, beautifully carved to include scrolls of wax that had been dragged down by the sculptor, to sit around its base like some sort of medieval ruff. It had Celtic patterns inlaid in different colours, criss-crossing each other several times over which would have any viewer utterly bedazzled.

"Wow," said the delectable Lucy of 'Juicy Lucy's Knickers and Bras' at stall number two, as she hung another pair of frillies on the washing line suspendered overhead. "That's fantastic, I could just see that in my fireplace at home."

"Or on the mantel piece over a raging fire, well pr'aps not raging, in case it melts," laughed Tubby Smith her portly neighbour, in his white coat and trilby with knife in hand, manning the butcher's van in plot three.

"We might well be getting married, Tubby," said Lucy with her eyes in her head, "but you have no sense of where things should go, no idea of interior design and you're colour blind. I've told you before, you do the building and plastering and leave the decorating to me!"

"Yes, dear," Tubby said with his hands together in prayer, hoping for some assistance from the Almighty.

And so, boxes of miniature candles were the next to be unloaded, all modelled upon the larger one, but with different aromas, some subtle, some pungent, some that cut the air like a knife, but all designed to play tricks in one's mind. There were also tall candles twisted from base to tip, squat candles with multiple wicks, with names like 'Lovers Lament' and 'The Invigorator'. There were candles for lighting a room like a church altar, others to provide only a colourful hue, all for different moods and different occasions. All that should have provided an opportunity to create a work of art around the stall, but they were being placed apparently without consideration, blindly onto the table. This infuriated the budding interior designer in Lucy, who came out from behind the washing lines of knickers blowing in the wind and approached the stand.

"You'll never sell anything with a display like that," she said posing with one hand on her a thrusting hip. "You need a bit of creativity, panache, you need to be sexy with your styling!"

"Really?" said Joe, fresh from his last shift at the sewerage works. "Then I'm sure that a sexy lady such as yourself would like to come and help?" he said. This being like a red rag to a bull, Lucy shot around the other side of the table and took the box from him, envisaging herself as Clearwater's answer to Mary Quant. But it was then, just as her creative engine began to fire up, that the most awful smell fell upon her. Joe had come directly from the Clearwater sewerage works and hadn't had the time to shower or even top up his antiperspirant, assuming he had any on in the first place. "Oh shit, what a smell!" she said without any consideration for his feelings.

"Oh yes, it's lovely isn't it, Owen reckons it's called Ylang Ylang, but I think it's passion fruit," Joe said sniffing one of the candles, which Owen had suggested he took home with him to ease his way past the missus. But then, he could hardly criticise, after being told by his wife that he still stank of oil and saltwater nearly a year after being laid off the oil rigs.

"Well, if you put the small ones around the large one I'm sure you'll appeal to someone," Lucy said concocting an excuse to abandon her original mission and go looking for some fresh air. "Oh, I must go, there's someone at my stall." This was Tubby of course who had stood looking a little antagonised, seeing his intended flaunting herself for the sake of two uncouth jobbers and a pile of wax.

* * *

After his release from the police station the day previous, Teacher had found himself a grotty top floor flat, in the middle of Clearwater, within sight of the town's market. He had spent much of his time that evening sleeping, bathing and getting himself ready to face life again, to continue in his quest. With curtains closed, he sat in the lotus position with hands outstretched, palms upward to the sky. When instructing, he would advise that meditation be a tranquil thing, time devoid of all distraction, devoted to the gods in which one must believe. But he was a troubled man beneath his calm and composed exterior. His last two enterprises or missions as he called them, had failed and there seemed to be little chance of fulfilling his destiny, without copious amounts of cash. His father, he was told, had died from throat cancer, but there was always some secrecy around this and he doubted that this was the case. All this went back years and was probably due to the mistakes *she* had made. He was at least, re-focussed now and re-connected with the gods. "Oh mighty Belanos, here me now in sight of those that could and should have helped me in my quest. Help them to see the injustice we suffer and help me to enable the change, before she too passes over to meet you." He sat quietly then flexing his jaw, struggling to keep control and remain objective. "I have lost patience in some, my god, but I will no longer allow them merely to wallow in their own self-pity, attending my shops, buying my goods. Nooo! This time they will feel my wrath when I subject them to a plague of hypnosis."

* * *

At the offices of the Clearwater town council, the Mayor, Mr. Brian Woodruff, was pouring himself a third coffee from the machine on the top of the filing cabinet. This sixty-three-year-old man had been working tirelessly as a councillor for years but was seemingly passed over for the Mayor's job year after year. Until finally, probably because there was no one else and he wouldn't shut up about it, the board conceded and appointed him, even though several took early retirement rather than work under him. Sitting with his coffee, he took his beloved Scouting magazine from the top of the pile of mail sat on his desk, as in his spare time he was also a Group Scout Leader at the first Clearwater Group. Each week he would flex his muscles, somewhat insignificantly for a short man, and advise the leaders working in the Beaver, Cub and Scout sections on how best to run things, without doing anything himself. He was quite passionate about his hobby and would ordinarily take a good hour to read through the newsletters, programme planning advice pages and lists of those receiving awards for their long service. However, something compelled him to glance through the rest of the mail. Sitting in the middle of the pile there was a letter marked urgent, in a golden silk-like envelope, which got his attention immediately. Taking a very shiny stationery knife from his desk drawer, he opened it at the expense of the others and his magazine and read it; "Dear Mayor," it began officiously. "On this the first week of your testings, you will be minded preventing a calamity befalling Clearwater town. As the Lord said unto Moses, stretch out thine hand towards heaven, that there may be darkness over the land, a darkness that may be felt for three days and nights. Therefore, if you do not meet my demand of twenty-five thousand pounds, paid today into the Swiss account detailed below, I will stretch forth my hand and this darkness will fall over your town of Clearwater. Be minded that there were seven calamities that befell Egypt and that they may all befall you if you are inadequate in compliance." The letter was signed but in what looked like hieroglyphics.

"What the devil is this indeed?" Mayor Brian asked himself as he chortled away very much more amused than threatened. "Well, we know what to do with this," he concluded in an autonomic fashion, as he tore it in half and threw it in the bin.

* * *

Back on the market, Joe and Owen under Lucy's critical but distant eye, continued to open box after box of candles, which they piled onto the table set within their stall, until it bowed in the middle, which reminded Lucy of Tubby's antique pasting table. But despite this, they continued to remove stock from the apparently cavernous van storing it under the table and in large piles all around until they looked as if they were sat beneath an American sky scraping city skyline.

"Eh," Guido said to Betty as they stood still awaiting the arrival of the number seven bus, "wad da you think they is a doin'? They will never sella da candles in thisa summer weather!"

"Only if you use them when you have a bath," she replied.

"What! Dona talka de rubbish Betty, a candle in da bath will only be put outta by da water," he said not quite understanding her romantic methodology.

"But you're right love, they'll never sell that lot," she added as Owen, having finally emptied the van, then drove it away from the stall, which was finished with a sign proclaiming it as 'The Treasure Trove'. Joe was then left to sit on his own with the cash box on his knee, waiting for the customers that he had been told would arrive, to purchase the miniature candles at five pounds each. "Bloody extortionate if you ask me," said Sandra, in the sweeties stall.

"Too right, who would pay five pounds for a miniature bloody candle?" Susan agreed.

"Well, I might if…"

"If you were having a night of passion in with your man," Susan added finishing Sandra's sentence for her.

"In the bedroom, all dimly lit with candlelight flickering on the ceiling."

"As you take your clothes off ready to make love."

"Yes, well," Sandra said coughing embarrassingly, "no one wants to look at me in the nuddy, it's more of a good reason for not having any lighting on at all!"

Timings were everything to everyone involved in the market, as at about nine-thirty the bus finally arrived and the precinct came to life. First to benefit was Johnny in respect of the early morning menu that was served with a free mug of breakfast tea, the same tea he would serve at dinner and tea-time to be fair, but more popular and less stewed. By ten o'clock there was then a quick shuffle as those that knew what would happen on the hour left quickly, whilst those that didn't came to investigate Sebastian's stall as his watches, clocks and the like struck ten times over. Susan and Sandra were careful to ensure that for the morning, their stall was fronted with penny chews and lollipops to appeal to the toddlers ferried into the market by mums and the occasional dad. Only then later in the afternoon, did they switch to Mars bars, Twix and grown-up chocolate bars, like Bourneville dark, as the schools closed and their pupils drifted past on their way home. Tubby would always find that his sales of meat started slowly every day and then got better and better until just before the next bus, as no one wanted to carry a chicken and six lamb chops around with them all morning. For the opposite reason, because they could be scrunched up into the corner of a shopping bag, knickers and bras went well for Lucy early on.

Midday had been put aside by Teacher, to open 'The Treasure Trove' officially. And so just as soon as the suffering from the almost unbearable midday chimes had subsided, his Ford Escort van returned to the market and parked up behind his stall. There was then a crackling from two disco speakers that had been bolted to the top of it, followed by a peel of trumpets playing 'Fanfare for the Common Man'. This reverberated across the precinct reflecting off every shop frontage and into every store with open doors. If this didn't get everyone's attention, the music according to Emerson, Lake and Palmer, an eighties rock band, then clicked in as the rear doors were thrown open and two big fat fireworks exploded into the air. Sparks were sent flying all around when at their highest point, they morphed into some spinning lights that whizzed loudly as they shot off at right angles ricocheting off nearby rooftops. There was then a calculated pause like the results at the end of the "X" factor, just enough to ensure that the public were tuned in, before there was another flash of light as Teacher appeared on the roof of the van, with glitter in his beard and his bright robes billowing about him. Owen then took the brakes off and the entire magnificence rolled slowly out into the centre of the market.

As the ensemble paused right in front of the stall, the engine fell quiet and Teacher settled himself by closing his eyes and moving his hands over and around his face, slowly, deliberately, and mysteriously. When, whether it was due to a dirty great cloud sliding across the face of the sun or not, everything became darker and in response everyone became quieter, focussing themselves upon this over dramatic crackpot whose arm movements were now getting quicker and quicker. Suddenly, timed to perfection and a drumroll from the van's loud speakers, Teacher opened his eyes wide, throwing his arms out in front of himself towards the huge candle in the middle of the stall, which sparked two or three times and then lit up obediently, to an audible gasp from the audience. At first the flame was only a glimmer of a thing, but as Teacher's face became contorted so intensely as he concentrated, he caused it to swell until it burst into a powerful three-foot tongue, flickering and dancing for all to see. Then, more probably due in fact to the travelling cloud above, the sun came out and everywhere, if only for a minute, was seemingly bathed in candlelight. Then with a continued hypnotic stare, the flame was brought under control and reduced to a modest six inches, just as people's sensibilities returned along with a round of applause that Teacher wallowed in. "Ladies and gentlemen, I give you 'The Treasure Trove'."

Chuffed with his performance, Teacher checked to see if his two employees knew what he expected of them; he felt that they should pay him some credit for whooping up the applause when required and quietening it down when not. "Quick," Teacher shouted expecting Owen to answer to his surname.

"What?" he replied.

"Yes?" said Joe also responding.

"No, not you Watt, Quick," Teacher reiterated.

"That's me," said Owen.

"Watt," Joe responded in question.

"That's right!" Owen confirmed, as Teacher walked around the stall banging the heel of his hand repeatedly on his forehead until his was eye to eye with both. They grinned, as silently he strained to keep a smile from breaking out on his face, pointing at the cash box and the gathering public without saying a word, to prompt them back to work.

Tubby had watched the opening with great interest, but as soon as it was over he went back to sorting through his cuts and sides of meat, all hanging forlornly along the rails in the top of the refrigerated box van, parked behind his stall. He was always disappearing to do this as he liked to keep busy, preparing fillets, joints and chops etc., but should Lucy not be looking after her own customers, he would have to cover and invariably miss his. As always, he had been in there far too long, day-dreaming with his head in the clouds, like some sort of giant eagle surfing the thermals, when abruptly, something flew up behind him and tapped him on the shoulder. He turned to see what or who it was, but there was nobody there. Unnerved, he was then acutely aware that his spine had begun to feel as chilled as the meat hanging around him and that he was covered from head to toe in a light dusting of frost. He also felt compelled to get back to his stall for some unknown reason other than to thaw out. Coming down the three wooden steps at the back of his van with half a dozen lamb chops in one hand and a flitch of bacon in the other, he was suddenly surprised by Teacher standing with his hands behind his back, bending over the white melamine trays set out on the table, containing the prime beef steak.

"Oh hello," Tubby said, "you're the new stallholder from number seven. What an entrance that was, let's just hope your sales are as good. But tell me, why candles?"

"I sell whatever the mind, my mind, dictates that I should sell. Candles this week, but maybe some new treasure next week, it's all in the hands of the gods."

"I see," said Tubby a little taken aback by the plural use of the word God. "Well, you are very welcome to be a part of the market here whatever your God and I'm sure we can become friends. I see you might be interested in a nice piece of steak?" he said with the friendly intention of giving away a piece free of charge.

"Hathor, the nurse of Horus our bovine goddess, would approve, so much so that the sun disc she holds between her horns, would be illuminated considerably."

"Is that a yes?"

"I shall require a full side of beef in its frozen state," Teacher continued.

"A full side?"

"Yes."

"But that's nearly three hundred pounds in weight."

"I'm sure it is," Teacher acknowledged with no change to his expression, "but it must be frozen."

"But that will cost you nearly a thousand pounds," Tubby said looking for further confirmation or for the revealing punchline to a joke he had just fallen foul of.

"Yes, but it must be frozen."

"Are you sure?"

"I am Teacher. Not Mr Teacher or your Teacher, just Teacher. And as such, you can trust me and the gods that befriend you."

"My dear man you can have it stuffed with bad boy pot noodle for that kind of money," Tubby said as he took a sharp knife from the rack above his head and disappeared back into the refrigerated van, to cut it down from the rail.

As the meat was delivered to the Treasure Trove, Joe emptied the back of the van of all the goods and resources required to keep the stall going, apart from two giant oxygen cylinders, a part of Owen's diving kit, but still found he couldn't get the carcase to fit inside without its legs hanging out the back.

"Ya know, there's only one thing for it Owen, we'll 'ave to get the butcher to lop its legs off," he said with a grin on his mucky face.

"Down't, ewe do that Bach! We needs it intact, so he does. We'll haf to tie the doors together with a bungy, isn't it," Owen replied casting one beady eye down the pedestrian area, spotting his boss sitting quietly at Johnny's mobile café with a cup of tea and a sticky bun. "And whatever ewe do, down't ewe let my cylinders go banging together," Owen added.

"Why? They won't explode will they?"

"Noo, of course not, rhoi nerth i mi, we'll just sing some Welsh ditties in tune as they make a loud clanging souwnd," he said looking unbelievably at Joe before saying, "of course they'll bleeding explode you barmy seisneg sewerman." So carefully, like a bomb disposal operative, Joe moved them around in the van, making room for the beef. As soon as this was done, whilst Owen hovered over him kestrel like, he took out the remainder of the diving gear, wet suits, face masks, flippers and all, and stashed everything under the front seat, finally having the room to push the side of beef almost all the way home, but for its two back feet around which Owen fastened the doors. "Well done Bach, and all before 'e finishes his pan-ed."

As another round of whirring and clicking gave rise to the by now mass exodus of stallholders with fingers in ears, the clocks, watches and digital garb of Sebastian's timepieces chimed and bleeped their way through the 6 pm milestone that signalled the closure of the Wednesday's trading. Meats and sweets, burgers and buns, knickers and ice cream whips, all were folded up and packed away before being taken to be stored overnight in two containers on the car park, that had quite literally at one time fallen off the back of a lorry.

Teacher, or 'The Hippy' as everyone had labelled him, was by anybody's interpretation, somewhat strange and so he seemed to be someone not to be trusted, especially when allegedly lighting candles with the power of his mind. However, he had realised this and in fact had a plan to deal with it. He wanted allies that were prepared to trust him and that would help him if needed, but for this to be the case he had to demonstrate his political and social credence, his credibility and approachability. So, as soon as the Treasure Trove had been packed away for the night, he drew seven packs of four candles and with the first made his way over to Betty's pet stall.

"And these are for you my dear. I and the mighty Belanos, noticed you working so hard today in serving all those obsessed pet owners, that I felt you deserved a get to know me gift." He smiled at Betty who melted in front of him beginning not for the first time, to try to imagine what kind of a husband he would make. "Well it's really nice to have you here, Mr …"

"Teacher, just Teacher," he said as he waved a little wave at her whilst gliding across the precinct to speak to Guido.

"Hello Mr Pavarotti," he said eluding to the musical interludes there had been that day at every lull in trading, "I have a gift of four candles for you, a thank you for having me here," he said again with a disarming and infectious smile.

"Well, a Mr …."

"Teacher, just Teacher."

"Well a Mr Teacher, it is a velly goot to have you 'ere. If ever you find yourself too 'ot, in all those robes, just aska me for the Tutti Fruiti ice creama." Teacher said he would as he went across to stand six and Susan and Sandra with the same introduction and same little gift.

"Thank you," the girls said in unison as they tried to reciprocate with a box of Turkish Delight, but Teacher turned it down tapping his conveniently dieted tummy as an excuse. One at a time he visited all the stallholders with the same gift, exchanging a few words that would play on their mind and in time secure them as friends and moreover allies, should the need arise. Finally, he left, after he had climbed into the front passenger seat of the Escort van, with Owen at the wheel and Joe squished in the middle, all being chilled by the half a side of beef still frozen hard in the back.

A MOAN OF CONSTIPATION

As the three men drove out of Clearwater, the day seemed as good as over, the sun was low in the sky and shadowy fingers stretched out across the ground, but the warmth of the day still lingered and the risk that the beef may start to thaw out was becoming a concern. "Get your foot down, quick," said Teacher knowing that he had to make the most of the carcass whilst it was still frozen.

"Now down't you worry, Teacher," Owen said, clearly in the know as to what was to happen next. "Just one thing, you wown't be asking me to go down there in the dark now, will ewe? I might be Welsh but I'm no bleedin' Superman all right."

"It'll be fine," Teacher said fixing his gaze upon the two men, who were then seemingly a little more pacified as if they had received a treat from their master to stop them barking.

"I don't understand what it is you're going to do anyway," Joe said shrugging his shoulders.

"You don't need to know," Teacher said calmly,

"It will be perfectly obvious by the morning." Owen turned off the main road and continued up a narrowing lane, populated either side with warning signs, saying there was no access, it being a service road owned jointly by the water board and electricity company. Going now begrudgingly uphill, the van slowed as it left the tree line, the weight of the two compressed gas cylinders and half a side of still frozen beef was starting to tell. As they got higher and higher they could look down right across the valley floor where many of the lights in the town were now flickering into life, as workers arrived home to cook the evening meal or settle down to an evening's TV soap opera. The vista was so impressive that as Owen pulled up before a road barrier Joe jumped down out of the van. "Wow," he said looking down the valley, "will you look at that!"

"Come on," Teacher shouted, "we haven't the time for dawdling." He continued to be concerned about the time, checking it on his mobile phone, constantly.

After they had passed through and dropped the long arm of the barrier down behind them, they travelled up and over the crest of the hill, into a cutting. All around them the sides of the hills became higher and higher until they were looking down on the three men, suspiciously from either side, as they passed into a deep and claustrophobic combe, which held the dark dark surface of a deep lake, glistening in the fading light. Alongside the shoreline there were two large tents, tables, chairs and all the paraphernalia of a working campsite. The van pulled up alongside. "Right, quick, get kitted up," Teacher instructed without delay.

"What?" said Owen.

"No, I'm Watt, he's Quick," said Joe with a sly grin across his face.

"Stop," Teacher said menacingly, fixing his eyes on the comedian, "just don't start that again!"

By the time Owen had pulled on his scuba gear, he had taken to looking like some out-of-place sea lion standing next to the water looking for a fish, which wouldn't have been so easy anyway given that the light was disappearing fast. Teacher however, had foreseen this and from under a tarpaulin he produced a giant marine lamp that he carried into the water, his robes floating on the surface as he did so. "Get the beef," he shouted to Joe.

"What for?" he replied.

"Just get it, before the hackles of Hathor rise to meet you,"

Teacher commanded whilst transfixing him in his gaze. Owen spat into his scuba mask to clear it of condensation, then after ensuring it was refitted properly, dipped briefly beneath the surface of the water to take a couple of breaths, testing the sweet air from the cylinder strapped to his back. All was well, so he then committed himself and melted away into the depths until all that anyone could then see of him, was a graze of light as he manoeuvred the giant lamp around until he found what he was looking for. Re-surfacing then, he gave an OK sign with one hand, inviting Teacher to drag the beef side into the water, after strapping a small specialist buoyancy balloon to it, which Joe inflated with air from the other cylinder. The beef was now floating just under the surface. Diving down again, the top of the little balloon was all that could be seen bobbing just above the water as it glided out into the middle of the lake until it stopped, sitting like some Second World War naval contact mine. "He's there," Teacher said more to himself than to Joe, who responded just the same.

"He's where? Other than being in the middle of the lake with arf a side of beef in the pitch black! There must be some bloody big fish out there if it's supposed to be bait."

"Quiet," Teacher demanded whilst trying to concentrate on the task in hand, as the light under the water could then be seen to be moving around until finally it stopped. Owen then let some air out of the buoyancy balloon and everything disappeared below the surface. "Now just to wait," Teacher said to himself before turning and wading ashore. "Watt!"

"What," was the questioning reply from the now disgruntled man, brassed-off and sulking at not being allowed to be included in the water team.

"Break camp and get everything into the van. I don't want to see any trace that we were ever here," Teacher instructed as he stood dithering on the shoreline.

"Right away Teach, you can rely on me, always me, always getting the crappy jobs," Joe said as he attempted to motivate himself. "Any deadline, any further instructions, performance bonus perhaps?"

"Not unless you want to exchange places with the side of beef," Teacher added with a grimace of temper in his voice.

With no more than money as his incentive, Joe took nearly an hour to tidy the camp away as activity on the shoreline indicated that Owen had returned from working in the lake, minus the side of beef, and was now changing back into his ACDC T shirt and damp Jeans. Teacher meanwhile, zipped around manically, trying to meet some self-imposed deadline, looking at his watch and issuing orders to remove any lasting trace of their campsite. Finally, as the darkness became total, the camp was broken whilst the scuba gear, cylinders and marine lamp had been sunk to the bottom of the lake.

The evening's work completed, everyone was sat squashed once more into the little van. "Five minutes, five minutes," Teacher kept saying. "Quick now, drive to the neck of the Combe." Owen knew for why and drove as fast as the overloaded van would let him, pulling up at the road barrier where the view down into the valley was now even more resplendent. There were glowing orange and red lights from the thousands of homes, road traffic and advertising signs. They all jumped out of the van, where they stood silently as Teacher lifted his arms to the sky and stars and began to chant:

"To Apsu, god of the Enuma Elish, hover over these waters with the power and strength you possess to teach our modern man of the folly he invests in his machinery. Ally yourself with Belanos and I, your Teacher, your one remaining disciple and revert this state to its humble beginnings." He stood then waiting, only to repeat the chant, to stand and wait again.

"What the bloody hell!" said Joe who was beginning to give up on the will to live.

"If you don't shut up boy, I'll come over there and battle ewe myself," Owen hissed under his breath, "we stand to get a huge pay out if this works!"

"To Apsu, god of the Enuma Elish," Teacher began again and then again whilst keeping his eye upon his watch, it was five past seven and Owen was beginning to believe that the plan was flawed. Joe stood thinking.

"By sinking that side of beef into the lake, was Teacher expecting it to block something?" Joe looked for confirmation of his theory.

"That's right Bach, once I unbolted the filtering grill o-ver the neck of the pipeline." Owen further explained with a beaming smile.

"Which is why you worked for over an hour under the water."

"Correct. Of course, once the gates to the electricity station below were open, as consumption demanded, the frozen lump of beef will 'ave been taken down the pipeline and probably lodged itself in the corkscrew within the turbine, most likely shattering the finials, soo crippling any further generating of power."

"So, what was all that Apsu, god of the Enuma whatever?" Joe asked.

"Listen Bach, I 'ave known Teacher longer than ewe, and can tell ewe that, we need to believe that there is noo reason why the turbine might fail at this time – other than by Teacher's fair 'ands," Owen said convincingly. "You'd do well not to allow your doubts to surface, keep them to yourself and I'm not being funny when I say, down't you argue with him!"

Then without any sound or warning, the lights in the valley from the forested borders in the north to the town of Chillborough in the west, right across as far as they could see to the east, flickered and then went out.

SCOWLING IN THE DARKNESS

The town of Clearwater was in terms of its resources, almost self-sufficient. In its recent history amongst other innovative schemes, it had built a hydro-electric power station. This clever gamble had cost the authority millions of pounds, consisting of a massive tunnel cut from a lake high in the mountains, which took water underground, down through a massive corkscrew turbine. It produced all the electricity required, before the water was finally discharged into a lower lake. The only problem in the master plan was in recharging the upper lake when there was insufficient rain collected by the surrounding mountains. Initially they called for support from neighbouring electricity grids, to pump it from the lower to the higher lake, overnight at periods of low electric consumption. However, they had now solved this and pushed the self-sufficiency ethic as far as they might, by constructing two supercharged batteries that stored enough power to do this in a flash.

Mayor Brian was working late when the power went out. He was infuriated that the word document he was working on, between chapters of playing grand theft auto with a Beaver Scout Leader from his local Scout Group, hadn't been saved and was probably now floating away on the ether. As steam was still blowing from his ears he grabbed his mobile and dialled the power station to find out what was going on; there were no scheduled stops for repair or maintenance that he knew of. But the phone rang and rang until his arm ached from holding it to his ear and he had to assume that the workforce at the station probably had their hands full. So, he made his way to his very luxurious Jag, which at least had an independent battery, heating and radio, and sat listening to late night chat shows whilst periodically telephoning, until he accidentally fell to sleep. At around 9 pm he was awoken by his phone, ringing and vibrating in his shirt pocket. It was the chief operating officer from the power station, finally returning his call.

"Brian, it's Henry Abbot here, from CPS, I'm sorry I've not been on sooner, it's been mayhem at the station here."

"So, what's the problem?" Brian asked still only half awake.

"It's the hydro turbine. It's been damaged, seriously."

"What, you mean you're being serious or that the damage is serious?" Brian sounded panicked.

"Both," Henry exclaimed, annoyed with the Mayor's apparent pre-occupation with stupid questions. "But there's more, the finials in the turbine have been damaged by what looks like a body."

"What?" Brian said shocked, finally sitting upright and opening a window. "Are you sure?"

"Well, I'm not a bleedin' anthropologist, but they're definitely bones and a good deal of what looks like body parts. You best call the police as this is really sinister."

"You mean it could be deliberate?"

"Almost certainly, the grill and filter at the top lake should have prevented anything this size getting into the pipes. In fact, I'm surprised that the turbine didn't just chop a body up into bits and then let it pass through to the bottom lake," Henry explained, but there was no reply to his comments. "Brian, Brian are you there?"

Brian had left his car in the car park, still with its lights, looking like the site of some sort of alien abduction, as he ran back to his office with the aid of a torch from his glovebox. It hadn't dawned on him until now because he treated it so flippantly at the time, but having kicked his litter bin over, spilling the crumpled contents right across the floor, he found the letter he had discarded. He read it again, out loud. *'Stretch out thine hand towards heaven, that there may be darkness over the land, a darkness that may be felt for three days and nights. Therefore, if you do not meet my demands and pay twenty-five thousand pounds, into the Swiss account detailed below, I will stretch forth my hand and this darkness will fall over your town of Clearwater'.*

He smacked his hand across his forehead. "You bloody idiot," he blurted out, in language his Scouts would have lost points for. He turned again running back to his car, slamming it into gear and three-point-turning it around in the road. As he thrust his foot down, leaving enough rubber on the road to keep the local post office in elastic bands for a year, he headed for the power station whilst calling 999 on his hands-free. He was put through after explaining to the Chillborough nick, who as soon as they were convinced that they weren't being hoaxed, promised to send a Scene of Crime team.

By midnight, the main office was lit dimly by what power the station's batteries had accumulated during the last generating period. Things had been absolute pandemonium, with Henry running from A to B like the jack in a pinball machine, trying to make sense of the failure. Two of the station's engineers were now bent over some blue tinted plans spread across the desk along with the manual for crisis management, as an impatient Brian continually asked, "How long, Henry?" Not to be drawn into something he might regret however, as he perspired in what was no longer an air-conditioned environment, Henry bit his lip, only prepared to give a guesstimate. "Could take as long as three days."

Brian drew in a breath to keep his heart going whilst re-reading the still-crumpled message from his waste bin. "There may be darkness over the land, a darkness that may be felt for three days and nights!" He grimaced. "I'm obviously more than a bloody idiot!" he said as Henry took it from him and read it himself.

"What! You knew all along; you knew?" he shrieked, "What the hell happened to a Scout Masters' motto of 'Be Prepared' then?"

The Chillborough Police were no more chilled than the Mayor as they never reacted with blue's and two's to reports of dead bodies, unless they were linked to circumstances that might suggest the job to be ongoing. So, it was 7 am on the Thursday, before a large white police transit containing four constables, laboured into the power station's deserted car park, to cordon off the site and preserve any evidence. This was followed one breakfast later, by a smaller van emblazoned with the letters CSI, from within which two men with Scene of Crime Officers' badges pinned to their chests, began ferrying blue semi-transparent plastic bags, plastic overalls, masks and gloves into the reception area.

"This way, this way," Henry said as he met them and ushered them as quickly as he could into the turbine room, which always seemed to amuse the officers at murder scenes, as any dead body, least of all a pile of old bones, was unlikely to get any worse as the result of a delay. Even when being introduced to the engineers that had closed the system down and exposed the internal workings of the turbine, they merely sat on top of their equipment whilst waiting for the senior investigating officer to arrive. After two breakfasts, a white box van, swept sedately into the car park, from which a white-coated woman with hellishly dark-rimmed glasses, went to the rear and took out a large bag. Putting it momentarily on the ground she opened it and took from between various medical and forensic equipment, her ID badge which once pinned on her coat announced her as The County Pathologist. She was followed only moments later, in vivid contrast, by a Honda 750S motorcycle, appropriately known as a freedom fighter, which in a flash of black and chrome darted in through the gate and skidded to a stop, spraying the gravel from the budget car park, right across the road. The rider, heavily adorned in black leather with a mirrored visor to her helmet, began walking like Darth Vader on a mission, towards the reception, whilst pulling off gloves and un-popping press-studs. "Hiya, Caitlin," she said somewhat muffled having not yet removed her helmet.

"Well, look who it is an' all. Sally Reid," said the doctor in an Irish accent, not knowing of any other police officer who rode such a beast of a machine. As Henry met them and ushered them in with Brian in tow, the ladies introduced themselves as Doctor Caitlin Brannagh and senior investigating officer, Sergeant Sally Reid from Chillborough Police.

"Well then, gents," Sally began, "if I can ask ya to formally sign me log book, so I can keep a track of who comes and who goes across me crime scene, then we can get on." She held out the book with a black biro sellotaped to a piece of string threaded through the spine, whilst formally identifying herself by showing her ID card. Finally, she introduced the doctor as the pathologist on call that night, before asking what had happened.

"It all started just after 7 pm," Brian began, considering himself the senior government representative, which he also thought gave him the right to eye-up the two women, "just as I was lifting a Porsche Gt2 Rs from under the eyes of the cops."

Sally looked severely at him somewhat confused. "Grand Theft Auto," he explained as she smiled and nodded her head. "I was winning my way through part one when all the lights and everything went out."

"That's right," Henry said, "The power disappeared, right across the whole friggin' area."

"Just like that? No warning signs or 'owt?" Sally asked somewhat surprised but also somewhat smug, being of a neighbouring borough, which had been ostracised from any political union with the self-sufficient cronies of Clearwater.

"No nothing, only a bit of a hike in temperature, then as the turbine fractured and jammed, it went through the friggin' ceiling. There was panic then for most of the following three hours until we managed to cool it down. I thought at one point that the whole place was going to blow up!" He looked exhausted, Sally thought, but he was really to be thanked for his expertise in preventing a mini Chernobyl from descending over the entire Midlands.

"But what's all this to do with a dead body?" she asked as the party was shown into the turbine room, which was wrapped like a spider's web in police authority tape.

"Well, as the engineers realised what had happened, they stripped the lid off the turbine to find this," Henry said as he lifted the tape for everyone to pass under, prompting Sally to scribble away in her log book.

"I see," she said as in considering the still ringing wet turbine housing, she could see bone after bone after fragment after body part, strewn about the internal chamber amid the broken finials of the corkscrew. "This'll be your department then Doc," she added.

"Well 'tis very surprising an' all that," Doctor Brannagh said with her Irish eyes in the top of her head. "I'll be needing the help of the Almighty with this one, Sally," she said as she began to decant her very comprehensive medical kit.

Before Sally could blink, there came a hand upon her shoulder, which for just one minute, prompted her to imagine what a criminal might feel like when being apprehended by the police, but it was Brian with his irritating mayoral head on.

"Sergeant, before you disappear, I need you to see something else," he said as he handed her the blackmail letter he had received. She looked at him inquisitively before reading it for herself, which caused her mouth to fall open and an inordinate silence to fall across the room. "And for how long have you know about this?"

"Too long," he replied. "I put it down as a hoax and threw it in the bin."

"A twenty-five-thousand-pound hoax…are you serious? Do you not think had you said something, that some extra security at least, might have made a world of difference?"

"Well I realise that now and can't really forgive myself, I only hope that someone doesn't die or something."

"What, like the poor bugger in the intake pipe?" she asked facetiously, waiting for a response that never came.

* * *

It seemed as if there had been no dusk or early morning to speak of and no dawn chorus, as if all the birds had respectfully gone elsewhere. Clearwater and its surrounding enclaves may well have gone to bed none the wiser, but now there was no electric to wake up to, no alarm clock or hot water from a boiling kettle to make the coffee. And, if a person was up and about, no street lighting, traffic signals, buses or trams, just a free-for-all when navigating the way to work. Not that those managing to get that far were rewarded for doing so, as all the factories, shops and early morning cafés were also closed. By half past eight at least, the Thursday morning market was open. The Treasure Trove was already set up, dusted and polished, with stocks and stocks of candles on hand ready for the anticipated rush. The fact that the power had been off for thirteen hours was certainly unlucky for some of the stallholders, not to mention Guido's inability to manufacture new supplies of ice cream and Tubby's problems in keeping his meat frozen. Their absence from the market should have helped the Treasure Trove, however they weren't going to get away with it, as Guido had turned up to help Betty on the pet stall, with an archive of music scores tucked under his arms. Tubby was looking on the bright side too, anticipating working with his fiancée and getting his hands on her knickers. Sebastian, on the other hand, was totally unaffected by the power cut, as eighty-five percent of the items he had for sale were battery powered, the rest relying on old fashioned wind up mechanisms.

"Vat are ve to do today with no bratwurst or de Jagerschnitzel?" Sebastian shouted across to Johnny who had abandoned his petrol generator weeks ago, in favour of the new mains coupling that the council had provided. "Zis would not happen in ze fatherland, you know." Sebastian proclaimed.

"Then why don't you bugger off back there and leave us all alone," Johnny shouted letting the targeted banter get to him once again.

"Nein, it vil be far more fun to stay here, vit you!" Sebastian cackled.

"Well, come and buy a Coke or something, it doesn't have to be hot food."

"Vy do you not buy a big candle to cook on, from the Treasure Trove? Zere may even be a lesser chance of you burning ze burgers," Sebastian exclaimed before bursting into laughter.

"Bloody Kraut," came the predictable reply, whilst other disagreements ensued amongst other stallholders, whose alarms had not gone off that morning.

"Leave them alone Tubby and put that down," Lucy hissed at her intended as he systematically went around her stall, feeling and stroking each pair of knickers, frilly or smooth suggesting that he was just getting acquainted with the products. However, he then began holding each up in front of Lucy trying to imagine what she would look like with them on. "Oh yes," he said to the first pair of pink frillies, "Nooo," he said to the smooth, grandma long leg pants, "Oooh defo!" he then exclaimed as he lifted up a full length basque with see-through panels and a flower-adorned crotch. But without hesitation, he ran as fast as his little fat legs would carry him when Lucy advanced upon him with one stocking wrapped at each end around her hands, as she threatened to strangle him. Whether it was due to this lover's tiff or not, Guido envisaging a romantic scene in front of the Prime Pal, given that he was missing his beloved Gypsy ice cream van. He ruffled himself up, struck a pose and began, 'Save your love my darling, save your love', he sang in his very best Renato tone, as Betty shaped up to deliver the next line using a plastic dog bone as a microphone.

"Oh, bloody hell, here they go again," Sandra said putting her fingers in her ears.

"I've told you, I quite like it! We should buy some sweets to put on the stall to complement them, some of that plastic spaghetti or what about some of those candy pizzas," Susan replied.

"What about some wine, some of that Chianti, the stuff that Hannibal the Cannibal likes; we could sell it to Tubby as an aphrodisiac!"

The fact that the Treasure Trove was set up so early, was possibly the reason for all the joviality, now that the market was again complete. It had the effect of motivating everyone, unless of course it was the fact that the sunshine was out after a night of enforced darkness, hooting owls and visits from the ghosts of long-dead relatives.

The trigger to the successful selling of candles, was an early morning text that had been delivered to the town's population of mobile phones, alerting them to the fact that the power could be off for another two days and that there was a stall in the market selling candles! Sure enough, people were arriving already with boxes and poached Tesco's shopping trollies, to buy half a dozen candles for a discount price of twenty-five pounds. One hotelier armed with two shopping trolleys left with two large and thirty-six small candles despite Joe refusing to accept his credit card, returning with one hundred and seventy-five pounds in cash from his ninety-year-old mother, who pathetically got only one small candle as a thank you for her trouble.

"So, where's the hippy this morning?" Joe asked Owen, who had shared a Premier Inn twin room with him that night.

"How would I know boy, probably in some five star 'otel if I knows 'im, isn't it?"

"It's *his* stall though, he should be here by rights," Joe went on, always finding all but nothing to moan about.

"Aye but 'e did talk about you boy, about not sharing a cramped van with ewe, comparing you to a bleedin' sewerage rat!"

"I had a shower this morning," Joe argued.

"In cold water presumably, what with the bleedin' electric being off! Why do ewe think I'm sat over 'ere and you're over there?"

"I just thought it was a case of us both covering the stand from all angles," Joe suggested shrugging his shoulders.

Suddenly, there came an over-revving of a nearby motorcycle, which irritatingly got louder and louder like the noise of a passing earth tremor. As the ground started to vibrate, candles fell from the towers of stock around the Treasure Trove stall as coincidentally, Sebastian's clock emporium celebrated the arrival of another hour in the day. This was just as Teacher charged into the market place on a white 700cc Moto Guzzi V7 racing bike, in a cloud of blue smoke with his robes flying all around him. He wasn't quite in control having refused to take the bike salesman's advice, who suggested that he took a less powerful machine as a beginner. His ineptitude was obvious as he clipped the plastic buckets at the front of Betty's stall, propelling tens of rubber bones and doggy treats high into the air, then crashed through a stack of scented six inch candles and shot straight into the container in the car park at the rear of Sandra and Susan's stall, with an almighty 'clang'!

"I just knew that was going to happen," said Susan with her hand to her mouth, whilst her sister looked up into the top of her head.

* * *

By midday a very bright Dr Brannagh had called for Sally to attend the laboratory room in the power station. In her white coat and thick protective glasses, she turned to face Sally from a table-top strewn safari like, with bones from the turbine. Despite the gruesome sight her Irish eyes smiled as she explained. "I have some very good news, so I have Sally."

"Good, I could do with some," came a very bleary-eyed reply.

"They're not human bones. Very definitely a cow or such-like," she said as she peeled off her protective gloves. "It must have fallen into the intake pipe an' all."

"Well, that's a bleedin' relief, we'd never have tracked down the owner had they been human," Sally said as she considered that any charge of murder or suspicious death was now null and void. There may be something along the lines of criminal damage, she reminded herself and so begrudgingly, she reported back to Superintendent Daniels at Chillborough nick. He listened intently and after a brief chortle to himself, downgraded the scene, leaving the other officers there only to tidy up but directing Sally to return to base. So, after saying goodbye to Brian and wishing Henry success with his already behind schedule repairs, she donned her leathers and black helmet and by four o'clock left in a cloud of dust and flying leaves. Pulling out onto the road in the same Knievel fashion as she arrived, she was surprised to see how pretty the countryside was. She had arrived after dark and had seen nothing of the abundance of green trees and fields, only the flare of light from her headlamp lighting the mundane road. Considered by some to be a bikers' paradise, her route took her through quaint little hamlets and villages resting quietly in the landscape, away from the sprawl of Chillborough. In fact, it was this that convinced her to divert from her route and turn tangent through Clearwater town, which despite its lack of electricity was delightful, even having its own market. So attractive was the idea of stopping, that when she noticed that the market was open, she pulled into the adjacent car park.

A DASH OF GUILT

It took only the morning for most of the initial stock of candles set out across the Treasure Trove stall, to be wiped out. This was probably due in no small part to the public bulletins that had been sent, like messages from the gods, to everyone's mobile phone right across the town, suggesting that the power may yet be off for another forty-eight hours. And so, by the afternoon, Joe found himself carrying box upon box of rattling candles from container to stall just about at the same rate as Owen was selling them.

"You have to be right switched on to be able to judge what will and what won't sell, even at the best of times," Johnny said to Tubby who had become bored with ladies' knickers and sat now with a can of warm Coke outside the deserted mobile café. "I've always thought that a hot cup o' tea and a bacon butty were a sure thing, but all my stoves and stuff are bleedin' electric! How this Teacher bloke has the knack of deciding to sell candles just before a power cut, beats me!"

"I know, I've got a shed load of meat in my refrigerated van, but I can't get any diesel to keep it going, because the garage's pumps won't work without electric! I daren't open it in case it thaws out. Candles I ask you. How lucky can you get?"

"Aye, but what they gonna do when they run out or when the power comes back on," Johnny said suddenly trying to look appealing as Sally wandered onto the market. "Hello my love, can I get ya anything?" he said as she considered the menu and then sat down at an adjacent white table and chair.

"Got any power on? Any burgers, chips or owt?" she asked, but of course Johnny shook his head offering her only a warm Coke. "What's occurring there, then?" she asked, looking down the market at the panic buying still gripping the Treasure Trove.

"Oh, they're selling candles by the bucket load. There's been a crowd around their stall all day, making a right killin' they are, at five pounds a candle. Anyone would o' thought they knew the bleedin' power was going to be off." Johnny tutted and smiled as he took a rare pound from Sally for her Coke. "Bloody beginners' luck!" he added.

"Beginners," Sally queried as her interest grew and fingertips tingled. Whereupon she stood for a better look.

"Yes," said Tubby assessing Sally's curves in her tight leathers and the snug fit she appeared to have in them. "They were only here a day before the power went out." Sally could feel her highly-tuned police sensibilities stir and tingling graduate until it prickled across the back of her neck. This prompted her to stand and amble past Sebastian's ticking timepieces to get a better look, becoming more and more suspicious as she got nearer to the now waxy fingered men who were pocketing mountains of energised cash. In fact, she was just about to buy a small candle for herself, to take back to the nick to be checked, when she saw him. She had to do a double-take at first, but under what sunshine there was, Teacher's white robes lit him up like the tops on a pint of Guinness, causing Sally to drop her half crushed can of Coke.

After the shock had hissed its way out of Sally's ears and mouth, she shook herself to kick off the last few shivers and at last, broke out into a run. This was a mistake however, a silly mistake that she, (as a trained policewoman) should well know! As instead of blending into the crowd she had singled herself out, drawing Teacher's attention to her. He should have been warned by the gods overhead, if he was to be believed, but in a millisecond, which only served to illustrate his guilty conscience, he flinched.

"Oh shit!" he said emptying in a panic, a self-fashioned pocket in the front of his robes, of five pound notes into the biscuit tin the boys were using as a till. "Sally bloody Read, I should have cast her down when I had the chance," he yelled as he made a bolt for it. For her part, she wasn't sure what Teacher had to do with the problems at the power station, but the fact that he had started to run upon seeing her was all the ammunition she needed. As Owen and Joe continued totally oblivious, a white flash behind them suddenly shot back into the container from whence it came. Sally had tried to keep her eyes on him, but in the melee of candle buying shoppers, who she now bumped into and jostled with, she lost him. He had the run on her though and she didn't realise where he had gone until the noise of his Moto Guzzi kicked into action. He then shot out of the container, growling across the market before pulling out onto the road, leaving a contrail of blue smoke behind him. "Ha ha," he screamed as he opened the throttle pulling a precarious wheelie as he took off like a Super Mario brother.

"Where the bloody hell is he going?" Joe asked. "He's always sloping off leaving us to do his dirty work."

"Aye Bach. To tell ewe the truth, he'd of done us beta nipping round the bank to get rid of some of this cash," Owen said as he tried to force shut the lid on the now over-full biscuit tin.

Sally went into full reverse, running back towards the car park whilst pulling her bikers' gloves on and trying to push her lid down over her head without running into any parking bollards or lost children. Finally, kicking up the Honda 750, she took up the pursuit, easily at first as it wasn't difficult to see which direction Teacher was heading, she just had to follow the fog of blue smoke that was still hanging in the air. Up the town's main high street they went, Teacher being a good twenty seconds ahead of her at this point, but his inexperience on his bike was starting to show. He had already knocked over two litter bins, a fish and chip billboard and a doggy-do station, when in trying to avoid a DIY'er leaving B&Q with a plank over one shoulder, he strayed from the paved area onto cobbles set in concrete. The bike bounced and reverberated up and down as Teacher's jowls shivered and his backside wobbled like two agitated jellies, becoming unseated, only to come crashing down again, leaving him grimacing with pain. Sally was obliged to be careful; neither she nor Teacher were supposed be riding up the pedestrianised area and she had a license to lose that would see her out of a job. Nevertheless, following the litter, obliterated billboard and copious amounts of doggy-do, not all still in plastic bags, she was in fact gaining on him. She could see him ahead careering from side to side as he passed the chemist and the pound shop, leaving pedestrians diving for cover after picking up their rolling groceries. It had occurred to her that if there was any truth in the psychic arts, telepathic ability and the like, then the staff at the Tarot Card shop might know he was coming past at any minute and try to help him. This of course was just more of the crap she had come to associate with the fraudster, at least that was what she told herself. Finally, as Teacher survived the rigors of the cobbles, he began to gain in confidence and twisted his wrist to force his bike to speed up to over fifty miles per hour, reaching the T-junction at the top of the pedestrian area and a speeding river of traffic.

Zooming down the side of cars, buses and lorries, in the ditch next to the pavement, Teacher showered his fellow road users with grit and gravel, some chipping the expensive blue tinted windscreen of the Mayor's Jag as it slowed to join the evening's rush hour traffic jam.

"What the hell's going on," he yelled as Sally came down the other side of him. "Sergeant Reid!" he shouted as he recognised her leather-clad bottom. But she heard no more than her own engine and the screeching of her brakes coming on and off and so ignored him. He smacked his hand on the steering wheel in frustration; he was running out of fuel and couldn't get a fill-up as the petrol stations were all closed having no power, forcing he and most others, to travel up to

Chillborough, blocking up the roads for miles.

Teacher had a full tank of petrol and with his chin on the handlebars, hair, beard and robes flying behind him comic book style, he pulled away out into the countryside. Sally did likewise, the growl of her 750 becoming smoother and higher pitched as the revs increased, whilst also becoming quieter as the wind streamlined around her helmet. Coming now to a long blind right hand bend, Teacher, as he had seen in all the rally bike championships on the early morning TV, leant into it whilst putting a foot down to graze the tarmac as he did so. He was intent on accelerating and disappearing, but didn't noticed the two deliberately placed police warning signs and was upon a tailback of traffic before he knew it. True to his wayward control, he rolled the bike over the other way, mounted the pavement and hurtled past the entire queue, only to come face-to-face with a grim looking traffic cop. With gritted teeth and black eyes staring out from beneath his peaked white hat, the cop thrust the flat of his hand firmly in front of the oncoming bike and commanded Teacher to stop!

"Just what on my bleedin' road, do you think you are doing," he yelled at Teacher who had no choice but to pull up in front of him. "You won't have even seen the signs about the accident ahead and truthfully, I'm amazed there hasn't been another one behind you. You are incompetent."

"Yes, Officer."

"Is that all you have to say for yourself?"

"Yes, Officer."

"Well then," the cop said, disbelieving of Teacher's sincerity.

"There hasn't been any problem, Officer and nobody's been hurt by me," Teacher said looking at him with eyes as wide as cow crap on a flat rock.

"However," the cop said not being able to look away from Teacher's determined eyes, there hasn't been any problem and lucky for you, nobody's been hurt."

"So, I may as well be on my way," Teacher said revving the bike's engine loudly.

“So, you may as well be on your way,” said the cop, “good day to you, Sir.”

“Good day,” Teacher replied as he opened up the bike’s throttle once again before screeching off down the road whilst laughing at the ease at which he had escaped. Ahead was the accident that was causing the traffic jam, a battered old milk float had a lightweight kit car embedded on its back where the deliveries should be. Copious bottles of milk displaced all around were still asking what had happened as Teacher mounted the kerb and skirted around the mess. He looked back to see if Sally had been detained too and was no longer following him, but she had merely flashed her police warrant card at the spaced-out cop and was closing on him once again.

Sally was probably nearer now than she had been since leaving town. Teacher looked again to try and estimate just how near she was to him and determine what he was going to do about it. However, this was fatal as in not paying attention to the road in front, he hadn't seen the approaching traffic island that stood in his way with cars, vans and lorries all stationary around it. “Nooooooo,” he shouted as he shot between a vintage bubble car and a pizza delivery van, hitting the kerb as he continued in a straight line, mounting the island with a Bond-style leap. This may not have been a problem in town, where all the little islands were merely circles of white paint, but here in the country it was policy to plant some trees and shrubs around a central feature, in this case a picturesque pond. There was a screaming of brakes from the bike as Teacher, still hanging on to the handlebars, ploughed through the shrubs shredding the flowers as he went, then with an almighty splash he drove straight into the murky water. How the bike didn't stop was a matter for debate but it slid instead through the mud and blanket weed until it emerged on the other side with a very green and muddied Teacher still hanging on for grim death, whilst spitting out mouthfuls of grass, gravel and frogs’ spawn. Sally couldn't believe what she had just seen. Picking her way through the traffic she was expecting to see him now wrapped around the metal chevrons or at least still wallowing in the pond like a baby elephant on some summer evening in the Serengeti. But she reacted instinctively and dutifully following the mud and detritus spread across the road, until she pulled away to continue her pursuit.

The road off from the island was more of a country lane with high hedgerows on either side that made it difficult to see ahead, especially as the route snaked about keeping Sally from increasing her speed, fearing the oncoming traffic that might be in the middle of the road. Not that this mattered as Teacher had gone through an open farmer's gate and was now hurtling his way through a field of cows as they bolted in every direction. Maybe not at the same gateway, but Sally as soon as she realised, pulled off too. She was slipping and sliding on the grass having lost all grip, until she coaxed her bike to point in the right direction and closed to head Teacher off, before he could get to the woodland he appeared to be heading for.

Fortunately, Teacher had pulled off one gateway sooner than he wanted and as Sally had now found her route better defined by some vehicle tracks, she benefitted from a better traction. Teacher did not and therefore found her gaining on him quickly as they came to the top of the hill. They began to close as they approached the woodland together, like a synchro pair of Red Arrows, albeit fifty meters apart. Passing a little dilapidated sign, Sally could just about make out that she was entering Leedly Woods, which she made a mental note of as she tentatively guided her now dirt-clad machine between the trees and off to the right on an intercept course.

It was starting to get dark, especially under the shade of the heavily covered trees and what light there was threw dark shadows out in front of her. The only relief she had from having to concentrate so fully, being the glinting reflections of the shimmering trunks of the silver birch trees. It wasn't a very big piece of woodland having been cut back over the years to make way for arable land, but it had survived as there was a protrusion of rock in the middle that perplexed even the sharpest plough. Sally was never one to be frightened by a criminal, armed or not, but she was nervous now as she found

Teacher's entrance point at the edge of the wood but nothing more. She revved the bike's engine guiding it in between clouds of gorse and vivid bracken, through the deep undergrowth, to where he might be hidden, but in this cover, it was anybody's guess.

Dismounting then, she walked around the woods' perimeter thinking that she might find an exit point and perhaps see Teacher riding off over some adjacent field. But she couldn't find any trace of him, which seemed too strange to be true and she was just considering what to do next when suddenly she put her foot down a small rabbit hole and fell, twisting as she did so until she was flat on her back. She cursed heavily as she tried to pick herself up only to find yet again, that she was stuck tight as if grabbed by a giant magnet deep within the bowels of the earth. She was angry as she knew this was all a state of mind, a result of Teacher's hypnotic staring as she fell onto the road in Chillborough. However, she still couldn't get out of the bath at home without dragging herself up on the shower hose!

So, she lay for an hour at least, looking up through the canopy as the sky darkened and the stars began to wink back at her. Until with no warning or comprehension she found herself standing at the top of the approach road, adjacent to the Leedly Woods' sign, right next to her bike, which had been started and was sitting purring ready for her to climb onto and ride away. She ran a curious hand over her head, looking for the stand out bump that must have given rise to a concussion she thought. Not finding anything untoward, she was still frightened and thought it best to withdraw and report back to the Superintendent. She had lost Teacher once again even though she could still hear him in her head, like a jackass on speed.

FELONIOUS EVAPORATION

By the following Friday morning, after spending a monotonous night at his mother's house in Chillborough, Mayor Brian made his way to the town hall. He knew his position was one of responsibility and that people were looking to him to solve the power problem, but despite this, he never expected the reception he received as he turned into the car park and came under fire from a barrage of objects, being thrown by an angry crowd. There were umpteen Coke cans, half rotten apples and several cuts of meat that had clearly gone off, all bouncing off his back and head as he ran for the entrance. Thank God there were no bricks or stones, he thought, but these had been thrown through the windows at the front of the still dark building, where police with wobble board shields and pepper sprays were thankfully faring better than he.

By 8:30 am, the electricity had been off for thirty-six exhausting hours. Shops were doing their best to bring in fresh produce from neighbouring areas and stay open, but the incidences of shoplifting had become so frequent and the nature of it so blatant, that many retailers had simply battened down the hatches and closed. Having no electricity was one thing, but having no gas or oil due to the logistical problems of delivery, meant that most families were struggling. The only exceptions to this, were those that had a Scout member, instructed by Brian when doing their campers' badge, that were cooking on portable stoves or lighting fires in the back garden. This was fine but there had already been several incidences that resulted in the fire brigade being called for, including one over-enthusiastic Patrol Leader that had managed to burn down his father's shed and 00-gauge railway. On balance, things were getting serious, serious enough for Brian to call an early meeting of the 'Tutelage' committee, his conceptual crisis group that was good and effective in many ways and would put measures in place to deal with such situations.

As the suited members gathered like penguins huddled in a blizzard, the talk was of nothing but the letter from the blackmailer, the one that Brian had thrown away. Some condoned him without so much as a glimpse of the content, others were more open-minded but just irritated as they had no milk for their tea. Some were quite philosophical, including his right-hand man, Joe, who commented that everything happens for a reason and so if he felt he had to verbally punch Brian, well at least it would be justified. But each in turn did finally agree that the decision not to pay was probably correct and that given the threat was for the outage to last at the most three days, which seemed to be in keeping with Henry's estimate at the power station, they would rely on the local police and volunteer services to brave it out.

* * *

By 10:30 am, back at the Clearwater market, Guido and Betty were both sat behind the Prime Pal and Bakers Complete, arm in arm singing away like two over-loved budgerigars. They had worked their way through The Barber of Seville and Semiramide, Rossini being a love of Guido's, but had noted that such classics were difficult to join in with and so were trying things a little more well-known and up-to-date. Betty stood to take the stage and sang with all modern vibe. "You know I hate to ask, but are friends electric, because mine's broke down, and now I've no one to love."

"I'll name that tune in one!" shouted Tubby from behind a line of blustery knickers, who was gazumped virtually immediately.

"Gary Numan from the album of the same name." Lucy scored a fist in the air, as Betty was off again on a rendition of the Electric Light Orchestra's greatest hits, as Guido provided the accompaniment on his air violin.

As the hilarity eased its way back down to the more usual boredom, the stallholders were becoming more and more infuriated at seeing candle after candle wrapped and despatched from the Treasure Trove stall. Teacher was questioning his workers, "Why is this half of the stall bare?" he asked pointing.

"We've no stock left Bach, tis all gone, isn't it?" Owen looked a little warily at Teacher, given that he was clearly thinking he didn't know what, whilst twirling his great white beard around his index finger.

"Give out the rest of the candles to the other traders and clear the stall," Teacher ordered acknowledging Owen's 'ok' sign with a slight nod of his head. He then made his way over to Sandra and Susan. "Ladies," he began, "I trust you have been making some good money during this period of power outage?" He knew what the answer would be.

"No, the only thing that's been selling around here are your bleedin' candles," Susan said as Sandra agreed, both with hands on hips, "unless of course you've come to put in a bulk order as you did with Tubby?" she added.

"I am keen to be a fellow trader in the eyes of the gods and not someone that would exploit the misguided," he said calmly and considerately, but still managing to offend Sandra, who was, she thought, by no means misguided.

"So," she said.

"I would like to purchase some bottles of water."

"What, the mineral water, still, fizzy, what?"

"All types please," he continued.

"One of each? Or we have some multipacks," Sue said taking over from her sister thinking that any sale was a sale at least.

"All of it," Teacher replied calmly as he took his oversized purse out from the swaths of robing around him.

"All of it," Sandra looked confused.

"Yes, every drop," he said which had Susan tapping away on her calculator until the ball of her finger began to blister.

"I've just over five hundred bottles at a quid each. I could let them go for five hundred pounds exactly, do you a bit of discount?" Susan was thinking that she had to be constructive to close the deal.

"Thank you," said Teacher as he pulled a bundle of notes from his purse and began counting twenties out in front of her. "There we are, five hundred. I'll have Joe come across and fetch them."

"Err well, thank you," said the stunned pair who even though they had been counting along with Teacher, gathered up every note to count it again.

The other stallholders had been watching Teacher's interchange with the girls. Some were pleased to see the nicer side of their new compatriot, but some were wary as was Johnny, who Teacher approached next.

"Have you any water, squash, or fizzy drinks?" Teacher asked.

"None for sale," Johnny said with a wry smile.

"I can see many cans, bottles and cartons," Teacher pointed out.

"Not for sale, my friend," Johnny replied as in studying the Treasure Trove stand, Owen and Joe, he had concluded that there was something a little bit fishy going on. He believed that he might be better allying himself to whatever strategy Teacher was working to, to perhaps ride on the back of it.

"Ah, do we have a smart man in our midst?" Teacher said wryly.

"Oh, I'm definitely a smart man," said Johnny standing proud like a veteran on Remembrance Day.

"Really," said Teacher. "Mighty Belanos may well advise you Johnny that the difference between a smart man like you and a wise man like me, is that you might know what to say, but I know whether to say it or not." He turned abruptly and began walking away as Johnny either couldn't think of how to reply or thought better of it.

As Joe and Owen began collecting the bottles of water from Susan and Sandra, Teacher returned to his empty stall, which was now looking quite forlorn amongst the others. But instead of trying to help with its re-stocking, he climbed up and sat upon it cross-legged with his wrists on his knees and hands facing up to the sky. As he closed his eyes, Betty jabbed Guido in his ribs. "Wouldn't it be better to wait until his stand's full again before going through another diabolical opening ceremony?"

"He's meditating," Guido explained having practiced a similar thing when a crisis of confidence hit him and his creativity in terms of new flavours of ice cream deserted him.

"Ommmm, Ommmm," Teacher began to chant as he searched for the mantra within him that would guide him and protect him and perhaps more importantly draw a crowd around him, thinking it was some impromptu circus performance. "To Apsu, my god of the Enuma Elish, Belanos is pleased with you and I, his one remaining disciple, for reducing the state of man to its humble beginnings. Never again will they trifle with the light that has been afforded them, never again will they trivialise a threat made on behalf of the mighty Belanos. And in conclusion, I beseech you Apsu, to release them." Teacher looked down now as if waiting for an almighty flash of lightning or crack of thunder, only to wait for seconds until the clock reached 11 am exactly when Sebastian's radio sparked into life and the lights in Johnny's caravan café flickered and came on.

"My good god, he's brought the power back on, how the hell did he do that?" Johnny blurted out, convinced that he had discovered the Messiah, with some sort of all powerful wizardry that had come back in time to manipulate the world and its future.

* * *

Also promptly at 11 am, Brian was rewarded for two hours of 'what if, maybe this, perhaps we should,' as the electricity came on and staff around the council building with tired eyes, broke into a round of applause.

"Thank heavens for that," Brian said, knowing that Henry had promised to turn it back on at the top of the hour, but he was under instructions not to say anything in case this turned out to be wrong. Woe be tied should the committee find out that he knew this two hours ago. This was however, somewhat immaterial in the eyes of his secretary, Miss Fulton, who had released the time over email, Facebook and text messaging as soon as Henry reported the fact to the office at 9 am that morning. The beaming debutant had also invited herself into the subsequent meeting of the committee, carrying the mail more as an excuse to flaunt the 'I told you so', glint in her eye. Brian tried as much as his libido would allow, to ignore this, but in finding his gaze wholly distracted by her sexy lines and rounded bottom, he took the mail from her with a wink in his eye. "Thank you, Miss Fullsome," he blurted out correcting himself almost instantaneously, "sorry, sorry, Miss Fulton!" he said but his mistake had been noted and recorded in blood as she left with a sexy grin across her powdered face. In truth, he really couldn't be bothered with the pile of letters bestowed upon him, but a little gremlin that had made its home in the back of his head was banging a veritable sledge hammer around his nervous system, to remind him of what happened last time. So, he glanced at it; what harm could it do he told himself? Then he opened it, tax office, parks and recreation, school closures and then in a silk envelope with urgent marked upon it, the words 'As the mighty Belanos said'...

As a sixty-three-year-old man, Brian had been so keen to collect the baton and take a greater part in the relay of council life. But he wasn't as fit as he might be and his attempt to react to the letter by shooting out of his seat as if it were a starting block, was only complicated by his full and failing bladder. "Shit," he said as his legs gave way and he sank to his knees. He couldn't really avoid being noticed now as all the members that had seen him fall and heard his expletive, had fallen silent. So, he shrugged his overburdened shoulders, stood and read the letter aloud: "*On this, the second occasion of your testings, you will be minded to prevent a further calamity befalling Clearwater town. As the Lord said unto Moses, take thy rod, stretch out thine hand upon the waters, upon the streams, upon the rivers, and upon all the pools of water, that they may become blood. As you believe you defeated me in terms of your first testing and did not pay my ransom of twenty-five thousand pounds, I will now require an amount of fifty thousand pounds, paid today into the Swiss account detailed below. Or, I will stretch forth my hand and a plague of the waters will fall over your town of Clearwater. Be minded of course that there were seven calamities that befell Egypt and that they may all befall you if you are inadequate in compliance.*" The letter was signed again in what looked like hieroglyphics.

"Oh, my very good god," exclaimed Joe, Brian's deputy. "Who is this man?" he said as the small, round pair of glasses ledged on the end of his nose, steamed up completely.

"Or woman," added Miss Fulton, who now fully informed of all the facts was strutting around as happy as a beach babe in St Tropez.

"Well then, Mr Mayor," the committee chairman warned as he rounded on him, "how much will this cost us if you refuse to meet these demands?"

"We shouldn't give in," Brian reiterated. "We shouldn't pay the money, but we should put out an alert to the water-board. He or she, must break in to one of their installations to affect the water from the tap. And," he went on, "we should call the police at Chillborough Police station again."

* * *

Superintendent Daniels, having received notification of the latest extortion attempt, was only more convinced in his own mind, that the shenanigans to do with the electricity going off, coupled with Teacher materialising like some returning alien abductee, were no coincidence. So much so, that he had already put together a contingency plan in readiness and ensured that those members on the team weren't working on anything else. And so, Detective Sergeant Sally Reid, Sergeant Jock McCall and Police Constable Susan Jetsome, known as "Jet" to the staff at Chillborough nick, were now sat in the briefing room awaiting their instructions.

Jet was new to the team and had little experience of undercover work before, being only the liaison between uniform and operatives in a recent over-complicated affair, to pin down a team of drug runners that were growing cannabis across the town. This clever little plan was perpetrated without the realisation of several partially green-fingered gardeners, that were underusing their allotments. They found on their rare visits to their plot, that someone had been digging and growing their own plants there, then harvesting and selling the product across the poorer communities.

Jet was well-liked by most of those that she worked with, becoming known as 'the girl with the smile', something she had originally developed to hide the abuse she received at home as a teenager.

Sally was on the team as it was her that had the experience of dealing with Teacher in the past. She liked to be recognised by those working under her, liked to be the senior person and was expecting to command the operation. She felt she had earnt the right. She knew already that she would have Jet follow her lead and handle things more by direction than on her own initiative, but also knew that in working with Jock, she would have to reason with him more, to get what she wanted.

Jock was as predictable and reliant as he was modest; he had been on the force since the big bang and commanded much respect, from the senior management to the new rookie. He was there, incognito as far as Sally was concerned, as the Super wanted a man to report back to him. However, if asked, Jock would insist it was only because he had been the last out of the Transit as it returned from the power station.

"Sally, I want you to lead the operation, for two reasons," Daniels began. "One, you know Teacher, what to expect from him and how best to catch him at it, but also from an undercover point of view. Two, you are compromised already, having been so heavily involved at Briars Brook and then again at the hospital the other day. Be warned though, I know your limitations young lady and am not convinced that putting a woman in charge is the right thing to do!"

Sally made a move to protest but was cut off as the Super raised the volume of his voice, "however, it is up to you to prove me wrong. You will have the security of Jock by your side, should you need a man to fall back on." Jock glanced at Sally and smiled; he knew only too well of the Super's predilection for a male-orientated force and was in actuality, as keen as Sally to prove him wrong.

Jet looked in anticipation at Daniels. "In this last respect, yes Jet, I am putting you in as the undercover officer. I know you wanted a role like this, so don't let me down!" Jet let out a little squeak of appreciation and punched the air, grinning at Jock who grinned back, but not before Sally lifted a 'back of the classroom' arm into the air.

"But I ask ya, Sir, do you really think she's experienced enough for this?" she said, firstly because she wanted the role herself and secondly because she hadn't been given the autonomy to choose her own undercover team.

"We all have to start somewhere Sally," Daniels said.

"But wi' Teacher," she argued. "I have all the experience, have worked hard over the years and know that she will not be able to handle a man such as him. He's manipulative, hypnotic, in an evil way, and positively dangerous. You can't put someone with no or little experience into this team, not without dire consequences!"

"Well that's where ye come in, isn't it," Jock interjected strategically. "Ye need to be imparting all that bonny knowledge an' all that bonny understanding, lass. I might suggest that the pair of yous spend an hour or two just chatting aboot things, before the main event."

"Quite right," Daniels said, "to formulate some sort of a plan for inserting Jet into the operation." Jet looked a little upset at Sally's protest, but was pleased, nevertheless.

"We should start Sir, by attending the water works in Clearwater, do yous not agree Sally?" Jock asked.

"No, we should start by having the scene of crimes' officer have a look at that letter. We have Teacher's prints here on file after he was arrested, all we have to do is match them with it and we've got him, simple as that!"

"Steady on, it only proves that he wrote the letter. You're going to need more than that, Sally," said the Super as he lifted his desk telephone and asked the records department to send up the results of the fingerprint test. "He was printed wasn't he? I did ask at the time, didn't I?"

"Aye," said Jock, "I did them mysen, ye canni rely on the rockies Sir, they're just numtees." The Super nodded as the little group sat waiting, asking themselves if they would be needed after all.

After a few minutes of trembling, scene of crime officers jumping through hoops to satisfy the demands of those on-high, the file arrived. The Super looked at it briefly at first, then closer, before his head sank into his hands. "It seems that the prints you took, you Scottish pillock, have been identified as belonging to a PC Jock McCall! You didn't chance to look Teacher in the eyes, did you?"

Sally said little, she believed she had been side-lined again, with Jock appointed to look over her, but his clear ineptitude had helped her to agree, all be it begrudgingly, to taking on the role. After all, 'the game was back on', she told herself, as the Super picked up the telephone to confirm all arrangements with Brian at the Mayor's office.

THE IMPURITY OF CLEARWATER

"What the friggin' hell is he up to?" Johnny asked himself from his café as he started to increase the price of his soft drinks by fifty percent.

"Vat is it to you? You Englishers are as bonkers as bumble bees trapped in ze green houses," Sebastian shouted across the tables and chairs.

"And how would you bloody know," Johnny shouted back, "although he might be right this time," he added under his breath knowing he had taken a gamble.

Guido and Betty were at it again, 'water' being the theme seeing as it was amassed as if some sort of African crisis was about to hit. "Like a bridge over troubled water," Guido began as Betty stepped forward to join him with some aquatic harmonies, followed by skits and pranks such as 'Water difference a day makes', which had even Sandra moaning at how corny the two impresarios were becoming.

"Do you think we should buy some water?" Tubby asked of Lucy as he too had been watching the Treasure Trove stocks swelling like blocks of ice stacked around Ice Station Zebra. She poo-pooed him at first, only then to remember how appreciative the two of them had been for the candles. They had only just reconsidered when there came a giant hiss of air breaks from a huge tanker lorry, full of chemicals with angry warning signs all over it, pulling into the car park. Teacher knew what it was and what was being said by the market stallholders, who he needed to keep sweet.

"Watt."

"Teach," Joe acknowledged.

"Deliver one of those supermarket twelve packs of water to every stallholder with my compliments," he said in all seriousness.

"Right away boss," Joe replied looking forward to doing a job where he might be regarded as one of the team, a bringer of gifts nonetheless, despite the slight aroma of sewerage. Teacher would have done this himself had he not upped quickly to receive the tanker. "Concentrated orange squash?" Joe asked grazing the limits of over-familiarity, not knowing just how close he was to the truth.

"You've well been told Bach, what be going on over by 'ere has nowt to do with ewe. And, don't ye be ridiculing the man that be paying your wages," Owen said as he heard his quip. "Now get on with your deliveries."

There was a pleasant mood sweeping across the market, along with another rendition, "Wa-ter you want to make those eyes at me for…" sang a shaking Guido, with Betty 'doo-wopping' on the side and Susan and Sandra hand-jiving across the way.

"Entertaining!" Joe thought as he completed his deliveries, but before he could sit down again, he was called by Teacher to join him in the car park. "Have you finished delivering that water?" he asked.

"No worries, Teach," he replied with a grin designed to ask for a thank you or well done, but none came.

"Come along here, another job," Teacher shouted. "I need someone to drive the tanker I have hired, as the driver has now left." Joe was relieved that he had been asked and as he had driven large lorries before, he jumped up into the driving seat as pleased as punch. After a short while, with Teacher in the passenger seat, the monster crept out of the car park. As Joe got more and more used to the large steering wheel and the power that was in his hands, he began cruising comfortably through the town and countryside, affording such a panoramic view from the lofty seats that Joe saw things he had never seen before. Teacher sat quietly until a change in direction was required, directing with a brief left or right which Joe followed explicitly. As they approached a large roundabout at the edge of town, they passed a police transit from Chillborough nick. Sally was sat in the front driving seat and had to slow as the tanker just having the edge on her came onto the island. She looked up to where Teacher was sat still composed, looking down at her, as good as into each other's eyes, but whether she was blinkered or just not as aware as she might be, she merely waved at him as if to acknowledge the tanker's right of way. Teacher laughed quietly to himself as he waved back, but the transit merely followed on behind before turning off to head towards the local water works.

Having built up speed to that of a charging knight on a great white horse, the tanker was at the point that if Teacher said stop it would take some distance to do so. But fortunately, before a turn to the left, he began asking Joe to slow down, until at a lazy twenty miles an hour they turned down a narrow lane, towards the river. As the trees around increased in number and size, sight of the sky above became patchy as the canopy arched over the road, until finally the water itself came into sight. Pulling up at a sharp left hand bend, Teacher directed Joe to climb down out of the idling tanker and open the double gates in the hedgerow just ahead. This he did, then climbing back into the cab he coaxed the vehicle through and across a field of meadow grass that sat up obediently as they passed over it, disguising their ground behind them. Finally, they stopped with a shock of air-brakes, tucked into a small cutting that the river charged through, just before discharging itself into the vastness of Lake Yaramar, the only recognised water board reservoir in the Clearwater area.

Joe, still enthused by the apparent new found faith in him, then helped Teacher in detaching the corrugated hosing from the carriers, suspended under the tanker. Joe's only clue to what was inside were the 'HAZARD' signs upon the fuselage which gave several telephone numbers or codes, advising the emergency services of how to treat the contents should they be spilt. It was obvious what was to happen now as Teacher threw the free end of the hose into the river and then proceeded to open a multitude of valves on the tanker. Joe sat down on the grass, his legs dangling over the cutting wall as with a whoosh the corrugated hose swelled and then spat a thick red food dye into the water. The effect was instantaneous as the bubbling water, foaming and splashing its way down the gradient, turned to the colour of blood, thunderously at first but then more diluted as it made its way into the reservoir and onwards to the water treatment plant and the town's residents.

"Fantastic!" Joe shouted as he turned towards Teacher and tapped the side of his head showing him that he understood what was happening. Teacher smiled a rare smile. After nearly half an hour the flow rate seemed to slow and a strange gurgling came from the tanker as it emptied itself of the last dregs. Finally, as the end of the hose was spluttering and intermittent, the last of the dye became more like sludge. "Right, pull it in then," Teacher commanded. So, Joe jumped up with his continued enthusiasm.

"Don't suppose Owen knows about this?"

"Need to know Joe, and he doesn't need to know," Teacher replied predictably, which humoured him all the same.

"Quite right!" Joe said swinging around to acknowledge his boss. Suddenly however, without warning, a good part of the grass cutting where he had been sitting, crumbled and he found himself skating down the cutting wall until he hit the liquid filled basin below. He should have splashed into the water, but with all the dye, he fell in with no more than a 'gloup'.

* * *

Meanwhile, Sally had arrived at the water works with Jock in tow, to assess the grounds and make any arrangements to prevent any break-ins. Mayor Brian had too and made himself ready to liaise with the water works staff. They started by explaining what does what and how. "These are the water inlet pipes," said an engineer, pointing to two great mild steel pipelines that emerged from their underground journey and entered the works, like two grey worms from a giant's garden. "They go across here," he continued as he walked slowly around the site, "into the filter bays, where the water is cleansed of all debris etc." He stopped and pulled open some metal panelling for the party to look down inside one of the tanks, which they did as a shock suddenly ran across their faces.

"Is it supposed to look like that?" asked Brian as he looked in. "It's got a red tinge to it," he said, making the obvious look totally obvious.

"What! Oh my God," said the engineer who, having not been fully briefed, broke out in a cold sweat. "It's never been like that before."

"He's beaten us to it," said Sally.

"I can't believe it, something's happened to the supply up-stream towards Lake Yaramar," the engineer said pointing, as Sally, overhearing the panic, grabbed her radio and called for additional support. There would be little or no time for an assessment.

* * *

Jet had started her undercover campaign by being dropped off earlier in the town and was now visiting the Clearwater market. She had sat for a coffee and a bacon bap, a lorry drivers' lunch, at Johnny's Café. By using her slim lines and brunette flush, she had him fussing about her like a pauper in the presence of royalty, her coffee forever being topped up and biscuits of all description visiting her saucer. "You do have some characters here, don't you," she said looking over the fussing stallholders, smiling in admiration at their community spirit.

"Too right, there's Tubby our butcher over there, who has a fetish for his girlfriend's knickers on the neighbouring stall, nice girl Linda. There's Susan and Sandra on the sweeties, Betty on the pets' stall and Guido on the musical ice creams."

"Musical?"

"Oh yes, sings as he whips his tutti frutti, all opera and the like, absolutely hysterical. Then there's him, the bleeding Kraut opposite me here, far too bleeding far from home and too bleedin' close to me!"

"Oh, don't be like that, he's probably a really nice bloke."

"Back in Germany maybe!"

"That's just being prejudice!"

"Whatever."

"What about him there?" Jet said changing the subject and pointing at Owen who was sat behind towers of mineral water.

"Bit weird, that lot. They keep trying, but I don't really regard them as a part of the market community. There's three of them normally, including what looks like the ghost of some Glastonbury hippy. They sell weird things, one minute candles, now water. Busy as bleedin' bees one minute, as slow as Christmas the next."

"Ah, that will be them, then." She made a mental note of the summary she had been afforded. "Do you know, I'm so in awe of your setup here and how everyone knows everyone else. Tell me, you got any jobs going?" she asked.

"I'd love to 'ave you 'ere darlin', you seem to be really nice, always smiling. Unfortunately, my overheads and bank manager are killing me and I couldn't. Your best bet will be to ask the hippies, there only ever seems to be one or two of them there."

* * *

Back at the water works, Sally and Jock had the maps of the local area, spread out on an oversized desk and were planning how best to cover the river, the lake above it and the river above the lake. Outside, the brilliance of the blue sky, on this Friday afternoon and the still of the water resulted in imagery that could be viewed either way up and it still not be possible to tell which was the sky and which was the water. Jock made himself comfortable; he was to remain behind at the works to act as radio co-ordinator, his battered legs from years of police patrolling and drunken mules on the late shift, dictated as much. Whereupon, another police transit pulled into the car park, with three extra support officers, who introduced themselves as PCs Neville Bryant and Andrew Nebley, clearly fit and agile, unlike PC Kylie Brook who far from her namesake was vertically challenged and rather overweight. Brian was keen to help too and so installed himself alongside Jock, where he could keep up with bulletins from the filter plant as to the current state and shade of the water.

"On a scale of one to ten, one being clear and transparent and ten being blood red, we are currently experiencing a three," he reported over the radio, to Sally and to the council offices. He was looking more and more worried as his back of the mind Gremlin began to beat its drum again, louder at each increment.

After only an hour, the water at the works was a true blood red, whilst water from the tap in town had already begun to be tinged red which, although people were commenting upon, did nothing to dissuade them from drinking it, even if some had resorted to boiling it 'just in case'. But as the Mayor's situation reports increased on the scale from three to five, questions were being asked by opportunist journalists, insurance companies and plumbers whose emergency call-outs had trebled. Brian had a plan already agreed with the members of the committee which allowed for a public announcement at a point when it was thought that panic might ensue.

"This is Billy Tremble at Clearwater 75 FM bringing you all the sounds and news from your area. This is Friday, top of the hour, 3 pm. Always a thrill with Bill, there's news breaking here and now; a minor problem at the Clearwater water works resulting in our tap water being tinged red. But Mayor Brian has assured us that this is not a problem and that it IS safe to drink!" As Brian heard this over the radio playing away in the little office at the water works, he was well chuffed and just about to relax his Gremlins when the DJ followed things up with a little quip. "Hey folks, this sounds like one of them Egyptian curses that Moses received from God. Awesome!"

"Jesus H Christ!" Brian answered in kind, "what's he gone and done now, he's probably got the whole Christian church claiming there's been a bloody resurrection! In fact, when I get my hands on him there will be blood!"

Sure enough, as soon as the news was out, the media leaders were off. As fast as they could, they re-worded everything for best effect, especially an analogy to the Egyptian plagues, firstly the power outage which answered the depriving of light, being first of the plagues, now this, the turning of all the water to blood, what next? Facebook and Twitter provided all the in-filling with photographs, the fifty greatest plagues, how to find yourself as man despite God's wrath, even alternatives to water (as if there were any). People were soon leaving houses with water tanks still full of clear pre-polluted water, in anticipation, to search every last shop and petrol station for packs of water, sparkling, diluted and in any other way shape or form, even Tesco's frozen ice bags.

* * *

Suffice to say, the water at the Treasure Trove stall in the market began to leap off the shelves, pouring itself straight into the paying hands of the public at five pounds a bottle. Teacher was off, making a killing once again, even without his main plot for blackmailing the local authority. "Can I have twelve bottles please?" Jet asked of an exasperated Owen.

"Just a minute Cariad," he said trying to serve everyone in the crowd that had just gathered and was now helping itself.

"When you're ready," Jet continued.

"As I said..." Owen replied, who had started to sweat, heavily abandoning any preoccupation of providing a pleasant customer service.

"No problem," Jet said, as Owen continued to struggle, a four pack, two singles and then a pusher-in that he had to deal with.

"I'll be over by there in just a minute."

"That's all right, when you're ready," Jet said again, seeing the pressure piling on Owen which gave her an idea.

"Just coming, just coming," Owen said again, when finally Jet put down the pack she had been standing with whilst awaiting his service and casually walked around the stall to the back where puddles of water from burst bottles were splashing underfoot and five pound notes were simply blowing away in the wind.

"Would you like some help?" she said as without his reply she reached over the stall and took the money that the crowd was trying to shove into his hands, sweeping it together like leaves from the trees in Autumn. He glanced at her; there was seemingly nothing he could do to stop her anyway and still there was no sign of Teacher or Joe, only a very definite need to sell as fast and as furiously as possible.

Johnny was as pleased as chips. He knew he was right, he knew there was something going down and he was now bringing out all his stocks of water, squash, and fizzy drinks, setting up a grand display in his café, in competition. Unfortunately, shrewd was not his forté and he priced up his stock at four pound fifty a bottle, undercutting Teacher by a full fifty pence. Clever, he thought, until a voice called to him from out of the crowd.

"He won't be liking that you know," said a man wrapped heavily from head to toe in anorak, tracksuit, hat, gloves and cling film... "make your price the same as ours," he advised. It was Joe, very much cold and shivering having bused it back from the lake after leaving Teacher and the tanker there.

Owen glanced up through the battle of customers having heard his voice. "What the hell are you doing?" he asked, noticing how red his face was. "You look like one of them prawn fishermen from off the telly!"

"I fell in the river!"

"Tell me another one," Owen said with a Cheshire grin forcing itself onto his face, "You best get them clothes off!" he said as the grin at the corner of his mouth spread rapidly like the rising sun and he began to laugh.

"I don't think so!" Joe replied.

"You'll catch a cold otherwise."

"I don't care!"

"Clothes off – or I call Teacher," Owen said opening the Star Trek cover of his mobile phone, whereupon the hilarity was complete. Standing behind the stall then with little cover, Joe peeled off his layers, revealing a bright pink crayfish with a pair of white eyes blinking on and off. Owen fell to the floor with laughter, holding his bursting sides as he went, lucky that Jet had continued to serve the continuing barrage of customers.

"My good god, I take it you fell into something more than just water?" said Owen wiping tears from his eyes, as Jet caught sight of him.

"Good grief!" she howled, "You look like Jacques the Shrimp, from Disney's 'Finding Nemo'," she said, bouncing off the quip that Owen had made.

"Ha bloody ha ha," Joe replied despondently. "Wait a minute, who the hell are you? I don't know you…" he said wide-eyed, as members of the public were now joining in with the laughter that was spreading like a virus. "Well?" he persisted, "am I supposed to know you?"

There was a slight break in the pace of sales as Jet found a moment to explain. "My name's Jet," she said with an outstretched, although maybe ill–advised hand, as another wave of water-crazed housewives advanced on the stall like zombies. "I was just giving your mate here a hand and seemed to get sucked in," she explained.

"She has been a help!" said Owen with a conciliatory tilt to his Welsh head.

"That's as may-be!!" Joe stated defiantly as Owen cast an eye over the rest of the marketplace. "Where's Teacher?"

"I don't know, he was still at the river last I looked, trying to extract the last of the dye from the tanker, said something about it being the most potent part of the delivery."

"That's as may-be but where is he now?" Owen asked. But

Joe merely shrugged his shoulders, as he didn't know and he didn't care.

* * *

Sally had partnered up with Kylie and taken the first of the police transits to cover the service roads around Lake Yaramar. Driver Kylie had been instructed to keep their speed down, thereby allowing Sally to point and focus her modest binoculars along the shoreline. This was quite difficult as Kylie being vertically challenged could barely reach the pedals and at every pot hole or disturbing twitch in the road, her rounded bottom shot off the seat like a jelly on ice and the van accelerated like a dragster until she managed to sit up again. It didn't take an expert to work out that the further they travelled from the dam at one end towards the river source at the other, the darker and thicker the dye became, so much so that it was now forcing up the algae from below the surface, leaving a matted material of tomato soup with hand-picked croutons floating on top.

"This is Five two to Five four, anything?" Sally enquired down her radio.

"Nothing here," came the reply from a breathless Andrew and Neville, who were half jogging along the far shore, as it was too uneven to take the second van. "Wait, there! I see something, there's a white figure coming towards us, quite quickly actually, yes he's dressed in white, on a bicycle believe it or not!"

"Grab him, just grab him, it's more than coincidence that he's here," Sally replied breaking radio protocol, as she instructed Kylie to put her foot down until they were leap-frogging the pot holes.

"Five two, Five four. He's heard your van and turned around, he's heading back towards the river, over."

"Ok, ok, we'll head him off, out." Sally encouraged Kylie to get back on her seat and speed up yet again as they began swerving two and fro down the dusty track.

The white figure was all over the place, still on the road-less side of the lake. The wiry briars and patches of nettles grabbing at his, now grubby, white robes as they stretched out behind him, tearing them wherever a substantial thorn persisted. Andrew and Neville were fit and running now over the plants and grasses that the bike had already flattened, as if they weren't there, gaining ground at every turn.

"Have you got him?" Sally was bawling over her open radio, which didn't allow for a response and only slowed the two men down. The bike was getting close now to the river and the heading off manoeuvre of the transit, just as Andrew was ambushed by a dirty great briar lying across his path and he fell entirely sprawled upon his face. The professionalism of the team was then amply demonstrated, such that his radio was snatched up off the floor and the chase continued by his partner.

As Kylie pulled the van around the corner with a hand-brake turn at the head of the lake; there he was, right in front of them. They continued to skid across the path blocking the way as Neville and a recovering Andrew now with burning thighs, closed in. Finally, the bike crashed up against the van's front fender and everyone fell to the floor.

Sally leapt super-humanly from the passenger seat, landing right on top of the pile of robes. "I am arresting you for the…." she hesitated not being able to see Teacher's gnarled old face and so began again, "Sir, I am arresting you for…Oh, good grief," she said looking under the robes, "he's gone, there's no one here!" She looked around as panic ensued and the officers began postulating like vultures around the van.

"He's here," shouted Kylie as she pulled a trailing arm out from under the van as Neville ran to assist her.

"I don't friggin' believe it!" Andrew cursed as he sank to his knees, seeing Kylie standing there with a twelve-year-old child caught by the scruff of his T-shirt, covered in sweat, cuts and grazes.

"He told me to Mrs! He did, really he did!" the child said as he opened a hand with a five pound note scrunched tightly inside it.

Teacher was in fact stood outside of the hire station, having returned the tanker, in nothing but his white underwear. He had given his robes to the boy at the lake, but managed to convince the receptionist that he was in fact a seasoned runner, which she seemed to accept given the odd things some would run around in. Of course, he was now stranded and so put a call into Owen at the market. "Come and fetch me in the van, Owen, and bring me a new set of robes from the container," he said, not expecting to be bombarded with more problems.

"All right Bach, I will be down there in just a jiffy, now that I have someone 'elping on the stall. Oh, without a word of a lie, we do 'ave a problem with Johnny at the café. He's undercutting us on the water he kept from selling to you; needs a bit of a slap isn't it."

"Just collect me, Owen. I will sort Johnny out once I get back," Teacher said, shivering as a runner would when just standing, waiting for a starting gun.

* * *

Mayor Brian had been keeping one eye on the state of the water in the filter plant and one ear towards Jock's radio and the unfolding chase around the lake. Both had been worsening to the point that any arrest was not forthcoming and the water had reached a seven on his scale of one to ten. What with the Facebook factor and radio gaff, the town was clearly going into some sort of melt down and drying up. The environmental agency, whose staff had a permanent office at the water works, maintained their position that the water dye was totally harmless and that the water was still potable. However, they had been making tests of the water entering the works at various points as the drift of the dye was more concentrated at the river end of the lake. Again, there was no more change to their conclusions except for one unusual thing. As the water became redder, more and more frogs had dragged themselves from the glouping surface of the water and were now sitting baking on the shoreline. There were comments at this point about a plague of frogs, but the creatures were clearly going nowhere, just settling down wherever there was a gap amongst their compatriots. Not only was this unusual, but the water having lost a lot of oxygen, was now experiencing a significant boost in the rate of algae production, all of which was very worrying and unheard of.

* * *

As Owen arrived at the tanker depot in the old van as instructed, Teacher's first concern was to put on the new set of robes and cover up his white vest and underpants. It was a surprise that the girl at the hire desk hadn't looked at him disgracefully or reported him for indecency, but Teacher blew her a kiss as he left, which in his opinion would make all the difference. Once dressed, he and Owen drove back to the market whilst the subject of the 'new help' and the challenge that Johnny had laid down by selling bottles of water, at less than the Treasure Trove price, were discussed.

Upon their arrival, Teacher couldn't stop himself from uncharacteristically laughing out loud as he clocked the now dry Joe with a crayfish suntan and contrasting bright eyes. "Oh, good grief. Give me strength, before the gods fall into turmoil," Teacher said through his laughter, taking a few notes from the biscuit tin and giving them to Joe. "For the sake of Belanos, and everyone else's sanity, go and get yourself some clothes." Having dealt with one employee, he then began to question who this new self-appointed sales assistant might be. He had no idea who she was or why she was prepared to help, being nervous of anyone he hadn't personally vetted. It was in her favour that she had offered to help and he understood that in the current economic climate, there were many down and outs scrabbling for a job. It was only a shame that her fidgeting face was such that he couldn't look long enough into her eyes to use his hypnotic skills to question her. In fact, he was just about to throw her across the precinct labelling her a sponger, thief or spy, after emptying her pockets of five pound notes of course, when he thought he heard a glimmer of truth in her final explanation.

"All right then, if you must know, I fancy the Welshman! A proper man, the tone to his voice is so smooth and he has this rough and ready way about him that is just so dreamy," she said as she looked at Owen and fluttered her long eyelashes.

"Well, it seems that Eros has spoken, and the gods finally have you sussed," the converted Teacher said looking to the heavens. "Ok then, you can come each day to help out on the stall, minimum wage though."

"Oh thank you, thank you so much," she said as she turned back to the stall to help a now blushing Owen, as Joe returned in a well fashioned 'Onesie', camouflage pattern.

"Have you seen what that creep from the café is doing, he's undercutting you!" Joe said. "Owen said you'd be furious."

"You look after the stall, sell the water and mind yourself over things that do not concern you," Teacher said.

"But you can't let him muscle in," Joe insisted.

"Thank you for your information Joe, but leave it to me," Teacher said his eyes flaring, which in this instance was enough at least to get Joe to back off and keep quiet.

After rummaging in some boxes under the stall whilst the sale of water bottles above was beginning to resemble the closing hour of trading on the stock market, Teacher detached himself from the melee and sat cross legged behind the container hidden from most of the stalls, except from Johnny's café and the towers of cut-price water that he had piled high in front of it. He composed himself, re-arranged his robes about himself and holding the flat of his hands upwards he began to search for his mantra.

"Ommmm, Ommmm, To Chalchiut, 'she of the jade skirt', goddess of the rivers, lakes and all waters, wife of the rain god, Tialoc. Send your serpents to aid a disciple of the mighty Belanos and cleanse the humans of their distrust of the gods. Allow only those that traverse your bridge to heaven to benefit from the cool waters." He raised both hands high in the sky and then in a flash pulled them down inside his robes leaving him sitting with eyes closed until in a flash the water bottles in front of the café began jumping all about, like skittles in a strike, splitting and exploding as water splashed everywhere, until the towers Johnny had created were flattened and their entire contents were gushing away down the gutter and into parched gullies.

The other stallholders looked totally shocked at what had just happened. The water bottles were self-igniting and spilling their contents like a waterfall, swamping the little islands of tables and chairs as if they were the paraphernalia of a Niagara café, seemingly shouting protests after being barged in the back. All this happened in the blink of an eye, even Sebastian put down the tools he was using to repair an old antique carriage clock and went to help. Jet was busily selling water again when out of the corner of her eye she too witnessed Johnny's misfortune, as he was now trying to save cupful after cupful from the puddles in the tarmac, rendering it more polluted than what was flowing red out of the town's taps. Jet felt sorry for Johnny and broke off what she was doing, just momentarily, to help pick up what undamaged bottles there were left. But there were few, the clear majority being totally shattered, not even dented or bent, and Jet thought she could tell why. All around in the gravel up against the kerbstones and in the dregs of the watery puddles, were grapeshot pellets fired from an air-propelled gun. Someone had done this deliberately, she deduced.

* * *

By the time Sally had gathered together the troops and taken them back to the water works, leaving the little sod that had led them up the garden path to find his own way home, Brian had declared the water quality to be at eight on his scale of ten. He knew too that blood red supplies were now arriving well into the centre of town, further frightening the population and accentuating the search and purchase of bottled water.

As the two met, Sally asked, "Have you made any movement towards paying the ransom?"

"No none, I couldn't. It was made very clear by the committee that we will not be subject to this sort of thing. If we give in now he or she will only come back at us and try again," he explained.

"Well yea, I agree with you now, but at what point would you draw the line, at what point would you pay 'im what 'e wants?" she asked in all sincerity.

"I suppose if things got that bad and someone's life was threatened, or if someone actually died."

"And you're prepared to wait until that happens?"

"What are you getting at?" Brian's head was working overtime.

"Ave you 'eard of the ten plagues of Egypt, where God speaks to Moses and tells 'im of great calamities that he is sending to Earth, to teach the people the rights and wrongs of society?"

"Yes, and?"

"Think about it, we've already had a plague of light when all the electricity went off, now a plague of water, what next? Plagues of flies, locusts, death of yer cattle and what about the death of yer first born, are ya goin' to leave it that long before you pay him off?"

"You think I should pay? And what makes you think the blackmailer is a he?"

"I'm only sayin' to be careful if you intend to continue with this policy. As for he or she, well we know it's a he, as we think we know who it is – we just have to catch him."

"So why don't you just go and pick him up?"

"Evidence, we need evidence as always." Sally sat for a moment thinking, "It might be a good idea if you agree to pay, if there's a next time, but not into his bank, pay cash, then we could set up a sting."

"A sting?"

"Yea, a handover where police and an undercover agent will be waiting for him."

"An undercover agent, are you putting someone in place?"

"Whoops - shouldn't have said really, but there is already someone in place."

"Who, what's his name?"

"Couldn't say, she wouldn't be undercover if I did?"

"So, it's a woman then?"

"Whoops, there I go again!"

"Well, I'll have to talk to the committee," said Brian attempting to pass the buck.

"You need to TELL them you need the cash, to appear capable of paying him off and provide the bait we need to catch him. If we're successful, you'll get your money back anyway."

Jock was sending a situation report back to Chillborough nick to keep the Super up to speed, especially given that they had missed another opportunity to catch and prosecute Teacher, but then as Sally said, there was still little evidence to go on. He was also concerned that Jet hadn't checked in since going undercover and so also asked the Super to send a message, something that would trigger a meeting with Jet and Sally, out of town. Sally didn't know if Jet had received the message she sent by text. She had in fact, received it but in Jet's opinion it would have compromised the progress she had already made in infiltrating Teacher's gang as a sales assistant, so she ignored it.

* * *

By 5:30 pm Owen, Joe and Jet were still being run off their feet, still selling water like it was going out with the tide. At risk of putting a downer on the figures, Teacher summoned 'Crayfish Joe' as he'd now been christened, for a job of his own.

"I want you to go up to Lake Yaramar, below the river where we emptied the dye, with the two-way radio to set up an observation post."

"To observe what?" Crayfish asked.

"You will know what when it happens, Belanos is keeping his eyes open for you and will let you know."

"But if I don't know what I'm lookin' for…" he shrugged his shoulders, "and who the hell is Belanos?"

"You would be wise to ally yourself with Belanos and even more wise not to blaspheme with him in mind. I am his disciple and just so offended," Teacher said, apparently calm and in a controlled manner, but with eyes that were flaring as he appeared suddenly several inches taller.

"Oh sorry, sorry," Joe said detecting frighteningly dark undertones. "It might be quite nice to get out into the countryside though, of course it might," he said trying to calm things down.

"Fetch yourself a takeaway and meet me at the van," Teacher said as he readied the radio and fumbled for the ignition keys from the depths of his robe pocket before ambling off leaving his exhausted sales staff, Owen and Jet, to tidy away.

"Woah, what's occurring?" Owen yelled mid-sale, as he spotted Teacher and Joe leaving. "Ok, bugger off then boys, leave it to the menials, again!" He shouted like a picket at the pit front gate, but only once he was sure that Teacher was out of earshot.

"Yea, bugger off," said Jet joining in the joke with a purposeful and over affectionate smile for the grumbling Welshman.

It seemed that Jet was going to have little opportunity to investigate Teacher, to talk to him or figure out what he was thinking, what progress he was making in extorting the council or even what he was planning next. She understood already that the stall made thousands of pounds selling bottles of water that kept arriving as singles, six packs and twelve packs all day long. But the only forward movement she appeared to have made, was in fabricating an affection for the thick set Welshman, to try and get him to divulge something, without however, having to resort to a James Bond moment with him in bed. She was beginning to believe that she might have made a mistake being so forthright, as it was he now that was making the running.

"How about a drink tonight?" he asked politely.

"Well, maybe just one, I do need an early night tonight."

"Not a problem, Cariad," he said with a smile, which Jet thought she could take one of two ways.

"Would Teacher like to join us?" she added, which had Owen looking annoyed or at least deflated.

"No, he would not," Owen replied, "I meant you and me Cariad, a bit of a date like."

"Erm," she thought carefully, "Ok then, at the Brewers Arms, 7 pm."

* * *

The Super was also concerned that Jet hadn't checked in since going under cover and so on the back of the report from Jock, he sent a text to her mobile and one to Sally's saying, 'Meet at the Crawl in fifteen minutes'. Sally begrudgingly left a half-finished pizza with stuffed crust, on the side of her plate trying to get to the meeting, but once again Jet was absent. Waiting a full thirty minutes certainly pissed Sally off and she was just about to leave when Jet finally arrived, ambling into the layby looking unconcerned about her lateness, which was infuriating. "Where the hell have you been? It was the Super that sent that text, not me, and that was nearly an hour ago," Sally said angrily, looking at her watch, "not to mention the message request I sent ya."

"I know, I know, I just couldn't get away, boss."

"One fing you have to learn young lady is the value of good support and that good support needs to be answered when it calls. Find an excuse to get away, time of the bleedin' month or something." Sally's irritated voice travelled to the top of the trees guarding the layby where it blew through the very tops until they answered it with a rustling of leaves.

"Ok! I'm sorry, it's just that it's all a steep learning curve for me," Jet said feeling that she was the one and only undercover cop ever to suffer her governor's wrath.

"I'm not asking you, I'm bleedin' telling you!" Sally said

slamming the door of compromise shut in her face. "So, what's been so important that you couldn't contact me?"

"Well, we were selling bottles of water at such a pace, if I'd have left, Owen would have asked himself why I wanted to help in the first place."

"And?" Sally wasn't satisfied and wanted more.

Jet however, was beginning to realise that whatever she said would be inadequate. Her years of living with parents that just didn't want her to grow up, didn't want her to leave the nest or have life experiences of her own, were rumbling in her stomach and she was shaking but finally reiterated, "In my opinion to break off merely to contact you would have compromised my position." There was a break in the conversation as Sally contemplated what Jet had said. She believed that she would say this again to the Super if need be, so thought it best to leave it at that.

"Look, we're expecting another of these episodes to hit the town shortly, and, it has been suggested to the Mayor that he agrees to pay next time, in cash, so in actuality, we can set up a sting. A sting in which you will play a part. So, watch out for texts, please, and meet me here again when next you're called!"

* * *

By early evening, Joe had been taken by Teacher to Lake Yaramar. He had been given an ex-military two-way radio, a pair of binoculars, of the type a twitcher would use in his back garden, and a cool box full of food. The binoculars were more for keeping an eye out for the police who had already found tracks from the tanker and the obvious site of discharge, than looking for clues to the next calamity. But being still ruddy brown in colour and wearing his camouflage onesie, he blended beautifully into the undergrowth like an army sniper, such that only the frogs, who were still vacating the now algae rich lake, could see him. Perfect cover he thought for some peace and quiet and frankly being less of a bleedin' embarrassment to the stallholders at the market.

The police had cordoned off the discharge site, although for who's sake it wasn't clear as there was no one around, not even the occasional hiker. There had been police patrols walking slowly around all the local roads and footpaths, whilst carrying big black bin liners and rubber gloves to bag anything interpreted as evidence. Jock felt himself well suited to the terrain around the river, being heath and moorland; he even felt like nipping home to fetch his kilt which thanks to the briars and thistles would tickle his fancy all day long.

It seemed, however, that all was quiet now and that the patrols had all but given up, which allowed Joe to hunker down with his MP3 and listen to his musical favourites for the evening and possibly the night. What it was that Teacher wanted him to look out for, certainly wasn't obvious and so he treated most of the experience like he did those years ago as a youth, when he would go on fishing trips with his father. In fact, he could see something in Teacher that reminded him of his father. It certainly wasn't the way he dressed, but maybe the controlled manner in which he dished out instructions, never letting his anger get the better of him, keeping himself to himself, to the point that Joe would now wait on his every word, hoping to receive a 'well done' or a 'thank you'.

* * *

Jet had dressed herself up, but not to restaurant standard, only café or bar. She didn't want Owen to think she was going out for the entire night as she was certainly not to be hanging on a line until he reeled her in. She had combed her black hair down from the ponytail she normally wore and what with her white tasselled top and jeans, she looked very much a 'Dolly Parton' fan, but for the boobs, she unfortunately told herself. Nevertheless, she arrived at the Brewers Arms earlier than she had said, so she bought herself a glass of house red and sat looking about the typical old-time photographs on the walls. Then, almost scaring the living day lights out of her, Owen tapped her on the shoulder. "Do you come here often?"

"Only to meet muscly Welshmen," she said turning to greet him.

"Well, Welsh I am Cariad, but more cuddly than muscly," he said optimistically as they both sat down.

"Another drink?" he asked.

"House red please," she said, as he waved at the bar-tender and mouthed the order.

"Oh, is this your local?" she asked.

"I 'ave a fiew," he replied relaxing into his Welsh accent, "but it's not yours."

"What makes you think that?"

"Well, Cariad, if I were female I wouldn't be 'ere. Not unless I were with a big cuddly Welshman," he replied, which amused her and confirmed that she did like the man, despite his dubious occupation and notorious associate.

"How did you come to know Teacher, then?" she asked.

"I down't really know. He came to me after I were made redundant from the pow-wer station and what with my qualifications in diving, he said I would be ideal. To tell you the truth, I don't know him even now, he's not someone you come to know. I believe he's not of this world, isn't it."

"He seems an amiable chap, a bit weird maybe," Jet said looking for additional comment.

"He's all right, beyond a smile a lot of the time, pretty well in control of himself, but I'll tell you what it is right, Cariad, down't you ever cross him. He had two foreign guys working for him a while back that were arrested when he just disappeared into thin air; they had some 'arsh words for 'im. There's been coppers from all over the world trying to get their hands on him, but not one that could make anything stick. He's a clever bugger!"

"What's he done that's so wrong?" Jet said continuing to pick over her subject.

"Oh, come on, surely you've realised, 'who else sells candles during a power cut and water during a pollution problem; he'll 'ave us diggin' 'oles right enough, if the crematorium breaks down!" She laughed to trivialise what she was hearing as she had to get to the point of being included, to provide the evidence the police would need if he was to be arrested.

"So why are you still here then, if you think so badly of him?"

"The money, what else. He's promising Joe and I a five-figure sum, plus a cut of the profits made from selling candles, water and the like."

"So, what's next, what's he up to?" she said, as the need for information became the driving force in her conversation.

"I down't know to be truthful, he has this sayin', he does."

"Yes, the need to know principle," she acknowledged.

"All I do know is, that Joe's his golden boyo at the minite, he hasn't even given me a cluw."

"Do you think you're falling out of favour?"

"Quite possibly Cariad, just so long as he has my money!" Owen replied with his fingers crossed.

"What would make you leave and go somewhere else?" Jet was gaining in confidence and starting to probe a little deeper, getting under his skin to the point that the itch could be scratched.

"A need to carry on the evening with a nice girl from the pub," he finally said, changing the subject like the damned Welsh weather.

"Oh yes?" she said quite matter of fact, "Do you play rugby?"

"Ah well, that's more a good'un. I can talk till the sheep come down from the hills about the rugby."

CLOUDS OF FEAR

By the Saturday morning, Guido and Betty were flexing their vocal chords once again as Sebastian's clocks and watches announced the arrival of the 9 am opening. The Treasure Trove came under bombardment almost instantaneously by parched persons that had put up with only one cup of tea in the last twelve hours and a house full of blood red water feeding their toilet and shower, which by now had tinted everyone's skin as it had Crayfish Joe. "I can't quite believe this, I thought yesterday was manic enough," said Jet craning over the stall to make another sale. "What happens if we run out of water?"

"Don't ewe worry 'bout that, Cariad," Owen replied as he handed a twelve pack over to a mother and five grubby kids. "I think Teacher's master plan looks set to move on; he's in the back of the container now and he's up to something! This selling water at the market is merely a sideshow!"

"Well, things can't get much worse," Jet said shaking her head as in the back of the container there came some muffled digital garb from over Teacher's radio.

"Teacher to Crayfish," he said as he clicked open the receiver. "Teacher to Crayfish, where are you Crayfish?" But the radio had gone dead as if switched off at the other end and so after sitting for a while thinking, Teacher stood forthrightly and barged his way beyond the steel door, out onto the stall.

"Give it a couple of hours Owen, then clear the stand."

"Here we go," Owen said looking at Jet, justified, as in the background Teacher kick-started his Moto Guzzi and shot out of the market with his robes flying about him as decisively as his change in mood.

* * *

Sally was on the telephone to Mayor Brian. "What, nothing at all?" she asked.

"No, just the usual bills, complaints and internal mail; perhaps he's realised we mean business, perhaps he's realised he's not going get a penny out of us."

"Perhaps you're blind! He's not going to stop until he gets what he's after! According to my undercover gal, he's running out of his stock of water and if I know nothing, I know you best be gettin' ready to be expectin' somethin' else, very soon!" Sally tried to frighten Brian given his apparent laid back attitude. "And I guarantee you this, he's going to be asking for more money!"

"How much more?"

"Well, how would I know? But if I were 'im, I'd base it on his first and second demands," she reasoned with police logic. "You'll probably be looking at seventy-five fousand!"

"What! We haven't got that kind of money!" Brian replied down the telephone such that Sally could hear his breathing getting heavier.

"Can't say I didn't warn ya! You're gonna have to pay up if we can't catch him."

"And whose fault is that? You're supposed to arrest him, not me!" said Brian. There was a protracted silence much like a Texas high street awaiting a shoot-off between a pair of gunslingers, when Sally fired off a shot.

"Would you be able to find it in cash? As a loan from the bank?"

"Why?" Brian asked, looking for an alternative.

"I think there's a chance 'ere to sting him up his arse," she said tantalisingly. "A good chance for an arrest, but it'll 'ave to be cash."

"Why?"

"Well, if we take away the option of paying into his Swiss account, then he'll have to collect it, by hand," she said logically.

"I'll still have to put it past the committee."

"Get real," Sally said shaking her head. "Take control, you're the Mayor!" She tutted before hanging up the phone, clearly annoyed.

* * *

Teacher was stood outside the Acme Fireworks factory just outside Chillborough when the two-way crackled into life. It was Joe, finally. "Calling Teacher, are you there Teacher, this is Joe, over."

"Go ahead, Crayfish!"

"No, this is not Crayfish, this is Joe. Message from Joe to Teacher, over."

"Go ahead," said Teacher with a slight grin on his face.

"Something's happening Teach, something bad, you best get over here."

"Is it the frogs Joe, the frogs?" Teacher asked very matter of fact.

"No, all the frogs have been leaving the lake over the past four or five hours, to escape the rise of a thick mat of algae all over the lake. Most have dragged themselves up onto the bank and into the woodland beyond, but there's hundreds more just drying out and dying on the beach. That's not the problem, but it might be the cause of the problem. You need to get here, get here quick!"

Teacher put his finger in his mouth to wet it before holding it into the sky, to determine which way the wind was blowing, deducing something from it. Then he nodded in understanding as he tucked a package under his arm, started his bike and screamed out of the factory yard on one wheel.

* * *

Before Brian could collect his papers to make his way to the committee meeting, Sally knocked and walked into his office. He looked inquisitively at her as to why she had telephoned before when obviously, she was just outside, but then he noticed she had an envelope in her hand which she was waving in the air. "I found this tucked behind my bike's windscreen," she said looking pensive, "and I think we know what it is."

Brian took one look at the silken envelope and the 'urgent' label on the front and nodded. He took it from her, with a flimsy smile and added it to his untidy pile of admin before making his way from his office to face the rigors of the committee. "Don't forget the option we discussed, but it 'as to be cash!"

As Sally left the building, her mobile phone rang; it was Jet. "I know I shouldn't phone ordinarily, but it's an emergency, something's going down, right now! Teacher has just had me and Owen clear the stall in advance of new stock arriving, but we don't know what that may be as yet."

"I should have guessed," Sally said as she took the bike down off its stand, started the engine and left leaving her trademark rubber tracks on the road.

* * *

Joe's feet were blistering and falling apart after sitting on his haunches in the bottom of a bed of dense and sharp bulrushes at the lakeside all night. The noise of the frogs, leaping and escaping from the dense algae had been deafening, and so the extra effort he had made to remain incognito was palpable. Worse however, was the sight of his cool box full of grub, chocolate and sweets floating off across the lake after the tether had come loose, which had him in tears. He remembered what Teacher's brief had been and was frugal in his anticipation of the great event, but he was sure now that the frogs were not it. If only Teacher would get here quick, he had no idea how he was going to brave this out without some help and really needed to escape.

Jock was making his way out of the water works to have a final tidy round at the site of the pollution. He and the team had extracted and reported upon every last piece of evidence, including plaster casts of tracks and plimsoll treads and he was now clear to close things down, but the sight that greeted him by mid-morning was a frightening one.

“Och my, will ye luke at that,” he exclaimed as he ran back into the water works reception area. “Ring for the fire brigade laddy, noow! There be a massive black cloud coming o’er the lake, there must be one hen o’ a fire oot there!”

Sally was driving back from the town hall when she too saw the smoke. She rightly assumed Jock would call the fire brigade, so merely put her foot down. PCs Andy and Nev had been making enquiries at the tanker company and had taken a statement of witness that suggested Teacher had been there recently hiring one of their vehicles. They were standing talking to one of the workers there when they too saw the black cloud, billowing from over the horizon, getting bigger and bigger, minute by minute.

“That's coming from the lake,” said Andy. “Call it in, then let's get back there quick.”

“Ok,” said Nev who started the engine and drew the van forward to the give way line, where he sat revving the engine looking for a gap in the traffic as one of the fire brigade’s ten wheeled engines shot past them, like the devil on tour. It was careering around bends and corners, from left to right with sirens wailing and lights flashing. Just as Nev was about to follow on behind, Teacher on his Motor Guzzi shot past them like a cotton ball caught in a gale force wind. The two PCs did a double-take looking at each other for confirmation that this was the guy that fitted the descriptions that Sally and now the tanker company staff, had just given them.

“That's that bloke, Teacher! It is, get after him,” Andrew yelled, as in leaving the tanker car park their brakes were screaming and clutch-plate steaming. “Call it in, quickly call it in!" Nev shouted.

Teacher was almost certainly more bike proficient than the last time he broke speed limits and abused other road-users around Clearwater, even whilst balancing a package from the fireworks company strapped to the rear of his bike, in a cluster of fabric netting. He had no idea that he was being followed at first, as he was more preoccupied with the ever-increasing cloud in front of him, that had now taken on the chilling shape of the Hiroshima mushroom. However, in coming through a sharp right hand bend and past a caravan site entrance with a huge convex mirror set to help disadvantaged motorists, he spotted them in the reflection. He slowed quickly and took a left down an insignificant road, as a test to see if he should be concerned. Sure enough the police van followed. "If all the bleeding gods in all the bleeding worlds were here now!" Teacher yelled as he opened the throttle.

"Shit! He's spotted us!" said Nev reacting with the self-control dictated by his police training, as the cat and mouse chase then screamed through the urban scrawl of the town. Under bridges and over crossroads they went, down wrong way streets, and over playing fields, whilst all the time Nev could imagine hearing the musical accompaniment from the Benny Hill show in his ears.

It was obvious after a short while, that Teacher knew which way he was going, his turns being decisive and quick and as a rule, in the direction of the cloud which was now towering over them all, cutting out the sunlight. Like a giant tornado on the plains in America it was now rotating in a clockwise direction, then within minutes it swung around, almost as if there were a solitary body from the heavens directing it from a podium within.

Before Nev had realised, the chase crossed from tarmac to dirt track and their van was now bouncing on poorly inflated tyres and soft suspension, violently at times, whilst only just keeping Teacher in sight. For his part, the dips and bumps in the track were treated more as aids to scrambling as his bike would fly through the sky with Teacher standing up in the saddle, laughing and having a whale of a time. But contrary to his expression his mind was working overtime, calling on the gods to help him in his quest and upset the chasing van dumping it into one of the sharp ditches on either side of the road. He didn't have to wait long, as almost in answer to his prayers the track, now punctuated by Forestry Commission signs, disappeared into a dimly lit woodland. It was so old that the bows of the trees met each over the track resulting in a tunnel that began to disappear into a black hole beyond.

"Will you look at him go, has he no fear?" Andy said to Nev as Teacher turned his whole body, except his hands which were still steering from the jarring handlebars and was now sitting backwards on the bike facing them, looking directly at them. "Don't look into his eyes!" Nev yelled.

"I know, I know…" Andy shouted back as in closing his eyes Nev had strayed from the track and was on a collision course with some of the forestry's grand daddies, all of six foot in diameter. He swerved violently, with the skills he had been taught by the force's advanced driving course, regaining the track, even continuing in the right direction. "Shit hot!" cried Andy who offered a high five which Nev, perhaps wisely failed to respond to. "Wait!" he shouted as he looked up to see the Moto Guzzi careering off down the track.

"Where's he gone?" he said realising that there was now no rider in the saddle. "He just disappeared right in front of me," Nev said.

"That's right, he was there one minute then gone the next," Andy agreed. "There's something paranormal about this bloke!"

Jock was making his way along the lake's service road, on foot now with Kylie in support. Both looked terrified of the massive cloud, that like some evil entity was poised over the lake. Still, Jock had his macho hat on and to be fair was reassuring Kylie who was shaking from head to foot. He could hear the fire engine now hurtling down the main road towards the water works, an obvious place to start but not helping them on the frontline. Sally was behind them with lights flashing and two tones burning a hole in the air, but she wisely turned off to make her way down the service road to where Jock and Kylie were standing.

"Get in," she shouted through the open driver's window. "I can't explain now, just get in." They threw themselves in through the side sliding door, which slammed shut of its own accord, as she hit the gas again.

Teacher climbed down out of the tree that he had hauled himself up into after grabbing a low hanging branch, just as Nev and Andy took their eyes off the road. He dusted himself down and sat on a tree stump, taking out his mobile phone to check the balance of his Swiss bank account. There had been no deposits. He checked his emails, there was nothing from the Mayor here either, not even a pitiful plea for clemency, so he tapped out a brief message: "If you do not make payment within the next few minutes, a third plague will fall upon you, one that will escalate beyond the decency of Belanos!" He was getting desperate and in his temper, he was almost hoping that there would be no payment, despite the implications, purely from a revenge point of view. He doubled back, seething at the obstinacy of the council, to collect the fireworks and netting from his bike that had buried itself completely in some dense bushes. He knew exactly where he was however, and took a small footpath leading down to the bulrushes on the shoreline around the lake. There would be nothing stopping him now.

Having skirted around the water, Teacher was pleased on one hand to find that Joe had done a good job of concealment, but irate on the other as he couldn't find him. "Joe, Joe where are you," he whispered as loud as he dared.

"Here," said the bedraggled man, now a luminous green from the algae, all apart from his face which was still crayfish red.

"Put this on over your head," Teacher said as he gave Joe one of the Nets he had been carrying and donned one himself. Then, opening the package from the fireworks factory, he extracted a short-barrel flare gun with a dense red, smoke grenade ready loaded.

"Fire in the hole!" he yelled as he pulled the trigger catapulting the grenade high into the sky, directly into the black cloud. He was laughing ridiculously whilst contemplating the dilemma the Mayor would shortly find himself in. "From the power that is Belanos…" he started dramatically but was too late to finish his mantra as an almighty explosion nearly one hundred feet above them ripped through the air, echoing off the hillsides all around and dispersing an acreage of dense smoke from the grenades. This daytime blitz had the immediate effect of shocking the millions upon millions of mosquitoes, gnats and flies that had arisen out of the acrid and predator-free lake and out of their co-ordinated cloud breaking their pattern into frenzied escapes that had most of them heading for Clearwater. Teacher pulled his mosquito net back over his head to load another grenade in to the breach, firing again to further drive the high-speed critters towards his intended destination. He laughed again as he had fulfilled his threat to subject the local population of Clearwater to a plague of flies.

* * *

Jet and Owen had received a large pregnant transit lorry into the market place and had begun to unload three bicycles, two hundred and fifty mosquito nets, six hundred insect repellent aerosols and six hundred sticky tape fly traps, not to mention nearly a thousand plastic fly squatters. Both had seen the thick black smoke on the horizon and both had wondered why it seemed so cloud like, until it fractured and started to break up. Then putting two and two together they wasted no time in pulling a mosquito net over each other, before starting to populate the stall with all the anti-fly products. In no time at all the sky darkened by degrees, as a cumulus of buzzing black, blood hunting mozzies, descended over the market like hail in winter. Without a good mozzie net people were instantly covered in hundreds and thousands of the crawling ticks, all biting and nipping those areas of uncovered flesh, whilst the rest began exploiting open neck collars, cuffs and trouser legs, ear holes and nasal passages. Once again people resorted to heading for cover, the majority back to wherever their car might be parked.

The Beaver Scout Colony from Brian's Scout Group were out collecting within the doors of Tesco's when they too were caught by the sudden influx of flies that covered them so quickly, their bright blue uniforms couldn't be seen. In fact, had it not been for a charitable till worker pushing them all one by one in through the shop's closing doors, being so nubile and fresh to the eyes of a fly, they would all have been consumed.

It may have been more challenging than a Rubik's Cube to figure out what the bicycles that had been delivered to the Treasure Trove were for, especially before the cloud hit, but it was almost a natural reaction for Jet and Owen to grab one each, as it was the only way to deliver the hundreds of mosquito nets, to anyone as they had all disappeared. Some however, had panicked and started running for the nearest shop, office or department store, only to find that staff inside wouldn't open their doors and compromise their sterility. Of those that did get caught in the open, Owen and Jet merely threw a net over them before telling them what the price was, whereupon twenty-five pounds was readily paid without them having to make a threat to remove it. More labour was employed as soon as net-clad Joe and Teacher arrived back on a slightly disfigured Moto Guzzi. Joe took the third bicycle from the container, as Teacher began to make up packs of a net, a can of aerosol, a sticky tape fly catcher and a fly squatter, all for thirty-five pounds. These were then loaded into the oversized wire buckets at the front of the bikes and delivered to customers, like early morning bread, across the town.

By the afternoon, Teacher began calling at the hotels and guest houses telling the proprietors that he had everything they required to protect their guests, whereupon every twenty minutes or so he loaded up the van and choked his way around town with packs of everything available as a one-off delivery or on the hour every hour. He was having a great time, even offering advice to those that didn't seem to know what to do with the pack. "Use the swatters on the male flies and the aerosol on the females," he advised, through a mischievous grin.

* * *

It wasn't long before Billy Tremble at Radio Clearwater was getting in on the act.

"That was a great number listeners, called *Magic Fly* by Space from 2009, and here at the head of our topical hour all the way from Pat Boone, *Flip Flop and Fly*... You heard it here first listeners from your trembling Billy Tremble, 705 FM."

Sure enough, as word spread through the town nearly as fast as the cloud of flies, recipients of a mosquito net, now bound up like a multitude of bee keepers, were making their way to the market stall to buy the thirty-five pound packs. Joe and Owen, already knackered, were therefore needed more at the stall than being mobile as sales then began to increase to the same astronomical pitch as the candles and then the water bottles did, only days before.

The other market traders had given up the ghost, especially after Guido swallowed a massive blue-bottle during the open bars of the Marriage of Figaro. From within their almost air tight camper van, Susan and Sandra could see, between windscreen wipes, the explosion in trade once again at the Treasure Trove.

"How does he do it?" Susan asked.

"He knows something we don't," Sally answered, as with a sudden bang, Teacher's face was imprinted on their windscreen. He had an ironic smile about him and his eyes were bright and large which sent a shiver right down Susan's back and into her feet.

"Oh my God!" she shrieked as Teacher hung a complimentary anti-fly pack on their wiper blades before waving and disappearing like a bucket of water thrown in the rain.

* * *

Having been bombarded by masses of panicked flies around the lake, Sally had abandoned any thought of further investigation without the kit needed and brought the police team back to the town hall. She firstly arranged for them to seek solace in the basement, put aside for such emergencies, as had other emergency services that had been caught on the hop. She then made her way upstairs to the meeting rooms where a meeting of the Tutelage committee was already taking place in the crisis centre. Mayor Brian was in the window reveal, sellotaping the gap between glass and frame now that the mozzies were arriving looking for a way to get in. Sally approached him already half covered in dead and live flies herself.

"Well?" she asked with an 'I told you so' look to her face.

"It's there on the desk in those two silver cases," he said pleased to see her and yet perplexed that they had to allow this third event to start at least. "But how's he going to rid the town of this, aren't we just too late?"

"And what's to say he hasn't got another batch ready to be released?"

"All right, all right, take it. There's five thousand in genuine notes on the uppermost layers in both cases, that's ten thousand in all, the rest is false, as the committee agreed."

"What!" She looked at him in disbelief.

"Don't, just don't. The genuine ten thousand is in there without the committee's knowledge!" he whispered carefully.

"Oh, well I'll give you that at least!"

"I've sent a proposal to the email address given on the letter, agreeing to pay in cash as we discussed. I've managed to make up some excuse about keeping it out of the official books. Oh, and I've given him your email and telephone number. All that remains now is for you and your police team to set up the handover, or sting as you call it and get the bastard!" He waved her to take it as he returned to his sellotaping, being scrutinised from all the now dark corners of the room by the eyes of the hungry wolves on the committee.

THE FLIGHT OF THE SCOTSMAN

With the two silver cases in hand it wasn't long before Sally, clad in a nuclear, chemical and biological war suit, including black gas mask with vertical filter strapped to her side, was sitting in the police transit at 'The Crawl' waiting to meet with Jet. The density of the cloud of mosquitoes this far out of town was less intense, but still unbearable without protection of some sort. As Jet arrived on her bicycle, she shook her net from head to foot after spraying herself down with her 'bug hunt' anti-mosquito aerosol, which she also used to fill the van's cab with, as she jumped in alongside Sally.

"Hiya, present for you…" she said with a beaming smile, as she dropped one of Teacher's anti-mozzie sale packs on her lap.

"What's this?" Sally asked.

"Mosquito net, anti-mozzie aerosol, sticky tape fly trap and a swatter. Thought you'd appreciate them," she said still smiling.

"You'd do better bringing me some info, somefin' to do with Teacher, somefin' that I can use against him, or do you not now want an undercover role?"

"So, you don't know what these items are then, or why I brought them to you? This is what Teacher is selling to take advantage of the current plague of flies," she argued.

"This is just chicken feed thrown around the yard by a blind farmer, not the main event, which is the extortion of the town council. The ransom demanded to avoid this scenario is seventy-five thousand pounds, that's where my attention is focussed and yours should be too!" Sally was clearly annoyed but then also devoid of any line management skills that might have provided some of the support Jet clearly needed. This was in fact, just something else Jet thought that placed questions against Sally's actions to date.

Having had her say and not expecting any reply, Sally opened the sliding doors behind her head, revealing the rest of the police team sat in the back of the Transit, quiet now having heard every word of Jet's telling off, jurors having heard the prosecutions closing statement.

"Right then, listen up," Sally began. "The town council has agreed to pay the ransom to stop Teacher from continuing his plagues."

"Thank Christ fur that lassie, can we be goin' home now?"

"No, Jock! They're making payment to give us the opportunity to 'andover the cash as 'e's demandin'. And of course, to arrest 'im and 'is cronies all in one go!"

"Och come on! It won't be as easy as that!"

"I know, Jock. I know. That's why we're gonna use seventy-five fousand pounds' worth of cash…"

"Away we yer lassie! If he finds oot, he'll damn near kill us all with his next paddy!"

"That's why we 'ave to get 'im this time. I've sent 'im an email saying the Council are gonna pay and 'e's replied. We 'ave to go to the old airfield outside of Chillborough at ten tonight and look for the old battered Ford van 'es got."

"Do we have a plan?" Jet asked accepting rather than arguing with Sally.

"Well firstly, you go back undercover. He may ask you to 'elp 'im and that might be invaluable. I'll go on me bike and co-ordinate everything. Jock you take the Transit with Kylie. Andy and Nev, you draw a marked police car from Chillborough nick."

Everyone acknowledged the arrangements so far.

"I want you, Jock, to do the handover as per whatever instructions Teacher gives you. Kylie can stay in the back of the van unless called for. I hope that Kylie and I can then get the jump on Teacher and manhandle him into cuffs and into the back of the Transit. Bring the cop car in through the gateway Andy, and stop anything coming out, but keep your engine running and radio open in case Jock calls for you urgently!"

"What about you?" said Jet.

"I'm co-ordinating."

"From your motorbike? But where will you be?"

"Around…"

"Don't you think we need more info than that?" Jet was pressing her, not happy at her level of involvement, but Sally turned on her, ready to put her down again.

"Am sure the lassie knows what she is to be doing," Jock said before Sally responded inappropriately, giving Jet a reassuring wink.

"Just one thing you need to know," Sally added, "the seventy-five fousand quid Teacher 'as asked for is short by sixty-five fousand; there's only five fousand in each case topping the false notes underneath." There was some laughter from everyone. "So, we meet 'ere six thirty, except for Jet, ok?"

"Roger," Jock said on everyone's behalf.

* * *

Chillborough airfield had seen no more aircraft since a World War II Shackleton bomber got lost coming out of a neighbouring RAF station and inadvertently dropped its payload right down the runway. This had left three huge craters that in part, were still there over seventy years later, still preventing the runway from being used for anything other than BMX and trials bikes, both ridden by glue-sniffing extremists. The state of disrepair was compounded by the MOD's refusal to repair anything, the Council's inability to repair it and Focus Filmmaking's unfulfilled promise to repair it. The film company was now the only resident, occupying some small offices, that were probably crew dispersal units during the war and the massive but dilapidated aircraft hangar, as dominating as a cathedral standing high over everything else. Unfortunately, it had never been best placed to join the Hollywood set as it was always too late to undertake the filming of a prequel, too early to tackle the sequel and always too skint to attempt the main event. But there were pieces of film set equipment, scaffolding and the like strewn all around the airfield, probably worth thousands of pounds, including now some huge mirrors on wheels that could be pushed around into place to reflect the sunlight or influence the landscaping of a certain film shot.

By the time the police team arrived, darkness was settling over the area. There was no escape of moonlight or pinprick from the stars as it was heavily overcast and being so far out in the sticks there wasn't even a comforting glow from any degree of light pollution. Therefore, a very nervous entourage paused at the crash gate entrance until Sally on her Honda 750 growled her way to the front, like medieval royalty standing before her army. As soon as she gave the Transit and the police car the pre-arranged A-OK signal, she revved the bike's engine and disappeared into the darkness, without a side or headlight to give her position away.

Andy, last in the queue, put on the police car's hand brake, leaving the engine running as instructed, right in the crash gate entrance. Jock then checking that everything was going to plan, pulled away slowly following the service road across the main runway, rattling his way over the bumpy tarmac, keeping to the bright orange markers that defined the road, away from the bomb-craters. He could see nothing in front of him except for the occasional rabbit and a pair of boxing hares. "A din't think I'd be out here the nict, lookin' for the Big Yin," he said looking about him and keeping his speed down so as not to un-nerve Kylie or anyone that might be watching. Then without warning, off to his left, a way down the main runway, a plethora of lights came on. Jock counted them; he could make out two red and three white, one of which was a very bright one. But, in trying to break the equation down he could only conclude that there were at least two vehicles. He stopped as the single bright light detached itself from the pack and started to come towards him. He clicked the radio on to send a message. "Five five to Five two," he began.

"Send," came Sally's response.

"Vehicles spooted doon the runway, south of the service road, I repeat south of the service road, plus one suspected to be a motorbike with single light which is heading towards me noo."

"Roger," Sally replied, saying nothing more as there was nothing to be said, despite the fact that the operation had clearly begun.

The bike became more of a certainty as Jock wound down one of the Transit's squeaking windows and found he could hear the high pitch revving of its engine. This then fell to a low grumble as it pulled in front of him and the white figure of a man sitting in the saddle, beckoned him on. It was Teacher or the Big Yin as Jock preferred to call him. Engaging the engine, the Transit pulled off the service road to follow the bike, as Jock found he could now decipher the lights that were left, two reds, as in rear lights and one slightly higher white light that had to be an interior of what he told himself, was probably Teacher's battered old Ford Escort van. As the Transit got nearer, the bike cut off its light and disappeared like a submarine on a deep-sea dive, into the earie darkness. It was obvious now what it was that Teacher wanted to happen and so in response, Jock slowed the Transit to find the time to update everyone.

"All units this is Five five. The cannie bike has left the scene. I see noo only the empty van with open back doors lit up by a tadgy lamp, which is where they are wantin' me to poot the cash."

"This is Five three, Roger Five five," came Andy's response, as it seemed Sally was not about to reply.

"Continue Five five," Sally said moments later, but the

signal from her radio had become distant and nearly inaudible.

"Get ready Kylie," Jock said over his shoulder to see his partner crouched in the back of the Transit with baton and pepper spray at the ready. "Ye show yoursen only if I shout," Jock said as he climbed down out of the cab and went around to the dimly lit rear doors. He opened them and drew the two super shiny cases out, which he then carried around to the front, keeping eyes to the left and to the right as he walked across the ten or so meters of tarmac between the vehicles. Placing the two cases side by side inside Teacher's waiting van, he then stood back and looked around for other instructions, but there appeared to be nothing more than a distant hooting of a blatant owl and so he slowly but surely retraced his steps until he found himself sat, as if transported back in time, in the police transit cab from whence he came.

Andy and Nev were sat in the police car, both fidgeting knowing from the radio reports from Kylie, that the delivery, as it was proving to be, was going down at that minute. "We should go and help instead of sitting here in a marked police car looking like an oversized pregnant penguin," said a very impatient Andy.

"Chill man, this is bloody preferable to an evening on nightclub duty in town, cosy police car, gate duty and…" Nev said as he lifted his duffle bag onto his lap and extracted two paper bags, one of which he gave to his partner, "Cornish pasties!"

"Well, when you put it like that," Andy said tucking in with a fever, "let him take all night!"

Unfortunately, any delay in proceedings were never to be the case as the radio sparked again into life.

"Five five to Five two, completed delivery and am noo sat back in Transit, noo further instructions and noo barmpots around, over."

"Five two here, pull your vehicle back twenty-five yards, leave your lights on and sit and observe, over."

"Roger," Jock replied as the radio fell silent.

"Well that suits me, sir," said Nev as he slumped back in

the seat to take a little cat nap, now that he had a full belly.

As Nev snoozed and Andy resorted to five minutes of searching for Pokémon across the airfield, Jet on the bicycle she had been glued to all afternoon, silently and carefully with no lights to illuminate her path, began to sneak past the sleeping policemen. She had been left out of the police team and left out of Teacher's operation and so defiantly planned to remain undercover until the last minute when she would pop up like a jack-in-the-box and nab Teacher with the ransom money in his hands. And yet at the first obstacle, rounding the back of the police car which was only six feet inside the entrance, her presence was nearly given away as she jumped when the radio within, crackled once again into life. "Five whit, whaur, whit, what," was the opening garbled message until Jock managed to compose himself, "Five five to all other units, d'ya see, the van has just disappeared like nessy in the loch! It were there two minutes ago and noo it has vanished, right in front a me." There was a pause, "Over."

"Five five this is Five two, it can't just disappear into thin air; pan around with your high beam on, don't let him get away." Teacher predictably, was getting the better of them and with Sally obviously a distance away, Jock was getting nervous as was Andy who commented on the whole event as being unplanned, unprofessional and typical of a woman, as he jumped out of the car and stood upright upon the door sill, to get a better look down the runway.

"He's right, I can only see the Transit's red rear lights; the other pair and the smaller white light have gone," Andy said as he focussed his modest horse racing binoculars on the tiny lights twinkling in the distance. We best get down there and take charge, someone's got to!"

"No, going down there is exactly what Teacher wants us to do; we must stay here and guard the exit," said Nev as he pointed with an open hand to illustrate his point. But Jet, having nearly been caught in the Transit's headlights as Jock panned around looking for Teacher's van, had taken advantage of the fact that her route was momentarily lit up and slipped away down the east side of the runway.

"Sit-rep, Five five," Five three called, as there was nothing to be heard from Sally.

"There, there he is och aye," the radio suddenly blurted out, "Five five, the canny bastart is off up the west side of the runway in his Ford Escort van. We're gannin' after him." But there was no reply from Sally.

"She had better be setting herself to head him off," Andy threatened, using the field glasses to get a better look at what he could see was a pair of headlights to the right of the Transit as the two vehicles were now racing back down the runway. Kylie was hanging on for grim death having lowered her weaponry, grabbing hold of the seat. She was now feeling more travel sick than she was ever sick in anticipation of having to tackle Teacher. "Just hang on lassie, ya uncle Jock is on the charge!"

* * *

Jet was watching what was going on whilst following the edge of the runway tarmac in the dark, feeling her way, by dangling her left foot from off the bike pedal. She was pleased to know that the money was being chased down, even though it didn't fit in with her very optimistic vision. And so, with the best principles of reviewing and reacting, which was a part of her incident management course, she elected to observe as she continued to outflank proceedings. Navigating by feel, instinct and nerve, she was never as sure as a rider that knows its horse, when the bicycle suddenly fell away handlebars first, down into the darkness, into a world of mud and topsoil, rubble and old aircraft parts. Jet was thrown clear of the bike but hit the ground taking the skin off each hand as she rolled, bumped and banged down into what she realised was one of the three old bomb-craters still littering the runway.

* * *

Jock was having a bad time of it. After getting the bit between his teeth, he was gaining on Teacher's van, until once again it disappeared, the two red rear lights being turned off before it was then heading at a tangent away from the runway.

"Ye damned sasanacs!" he yelled as went back to steering left then right scanning the route in front with the headlights on main beam.

"They've lost him!" Andy shouted from the police car as Nev got out and wandered onto the runway looking concerned.

"Five two this is Five three, come in," Nev said into the radio, "Five two are you there Five two?" But there was no reply from Sally, whose lack of involvement was beginning to infuriate him.

"She'll be in trouble if this goes tits up," Andy said as the two men got back into the car. "It's going to be a right cock-up!"

"We're just wasted, being sat up here."

"So, what do we do?" Andy asked revving the car up as if ready for a Grand Prix start, just waiting for Nev to give in and order them into action.

"No! calm down, we stay here and follow orders," he said with the experience he had acquired over the years.

* * *

Jet could see nothing at first, not until her eyes acclimatised by degrees, and even then, she could only just make out the sky from the ground. But her hearing had adjusted to compensate and she could now make out the sound of a motorbike slowing from its whining high revs to a grumble as it pulled up adjacent to the rim of the bomb crater.

"About bloody time," Jet said to herself, "she should be taking charge, we need her to take her finger out." But as she stood to wave and get Sally's attention, the bike was kicked over the rim of the crater to slide, with its passenger still in the saddle, down the slope to the bottom of the hole. This unnerved Jet, so for whatever reason, she remained crouched for a moment longer. Just as well as the rider climbed off the bike and pulled it up onto its stand, the main light illuminating him: it was Teacher. He stood looking around as if his inner mantra had detected a presence. He was certainly looking for something or someone.

* * *

"This is Five five, wait one, we have the canny bugger again! I see his headlights noo directly in front o' me. Be Jesus, he's getting nearer and nearer, he can't be… he is, he's playing chicken with us!" This, if anything, merely enthused Jock, who could remember the chicken games he used to play as a kid in Glasgow, on his chopper bike. The gang leaders would issue challenges, usually down by the canal, to ride towards each other like maniacs until one would chicken out and turn to avoid the other, falling straight into the pungent green water. However, he was always dry at the end of any confrontation.

He dropped a gear and slammed his foot back down to the floor; there was a look in his eyes that suggested he had been looking for a hero moment since joining the force. He started to swing right and then left to see if Teacher's van would do the same, which it did immediately. He switched his lights out; the van did the same. He switched them back on; the van did the same. He tried high beam to blind the driver, but his opponent only did the same and blinded Jock. As the speed built, the Transit began to rattle, the front passenger window started to work itself open as the door on the glove box fell down spilling out sweet wrappers, fish and chip forks and all the garbage it had swallowed up when used for hours of surveillance. Kylie was being thrown all over the place as clearly Jock had forgotten about her since going into racing mode. Then suddenly the back doors of the Transit, in response to hitting a rock or wayward bunny rabbit, flew open. There were police traffic cones, bullet proof vests, cooking stoves, utensils, pots and pans spilling out the back and then with her legs in the air, Kylie, who had lost her grip of the seat in front of her. She crashed down onto the tarmac and went rolling away like tumbleweed in the desert until coming to a stop in a battered heap. As she looked back there was the sight of Teacher's van hurtling towards the Transit. It never swerved, it never hesitated, never deviated and followed every trick that Jock had to unnerve it.

"Jump! For God's sake Jock, jump, he's not going to stop!" She could see what was coming, so frightened by the speed, as the Transit started to fade into the distance and the headlights on Teacher's van got closer and closer.

* * *

Jet's cautious approach had served her well; she was now curled up in a little ball, in the mud and water at the bottom of the bomb crater, shielded from view by an old aircraft engine casing. She should, she told herself, jump out and confront Teacher as he stood alongside his idling bike, thrown into silhouette by its still bright headlight, but she had no reason to arrest him; he had no piles of cash stuffed in his pockets. She was as much at fault, not carrying a radio when right now calling for backup would have been sensible. So, she settled to do what Sally said she should, observe and report from an undercover point of view. With a little more purpose then, she sat up on her haunches joining the hares on the airfield and found herself a comfortable position to sit, in case it turned out to be a long job. She didn't have to wait for long, as confused at first by Teacher's idling bike there came the noise of another more powerful machine. This too dipped over the rim of the bomb hole and slid, with more control than Teacher, down to stop alongside him. The rider of this bigger machine was all in leather, with a helmet sporting a mirrored visor that glinted and flashed light wedges around the sides of the crater. The rider then took off his gloves and as he began to talk to Teacher, pulled off his helmet. This gave Jet the shock of her life as the rider was not a he, but a she. It was Sally, obvious as soon as she tipped her head back and shook her long hair down from its grips as she leant across Teacher to greet him with a brief continental kiss.

* * *

Suddenly, there was the noise of a massive crash which echoed across the airfield, off the dispersal buildings on the west side and slightly later booming back from off the walls of the giant hanger, whose doors had been left open, acting like a giant boom box from under the television. Surprisingly there was less of the dull thud associated with crashing vehicles, but more of a sound of splintering and falling glass, which eventually fell quiet, but for the now continuous sound of the Transit van's horn. Sally and Teacher both stopped in their tracks and scrambled up the side of the bomb crater to look over the runway to the now carnage where last there were the two vans playing chicken. Clearly neither of them had pulled out, both had been staunch or stupid and both were now gone. Sally drew her radio, "Five three, Five two, come in, Over," she said.

"Err, this is Five three, there's been a crash," Andy said with a trembling voice, "and it's probably your fault Sally," he said as he fired off like a loose cannon. Not rising to him, Sally replied forcefully, "Get down there quick. Leave the gate, there's going to be no point you staying there now, find Jock and Kylie," Sally said turning to smile at Teacher.

"Roger, on route," Andy replied as he revved the police car, activated the search lamps on the roof and headed for the crash site.

Teacher also smiled as he pulled a two-way radio out from within his robes.

"Are you there, Joe?" he asked.

"Right here Teach, we heard the crash, it worked then?"

"I told you it would. Now get on," he said as Sally and he both scuttled back into the crater to collect their bikes.

Kylie had watched the crash right up to the final impact as

the oncoming headlights finally hit those of the transit. She threw herself back onto the tarmac expecting an almighty fireball at least, but as she got closer she realised that the Transit was still largely intact. As Andy and Nev approached from the other side of the crash, they were confused too. The transit was sitting there, dented and scraped without a doubt but not looking as damaged as it might have been, if it had been in a head-on collision. There was also a large conglomerate of scaffolding, constructed to hold something that wasn't there any longer, just free-standing alone now in the lights from the police car, which in arriving was causing something to crackle and crunch under their wheels.

Nev was the first to realise there was glass everywhere, twinkling as if it was mirrored. "That's it!" he exclaimed, "Someone's dragged one of those massive mirrors from the film studios over here into the middle of the runway. There never was another vehicle, no game of chicken, no crash to speak of. Jock couldn't possibly win this battle!"

"Away wi' ye," came a voice from the darkness. "Ya dinna think I would be so stupid, did ya? Noo I jumped just after the wee lassie. But I didn'a sees it as a bastart mirror," he said looking around trying to work out where the other vehicle was.

"Over there," Andy said pointing as the old Ford Escort van and Teacher waving from off the back of his motorbike, were now on the service road leaving through the unguarded crash gate.

"Oh no!" shouted Andy, "quick, let's get after them."

"Wait one," said Kylie as she arrived with a broken wrist, cuts and bruises, "you'll not be going anywhere with those four flat tyres!"

A PLAGUE OF SCOUNDRELS

The following morning saw no let-up in the cloud of insects swarming over the town. Apart from the absence of building rubble and fires burning at every corner, the view from anyone's window was totally devoid of humanity, like the aftermath of a nuclear strike. There were no birds singing, no hum from local traffic or chatter from those waiting at bus stops, no earthly life other than the blaze of insects. In terms of human life, it was as dead as leaves on a painted canvas.

After being on such a high, thinking that he had successfully dealt a blow to the Clearwater authority, something had revealed itself and Teacher was now looking angry. His quirky smile and wide eyes had deserted him and he was already planning umpteen plagues, each to be more vicious than the last.

As he arrived at the Treasure Trove on the Sunday morning, Joe and Owen had no problem in deducing that something was wrong. They didn't know what was in the suitcases, but they had assumed that it was the massive pay-out that Teacher had promised and so couldn't imagine that money was the issue. "Is everything all right?" Tom asked his boss.

"Nothing to do with you," came the reply.

"Well, it is if we don't get paid," said Joe a little more explicitly. "I'm not going back up there," he said meaning Lake Yaramar.

"Need to know, and neither of you need to know," Teacher said succinctly as he turned to Jet. "And where were you last night?" he asked, dragging her into the conversation.

"Me?" she answered.

"Yes you, last night. I needed to talk to you after we got back from the business at the aerodrome." He glared at her but she looked away.

"I went out on my bike," she said simply, "I worked most of the evening delivering mozzie nets as you asked, but you didn't show, so I went out."

"You went out, in this?" he replied eluding to the still dark morning, clouds of flies in the sky and a carpet of their dead bodies lying everywhere, the exact opposite of a picturesque early morning snowfall.

"Yes," she said, sensing that this was the time to reveal a part of her hand, "I went out of town, quite a way, saw something I never thought I'd see, something that put the rat right in the pack!" she said smiling an ironic smile, trying to illicit a reaction, which never came. However, Teacher had perceived what he had just heard as suspicious, almost challenging and so he made a mental note to fix Jet for good, just as soon as the occasion arose.

* * *

Sally's mobile phone was ringing incessantly and much as she didn't want to answer it, being still in bed, the caller ID showed it to be Brian, the Mayor. She sat up and prepared herself as if the little phone was posting a picture of her as well as relaying her voice. "Good morning Mayor, I was going to call last night but didn't have any signal," she explained.

"Well, I called you, several times and got no answer."

"Well, there we are then," she said belligerently prompting a conclusion.

"I haven't finished yet, why didn't you call?" he enquired of her, expecting to hear more by her own volition.

"Well, I'm sorry Brian but there was quite a major accident

last night!"

"That's of no consequence to me. Did you catch him?"

"Two of our PCs are in hospital this morning!" she went on.

"Did you catch him?"

"We were tricked when he used some large mirrors belonging to the film company, to confuse us when trying to make the drop."

"Did you bloody well catch him?" Brian reiterated getting more and more impatient.

"No!"

"No! Why the bloody hell not?" he said, finally losing his composure. "You said it was a certainty."

"It didn't work for the reasons I have just given you," Sally said sucking a wasp.

"And how do I explain the loss of ten thousand pounds of taxpayer's money?" he said so desperately that Sally thought she could hear him kicking himself like a suicidal ass.

"I thought you said you had found a different source for the ten thousand?"

"Why do you think I'm so angry?"

"Well, we don't know yet, if ten thousand was enough or not. I know he asked for seventy-five, but beggars can't be choosers you know!" This statement was the final straw.

"Quite frankly, PC Reid, I don't know what you are doing to be so ineffective. Just look out of the bloody window, no responsible person wants to have that lot descend upon them, least of all when they are Mayor of the town. Frankly, I'm not happy that you are in charge, I'm not happy that you haven't had some success at least and I'm not happy that you lost my money. I shall be ringing the Superintendent forthwith!" he said and was poised to slam the phone down when a little more sensibly, Sally replied.

"Mr Mayor, there's no need to do that. We were just unlucky that's all. We know our target better now, we know we need to be mob-handed and we know that dangling cash in front of him will flush him out. Frankly, if you had followed my earlier advice and paid him his twenty-five or fifty thousand, this would be over."

"Well, I'm not convinced; all I can say is that I'll have to think about what I do next."

* * *

Teacher was sat in the container trying to contemplate his next move. He had arrived there last night and opened the case to find it full of fake notes and only to the value of sixty thousand, whereupon his elation at having outwitted the authority turned quickly and violently into anger as he threw the cases down the length of the container. He couldn't let this stand and would be somewhat in trouble himself if he couldn't find the money. He knew his mother wouldn't listen to any excuses and didn't want to continually be banished to the lower echelons, never managing to return to where he should be sitting in life. Whatever he decided to do next, it would have to polarise the Mayor into paying the money, irrespective of the amount.

All the stalls in the market, except for the Treasure Trove were closed, as they would be on a Sunday, even if they could bear the conditions. Nevertheless, Betty had called to visit out of a sense of responsibility.

"When's it going to end?" Betty asked Jet tearfully, as she stood covered in empty dog food sacks secured by lashings of gaffer tape, wrapped several times around her and a purple hair net over her head.

"I've no idea," Jet replied taking another thirty-five pounds for another anti-fly kit.

"Rumour has it that you know," she said.

"Oh, Betty you shock me; do I look like I have control over thousands and thousands of little black flies?" she said.

"No," she replied, "But he has…" she pointed at Teacher who came out from behind the container to stand right in front of her. With his mosquito net pulled tightly to his face, he could now be seen clearly as he leant forward over the table, to look right into Betty's eyes, difficult given the larger flies landing on her hair net.

"But Teacher is a very nice man," he said.

"But then that Teacher, always seemed to be a very nice man," she echoed looking at Teacher, but apparently carrying on the conversation with Jet.

"He has the best of concern for all his customers," Teacher said still focussed.

"As a customer, I always feel he does his best for me," she replied robotically.

"Never capable of controlling a cloud of flies or mosquitoes."

"But he wouldn't do such a thing, would he? He's surely not capable of controlling all those flies, who would be?" she echoed as he leant forward and whispered something in her ear. "I have to be going now," she replied still glazed over. "Guido will be wondering where I am. I always go around for tea and tiffin on a Sunday, you know."

Teacher's show of hypnotic genius was the opportunity he was looking for, to retaliate against the challenge he perceived Jet to have made and by the look on her face he had done just that. Owen watched, resigned to Betty's fate; he had seen Teacher practice his hypnosis before on several people including Joe and wasn't surprised at Jet's reaction. Finally, Teacher turned with a smirk across his face as he wandered back into the container, collecting his shoulder bag and starting up his Moto Guzzi. He had some business to take care of whilst still in the right frame of mind and so pulled away with a purpose.

Seeing him leaving, Jet turned to Owen, "Did you see that, that was hypnosis that was. I'd been told not to look into his eyes."

"By who?" Owen asked.

"Oh, Joe I think, yes Joe."

"Well, he's right, Teacher has some hypnotic powers, but more than that he has a presence, something ancient, something lost by other men."

"Is he some kind of god or something?" Jet said in jest.

"It wouldn't surprise me if he was, Cariad," Owen said resignedly, but Jet began to probe him a little further.

"Do you think there's something wrong, something to do with the money you were supposed to collect last night?" she said knowing full well that it was sixty-five thousand pounds short and that she'd heard Owen and Joe questioning Teacher earlier on.

"There be something that's not right, isn't it," he said, handing another fly pack over the table, to an ill-prepared mum who had braved the trip from home in an upturned nighty.

"The thing is Owen, well I think I can trust you on this," she said which made him look up, a little surprised that one date with him could be so assuring.

"I was out last night, as I told Teacher; I followed his van which was somewhat slow through all the evening's traffic and poor visibility, as far eventually as the Chillborough airfield. I was there when the exchange took place and that police transit crashed through a great big mirror."

"Oh, Cariad!" Owen said. "Do you know what Teacher would have said or what he might have done had he caught you there? I've told you before down't you goo messing with 'im, he can be extremely manipulative and sometimes as dangerous as a whiteout on Snowdon." He wiped the flies from his face net to be sure that Jet could see how angry he was.

"But I haven't told you what else I saw there," she said dangling him on her hook.

"But you're going to?"

"Yes. I saw Teacher meeting incognito, at the bottom of one of those bomb craters, with a police officer."

"A police officer, are you sure?" he said as his brow ran into deep furrows.

"I can't tell you why, but yes I'm sure. They even kissed as they met each other."

"Kissed, what girlfriend and boyfriend like?"

"The only downside was that I couldn't quite hear what they

were saying to each other and then the crash happened before I could get into a better position," she explained.

"Perhaps he has a police informant and he is helping us."

"It's a she."

"Well, perhaps she's helping us, keeping the police from finding out what we've been doing."

"It's possible I suppose," she nodded acknowledging his thoughts and smiling, leaving him with grave doubts about his security and whether he was about to be brought to book and jailed for his involvement. He put his head down for that moment as the buzzing of the flies and the itching around his extremities seemingly disappeared, then he brought Jet fully alongside.

"Come and see this!" he said leading her by the hand into the container, which at first panicked her.

"Oh my God," she said as she entered, looking at rows and rows of hypodermic syringes, and wondering if she had taken her trust thing a bit too far.

* * *

Teacher was still seething as he pulled his little van into the half desolate council car park that was now near ankle deep in dead flies. Many of the workers there had left for home the evening before and not returned this Sunday, but the Mayor's Jag still sat in its dignitary bay. Parking next to it, Teacher negotiated the double door system constructed of mosquito netting, purchased from the Treasure Trove, and stood in front of the reception desk. This seemed to be for what he felt like an eternity, as a very well-dressed woman answered telephone calls and completed those jobs on her tick list that had a higher priority. Eventually, he leant over the countertop and put a hand across the telephone she was talking into, which reported back with an unavailable tone. He then turned to a second phone that was ringing incessantly and waved away the caller, until it was silent. Having her attention finally, he placed a parcel wrapped in silken paper and marked 'URGENT', right in front of her. She was just about to argue with him until she caught him looking into her eyes, whereupon she was as helpful as the obligatory nun in a plane disaster movie.

"You will see the Mayor gets this parcel, without delay," Teacher said whilst keeping her in his gaze.

"Without delay," she acknowledged and was off across the marbled floor and up the grandiose Roman staircase as if she had gifts for Caesar, to take it to him by hand before Teacher had even reached the door.

Mayor Brian was sitting in his darkened office as flies and mosquitoes swarmed against the windows, which thankfully were all tightly sealed with black gaffer tape. This latest "testing" as Teacher called them in his letters, had ground him down to the point of exhaustion. Knowing he had to confront the pack of dogs that was the Tutelage committee was particularly stressing, even his beloved Scouting magazine lay unopened in his in-tray. As he sat thinking about what Sally had said, his secretary barged in and stood po-faced, waiting for him. He ignored her at first until her persistence became an irritation, whereupon he snatched the parcel from her hand and shooed her out of the office.

"Oh no!" he said then, realising it was wrapped in silk, with 'urgent' written all over it, the very definite MO of the blackmailer. All urgency and pace of work seemed at that moment to slow in front of his eyes as his thoughts rearranged themselves and his responsibilities tapped him on his shoulders with all the weight of a builder's lump hammer. He sat looking, contemplating the parcel's purpose, until finally he began to open it, just as his telephone rang which for some unknown reason, he picked up.

"Hello, County Mayor here."

"You choose to send me fake notes after the local police made such an effort to deliver them. I thought we were friends; I thought that you understood me and the responsibilities I have to the gods. You are playing with fire, Mr Mayor."

"Who is this?" Brian demanded to know, although he could guess easily enough.

"Your interruptions will only delay my message."

"But I need to know to whom I am talking," Brian insisted.

"Teacher, not Mr Teacher, not a Teacher, just *Teacher.* You knew I would call after your blatant attempt to defraud me and then catch me. This was very unwise as you will now pay a greater price," Teacher said. "You have a parcel there delivered this instant, open it."

"Why, what is it?" Brian asked.

"Just open it," was the reply. As the paper fell away, the facial features of a glass Sanxingdui mask sat looking up at him. Its bulging eyes, huge nose and square face with a deep frown had all the facial features of Caucasian origins, probably from either of the ancient civilisations of Babylon or India. It was gold in colour and as it caught the office strip lights above, it sent a cascade of northern lights across the ceiling and around the walls, that were mesmerising to look at. But it also drew Brian to look back at it, into its deep dark black eyes which stood out in complete contrast to the yellow gold, until he could see nothing but pyramids in a sea of sand, as his mind wandered away from his office. Eerily then, the eyes in the mask reciprocated as a dull red glowing began to colour each of them, increasing and decreasing until flaring to a brilliant orange. Brian became more and more entranced. Then in tones designed to hypnotise him, Teacher, still on the telephone, spoke.

"You have offended the mighty Belanos, failed those that depend upon you and you have trivialised the lessons the gods chose to bestow upon you. May the wrath of Sekhmet fall upon you now and her lioness image remain in your eyes until you appease her. You will be subject to her breath and a re-energising of the plague of flies. You will no longer pay credence to your poxy committee, no longer be at the beck and call of the police. You will find the anger resting in you to become of immeasurable proportion. There will be no more favours, Mr Mayor, no more cash deals or credit!"

"No more cash deals or credit," Brian repeated in a monotone as both his and the mask's eyes flared brilliantly.

Then as soon as it began, the lights faded back to blackness and there was a click over the telephone as the line went dead. Brian sat shocked for a few minutes until suddenly, with an instilled shift in his mood, he threw the mask violently to the floor. It shattered with an almighty crash, leaving thousands of tiny shards of glass, a battery pack and light bulbs littering the office. It was almost as if someone had snapped their fingers in front of him, leaving him feeling angry and abused.

"What about the ten thousand?" Brian shouted at the now vacant receiver. "Surely that was enough!" he yelled in desperation.

* * *

Superintendent Daniels was sat at his desk at the Chillborough police station, making a concerted effort to blow each nostril free of the night's debris just as the phone rang. He gave a grumpy growl, but picked it up all the same.

"Superintendent Daniels, Brian Woodruff here. I am ringing you this morning as I am absolutely irate; things here are going from bad to worse. The town has been engulfed by dead flies, mosquitoes and insects, which the blackmailer promises me, will now be worsened. The police operation, a virtual certainty I was told, was about as effective as an ejection seat in a helicopter. And as for my money, ten thousand…"

"Wait a minute Brian, just calm down. I can't make head nor tale of what you're saying," the Super said calmly but as firmly as he could.

"I blame your officer Sally Reid, she has done very little since arriving here and what she has done has either backfired or been a right cock-up!"

"Such as?"

"Well, she convinced me to put a large amount of cash together, ten thousand pounds, to top off the fake cash we sent to the blackmailer in payment of his ransom. This was just so she could execute her so called infallible plan, arrest the man and return the money, neither of which she actually managed!"

Brian had the bit between his teeth, as his eyes imprinted with the image of the Sanxingdui mask, were still wide and angry. "The blackmailer, Superintendent, name of Teacher, was on the phone to me just this minute, promising retaliation after not getting his money. He is now intending to send another more intense wave of flies, just as the first lot seemed to be fading. Frankly Superintendent, my Scouts could do better," he said resorting in comparison, to what he knew so well and was obviously more confident of.

"When was this operation you talk of?" the Super asked, somewhat in the dark.

"What! You didn't know? Surely, Sally should be informing you, if not ahead of such a 'sting', certainly after its dismal failure."

"You're quite right, Mr Mayor," said the Super conceding.

"Well, I've decided, bugger the committee, we're going to pay him off at the next opportunity, before things get any worse. He wants his money by bank transfer, no cash no credit," Brian said, as just for a moment the pupils in his eyes enlarged and he looked glazed over again.

"Look, there has to be an explanation for all this. Maybe it's the mere fact that Sally is a woman, who doesn't seem to have a propensity for this sort of thing. I will be in contact with her right away, rest assured I will get something sorted." The Super was trying to conclude the call to avoid any admission of culpability.

"Right then, I will be hearing from you." Brian finished, putting the onus on the Super as surely as the deep breath he then took to calm himself down. "Goodbye Superintendent."

As soon as the telephone clicked at the other end, the Super tried to telephone Sally, but predictably, there was no answer. So, he left a terse message and instructed the operations desk to try to contact her by radio. This was as far as he was prepared to go, without a response from the officer on the ground. Besides, Clearwater might have been a good distance away, but from his office window he could see the black cloud of what he now knew were flies, mosquitoes and the like.

* * *

That afternoon in the shadow of the trees in the little woodland at Leedly copse, Sally turned off her radio and continued to ignore the frantic ringing of her mobile phone. She pulled her bike onto its stand and stood looking around. It was brighter than the last time she was there, which seemed such a short time ago. She actually believed she could still see the indentation in the grass where she had slept. It was beautifully quiet then and reasonably so now, being well away from the buzzing flies and zinging mosquitoes. As she stood taking it all in, the birds and rabbits began to show themselves, trusting in her, but before they could relax and get back to whatever they had been doing before, they froze, fell silent and then made a dash for cover. Sally didn't know why until in the distance she saw Teacher's van bouncing up the track over the field, her own more inadequate ears only hearing it as it got nearer.

It eventually drew up with a ratchetting of cogs from the hand brake and Teacher got out, seemingly gliding over the woodland floor around clumps of grasses, new shoots and old stumps as if he were skating on ice. He came to stand right in front of Sally with what could only be described as a look of expectancy on his face; there was no kiss this time. She felt that she had to acknowledge him somehow and so nodded her head, almost as if she was bowing to a member of royalty.

"Belanos is confused, as am I," he said apparently as calm as the little woodland around him, but he was seething underneath. "After our magnificent humiliation of your police team, I found that the Mayor has deceived us once again by failing to pay the ransom. I will not be fobbed off like a retired donkey locked in a barn!" Sally made an effort to immediately drop her jaw and open her eyes wide.

"What! I thought you collected the cases, both of them."

"Yes, but there was nothing in them, only fake notes," Teacher replied as the pitch in his voice began to climb.

"The dirty, dirty bastard! When I get 'old of 'im! 'E assured me that 'e would pay every last penny," Sally said, as she thoughtfully added, "I wonder if this were dictated by the Tutelage committee or if that creep 'as pocketed the lot!"

"You are talking about the Mayor I presume?"

"Yes, but I never expected there to be any sort of corruption within the council, or the police for that matter."

Without the steam that was still boiling up inside of Teacher, reaching a pressure such that it would blow the top of his head off, he managed to remain calm, closed his eyes and delivered his practiced ultimatum.

"Belanos knows to follow the fault lines and he will have me converge the dominances of all of the gods, down so cripplingly upon the perpetrator and his wards, by extending the current testing, before the delights of the next, most horrific one!"

"How will we do that?" she said.

"I'm going to recharge the wave of flies and insects descending from the lake. There will be no letter, no opportunity to get out of this; Belanos wants nothing but revenge. Your chance will come upon the final testing, if what you say is true!"

"I want revenge too. It's not so much the money, it's the bloody principle of the thing. His total refusal to recognise a woman within the police force, as if we aren't bleedin' capable or something."

"Where I come from," Teacher said thoughtfully, "women in high places are as revered as the man, especially when being addressed by someone younger than they."

* * *

Back at the market, sales of fly netting and other paraphernalia were keeping Owen as busy as the mosquitoes that had landed in the Clearwater nudist club. It seemed as if the atrocious conditions were motivating some people into devising innovative ways of getting around, such as the man from the diving school who would arrive in full scuba gear and the local bee keepers who seemed to think that walking around in netting and gloves wasn't unusual. But the bicycle deliveries were becoming more in demand, even to the point that as one delivery was made, another order was received. As it was Jet's turn to do the bicycle run, into the thick of it back towards Lake Yaramar, she packed up the basket and left with half a mind to spy on what was going on up there. She felt a growing responsibility to look for the more key evidence, before she was replaced as the undercover element, which had to be coming, given the strange meeting between Sally and Teacher at the aerodrome. And so, she firstly delivered twelve fly papers and a kill-a-spray to Askwith House in Yaramar village, where an old man clearly revelled in extinguishing every last mosquito that that ever plagued him. Then, she ditched her bike and under the cover of the over-grown hedgerows and country twitchells thereabouts, she climbed over the ridge at the top of a field, black with the dead bodies of insects, and climbed down the other side to the lake.

A SHIMMER ON THE WATER

Having dealt with the Mayor, Teacher didn't delay in delivering his revenge attack. In his little van, he pulled into the public car park at the top of the lake and clad from head to foot in netting, he then began to carry firework after firework to the water's edge. He positioned himself once again, exactly beneath the cloud of flies and mosquitoes that had re-established itself there after the last explosions. He was still boiling underneath his calm exterior and had a mind to use twice the number of fireworks, ensuring that the Mayor would think twice about double-crossing him again, come the occasion of the next testing.

As the first rocket was set and ignited, it flashed from the ground spiralling through the air, for anyone within a half mile radius to see. Jet had just emerged from the silver birch saplings that surrounded much of the lake and realised this immediately. She had just about got her head, hat and associated netting gathered about her when it exploded as it reached its target height, throwing arms of crackling candles in every direction, including some that shot straight into the cloud. The buzzing and whirring of fly wings increased instantly as it fractured, as if parted by some ravenous dolphin ploughing through a ball of sardines. But the cloud only knitted itself together again in self-defence, so Teacher then sent a second and third rocket into the sky at differing angles, whilst chanting and wailing a mystical prayer, until on the back of the prevailing wind everything began to disperse and head off in the direction of the town for a second time. The density on this occasion was considerably less than on the first, which Teacher thought was unfortunate, but the flies and mosquitoes seemed to be humming their appreciation as they passed over his head and he in true style, thanked them and their gods for their response, still with a firework or two in hand.

Jet was watching all of this and now understood the methodology that had gone into the creation of this calamity. Looking at the green-covered waters of the lake and the corpses of the frogs and amphibians that littered the banks, (the true link in nature's predatory chain, that would have consumed the flies) she now understood why there was a cloud of flies in the sky in the first place. Nevertheless, she was so startled by the multiple bursts of fireworks overhead and wave after wave of displaced critters flying all around her, that she stood up, forgetting who was instigating things.

Teacher for his part, had been concentrating on the cloud of insects as they sat a hundred feet or so over the lake surface and wasn't looking to his front. In fact, he wouldn't have seen Jet at all, had she not let out a shriek as she saw him apparently glaring at her through the biological fog. Now the damage was done and what with his own promise to deal with her the very next time he saw her, he sent a perilous message with blessings from the gods. Launching a firework straight and level, it skimmed the water looking for Jet as its target. She hardly had chance to move being transfixed by the changing lights as it closed on her balancing in the reed beds, until at the last minute she abandoned her precarious perch and threw herself headlong into the water.

As the bubbles rose all around her she continued to dive for the bottom fearing the rocket above her, until it hit a half-submerged log sending showers of multi-coloured sparks all over the surface.

The water was deeper here than Jet had imagined. She couldn't see the bottom at first for all the stagnant green weed that had accumulated on the surface. Only after her natural buoyancy saw her dive level out ready for surfacing again, did she find herself about ten feet down where the water was clear, albeit still somewhat dark. Coming up through the weed still half clad in fly netting, she looked from the surface like a methane bubble about to pop or some marine alien escaping a spaceship stuck in the mud at the bottom of the lake. She opened her eyes and looked towards the bank where she had spotted Teacher only moments before, but he had gone, in which direction towards her or away from her, she couldn't tell. And so, clearing everything from her face and eyes, whilst treading water as she was taught in her schooldays by 'Dishy Dave' the school lifeguard, she scanned the banks on both sides to see if she could spot him. The only thing that gave him away was another horizontal 'starlight parade', that bounced on the water's surface before smashing into the undergrowth above her, with all the best wishes of Barnes Wallace. Jet dived again; she had calculated that he had come half way towards her on the eastern bank, which was where she saw him originally and she knew it would only be seconds before he was in the reed beds right above her. But knowing he couldn't see her through all the weed, she kicked firstly to rid herself of the clinging netting and then to swim nose down, towards the bank on the western side.

She hadn't got far when there was an inevitable and almighty splash. "Oh God," she thought, "he's coming after me." As panic ran through her, she rallied her breast stroke to pull like there was no tomorrow. Not daring to surface, she continued to swim along the bottom of the lake until her lungs heaved in pain and her heart slowed to a struggle. She glanced back realising with great relief, that the splash was in fact a huge boulder that Teacher had dropped from the reed beds. It came crashing through the weed that grabbed it, flaring out behind, as it hit the bottom, the shock forcing Jet finally to breathe out some of her valuable air. There was no alternative now, she had to surface again, but this time and as a shock to her, it was into waist deep water, which at least allowed her to stand up.

He was nowhere to be seen, east bank, west bank, she was looking everywhere, intently gasping in the fresh air, but for the flies that she spat out like pips from a grape. She told herself not to drop her guard but continue to walk backward through the water keeping her eyes scanning the eastern bank.

"There was no way he could have run all the way around to now be on this side," she told herself, "but where could he be?"

Suddenly, something grabbed her leg, which put her straining heart into her mouth as it countered the momentum she had begun to create in increasing her backward speed through the water. It caused her to unsettle from being upright and fall, with only a fraction of a second to snatch a large gulp of air, the buoyancy from which just about kept her head from going under the water. "Leave me alone," she shouted gargling lake water and flies as the grip tightened and she kicked whilst changing direction in an attempt to fool him, but to no avail. Slipping once more she was finally pulled under the water as she felt his full weight on her leg pulling her down a slope at the bottom of the lake, into deeper water, the cold about her head increasing. Kicking out frantically her panic was only making things worse and confusing matters. She was churning up all the dirt from the bottom and dragging down all the weed from the top such that her visibility became so poor that she couldn't even tell which way 'up' was. As the strength in her limbs slowly started to desert her, feelings of apathy and defeat inevitably ran through her. "Is this the time to focus on my life to date," she thought. "Should I dredge up my memories from the bottom of this god-forsaken lake, before I release my last breath?"

* * *

As the shock of flies began to swarm comprehensively into and over the town, the emergency crews of fly-fighters that were still working, all in breathing apparatus and copious amounts of netting supplied by Teacher, watched the fight the sun had been putting up, be squeezed away and a troubled darkness descend upon them once again. All of them knew that this latest influx was set to be more damaging than anything that had come before and so they gave up the ghost without even putting their shovels and pans back on their two wheeled carts. Mayor Brian was devastated; he could just about see an end to it all, had just about rid himself of the constant buzzing in his ears, only now to be challenged once again without any offer from his nemesis to allow him to make a payment.

Even Owen and Joe had abandoned their posts, locking themselves in the container behind the market stall. "What the hell is occurring, Bach?" Owen shouted over the buzzing and rattling of flies crashing into the metal sides of their refuge.

"Seems someone, and I bet I know who, has succeeded in re-energising the cloud," said Joe, who knew what Teacher had done and now repeated.

"Must 'ave been a problem with the money, as sure as I is a Bally Welshman," Owen replied whilst still pulling flies from his hair.

"I wonder where Jet is in all of this?" asked Joe.

"I'll be buggered if I know boyo, but she'll be fine if I know Jet, just fine."

* * *

Jet was lying limp in the water, her left foot was still being dragged down whilst her body with arms out to her sides, floated above, ghostlike. But there was still a flicker in her face and a twitching of her cold blue fingers as she was calling now on her police training, doing what her course Sergeant would tell her to do when in trouble, to call for backup and then calmly think, not allowing the panic to dictate her actions. With his stern face in mind, she re-animated herself and reached down, working her way along the seam of her now inflated trousers, to her foot, to prise Teacher's fingers from the material he had such a grasp of. But there was no warm hand, no soft flesh just a knot of fabric, caught amongst the snarled spokes of a rusting shopping trolley full of rocks and rubble. She was relieved, she didn't know what she was going to do once she had Teacher in her sights, but the job of untangling herself from the fingers of the trolley caging was just as challenging. She couldn't simply rip the material, as the seams from the side and across the bottom of her trousers were providing some strength, especially when wet. She couldn't unload the trolley, she didn't have the strength left and couldn't bend and break the spokes, rusted as they were. The end seemed to be in sight as she straightened up, letting go of her foot, slowly returning to the position of a floating crucifix, maybe to apply for some spiritual help.

* * *

Sally was on her way back to Clearwater, when she pulled her bike over, to answer the screaming and now so irritating radio, that she had switched off. It was the police control room directing her to attend the station and the irate superintendent without delay. "Roger," she acknowledged, finally breaking her silence, whereupon she put her thinking head on, needing an excuse. "Jet didn't know what had happened at the airfield and could only guess why the sting failed to arrest Teacher," she told herself. In fact, she could use her as the reason why it didn't succeed. She called Jets's mobile, but there was no reply, left a message and sent a text. She needed to know where Jet had been at the time of the sting and what she had being doing since. It would serve the little undercover do-gooder right, anyway!

* * *

"Trousers – it's my all-in-one overalls that's the issue," Jet thought, as very slowly now with only seconds to live, using the heel of her right foot, she forced off the training shoe on her left. She then undid her belt, unbuttoned her trousers and slid out of them as what buoyancy she had left, pulled her from her shell. As her ascent from the depths neared the surface, the temperature increased and the sound of buzzing flies returned, not that this was going to stop her now. As she burst through the floating weed and debris, she blew out the stale air that had served her so well and screamed in a new supply that she took in deeply, allowing her lungs to re-inflate and the colour to flood back into her face. It was close, very close, she told herself, relaxing her body to lie in the shallow water until the cold became her next concern, forgetting however, the fact that Teacher was still at large.

* * *

It was four hours after Superintendent Daniels had called Sally, when he found himself still pacing up and down behind his desk until the carpet groaned for being singled out. He had left standing orders at the reception to send her directly to him as soon as she arrived, dashed with flies or not. He had all the case notes spread out across his humungous desk and was reviewing matters in his own head, when finally, there came a knock on his door. "Come in," he shouted, not expecting Sally to walk in and sit in the chair opposite his own, as he fell into a shocked silence.

"I have had a totally irate Mayor bawling down my phone about you, reckons you're good for nothing and the reason for him losing seventy-five thousand quid! What have you got to say about that, my girl, and this better be good!" he said as he began to shake in anticipation of his blood boiling.

"Yes, we lost it, or at least you were told we lost it. It was in fact all fake, except for a thousand pounds which was real, some crazy idea of the bleedin' committee. But we lost it none-the-same at the handover; it was just a repeat of the fact that Teacher outwitted us, yet again."

"You mean he *did* receive it?"

"Yes, I watched Jock put it in the back of Teacher's van."

"But that's not what the Mayor said, he was visited by Teacher who didn't mention any money at all…not even one thousand pounds, he said it was all fake!" the Super pursed his lips and threw the conversation back at Sally.

"But there was no time when the money was out of my hands," Sally reasoned until her furrowing brow led the Super to look at her inquisitively.

"What? What is it?"

"I've just realised, it must have been Jet! She had the cases in her possession just prior to the sting. I said all along she couldn't be trusted, said all along her heart wasn't in it. We have to speak to her without delay!"

"Right, I'll try and call her, you go and bloody find her, pick her up, I want her here!"

* * *

Jet had climbed up the embankment surrounding the lake and was now sliding down the other side, still wet through, with only a clinging t-shirt and white knickers left on. She was shivering from head to foot and knowing the dangers of hypothermia was heading directly for the house she delivered to, only that morning. She banged at the door as a puddle of water with a swim of flies gathered below her. There was movement in the frosted window as a hunched figure came shuffling to the door, "Who's there?" came a haggard old voice as a man stopped just short of opening the door.

"I need help!" Jet shouted back.

"Bugger off," he replied.

"No, seriously."

"There's nothing here, nothing an old man like me can help you with," the man replied, either afraid of strangers or fed up of letting in further squadrons of flies and mosquitoes.

"Seriously, I nearly drowned in the lake, I'm cold and I'm shaking and I need to get warm, quickly!" There was a desperation in her voice.

"There's nothing I can do, clear off."

"I'll make it worth your while, I can pay," Jet pleaded.

At this, the letter box flicked open and a beady little eye

scanned the front doorstep, a part of the security rigmarole its owner had developed over years of living alone. However, on this occasion there was an audible gawp as Jet's bare legs and her now not so white knickers came into view and piece de resistance, her wet T-shirt clinging to every contour. The bolts on the door then shot open like the cannon at the Queen's birthday, as the Yale lock turned and the door was yanked open to reveal a drooling eighty-five-year-old pensioner standing wide-eyed in front of her. "Come in my dear, let me help you, I'm a trained first-aider you know," he said as she stepped into the entrance hall. "Shared bodily heat, you know, that's what's needed, shared bodily heat."

At the bottom of Lake Yaramar, lying alongside the shopping trolley and Jet's trousers still caught in its spokes, was her mobile phone. Resiliently, it was ringing away with all the technology required of a black box flight recorder, shedding little bubbles with each beep that escaped and shot upwards towards the surface. Every now and again a passing minnow would investigate by poking its nose into the bubble stream until it realised that it was inedible and in fact just another piece of human junk. But try as it might, the signal to prompt Jet into contacting Sally was ignored until finally with a splutter and greater expulsion of air, it stopped.

ARCHITECTURAL HANDS

Jet opened her eyes on this Monday morning with difficulty, as they were encrusted with sleepiness after she had been out cold since Sunday afternoon. She found herself under the heavy covers of a giant double divan bed, not unusual as sleeping three quarters the way down beyond the pillows, was what she would do at home. She was relaxed, warm, dry and apparently safe and was almost enjoying the opportunity of a lie in, until a jolt to her system made her realise she was also stark naked. Being not nearly as much out of the world as she might have been, she remembered the struggle at the lake and banging on the door of the old house looking for help, but the rest was as cloudy as the sky, nothing more than a blur and something told her she had been there for some considerable time. Listening intently, not moving, not wanting to alert whoever it was that had facilitated her nudity, she assessed her situation. She was in a double bed but had adopted a diagonal pose across it, as if she had passed out where she fell, hopefully this was the case and that she hadn't been sharing it with anyone else.

Tentatively she slid out of the bed, looking around the room for her clothes, or what was left on her when she arrived there. But they weren't there. She tried the wardrobe, which was empty, the cavernous chest of drawers, also empty. So, after pulling a sheet from off the bed and wrapping it around herself like a Roman goddess, she made her way down the stairs. There was a whistling of a kettle, spattering of fat from a frying pan and the melodic singing tones of the old man that had eventually let her in the day before. She still couldn't remember what had happened since, but instead of confronting him she made her way to the front door and escaped as a whisper, only then realising that the flimsy cotton sheet was blowing away in the wind and she was already covered by waves of flies and mosquitoes. "Telephone!" she said to herself as she began to run down the lane trying to think where she had last seen one for public use, which were now about as rare as superintendents at a crime scene.

* * *

The new influx of critters had now established themselves across the centre of Clearwater town, especially as a prevailing wind helped them escape the lake after being mobilised by the fireworks. Many of the weary population had taken the opportunity as the first injection of critters eased, to venture out for shopping and to check on relatives when their hearts sank as the buzzing intensified once again. Would they like to get their hands on the perpetrator and possibly those at the council who had some control of the situation; would they like to subject them to some form of violence? Mayor Brian was playing the differing scenarios through his head.

Importantly, Mayor Brian was asking himself why he hadn't just paid up in the first place as he began applying more sellotape to the gaps around the window in his office. But he had pledged to himself, or at least he thought that to be the case, to do whatever he had to do, to make sure that the insufferable Tutelage committee paid Teacher what he wanted, at the very next opportunity.

He thought of the last time something similar had happened to him, but a lesser scale. He had taken the Scout troop out to the local campsite. It was on a summer's evening, when for all the humidity, there was an attack by a legion of mosquitoes from the local fortress in the woods. He gathered the patrols together for a brief instruction on applying anti-mozzi cream and what to do if they did get bitten, but this merely deteriorated into a tearful session, where all but the hardened patrol leaders, were asking to go home to mum. He didn't like to lose control like that and felt so guilty, a bit of a failure, when parents began arriving to collect their child, after already partaking in a night of steak dinner, surrounded by a romantic burn of candles and flowers. It was no wonder that they were disappointed, they would have been quite happy for their Billy or Belinda to get eaten alive and it was this kick off, on such a greater scale, that he was now worried about.

* * *

The effect of the re-energising of the plague of flies was a great success in Teacher's eyes. It only took about an hour for the streets to be unbearable once again and sales at the Treasure Trove to pick up once again. As he drove back towards town in his battered old van, now empty of fireworks, he looked up overhead and was pleased to see the trails and contrails of Lake Yaramar's finest, following him down the road. Revenge was sweet, the gods would be pleased. But the failing light and oppression from overhead were not due entirely to the insect cloud and it seemed that not all the gods shared in Teacher's delight, as with a sudden flash of lightning a large drop of water splashed on the windscreen. "Oh no, oh God, not rain, please don't let it rain!" But the first drop was indeed just a precursor as it was followed with another, then several, then a shower and finally as the heavens opened, rain that had been weighing down the genuine clouds for nearly a week.

Someone's god, not his own, Teacher told himself, had arrived on the scene with a vengeance to challenge him, as their architectural hands now began clearing away the land of the piles of insect bodies and intercepting the squadrons still arriving overhead. He didn't have to be told, he knew that this was the end of his spiteful escapade and that Mayor Brian would never now choke on his own failure to pay him.

In the centre of town there was a silence, something that often precludes a good shower. Normally the birds would stop singing, but they hadn't been heard from since the original cloud descended; people would stop chatting, making for cover, swelling the clientele in the café's and bars. But the silence this time was different. As the rain fell the buzzing stopped, the cloud of insects began to clear and a freshness settled over everything, a new day shining through the rainclouds.

By mid-morning people were coming out of their homes, buildings and cars, stripping off their layers of netting, feeling fly-free for the first time since the plague started. They were turning on their hose pipes and sweeping away the banks of insect bodies out onto the roads and streets to be washed away down the nearest storm drain. There were children coming out to play, people going in to work and people coming home from work having been stranded there. The mood of the day was changing to one of optimism.

* * *

By midday, Guido and Betty had arrived back on the market, ready to make a new start. "Sunshine you are my sunshine," Guido began with a song.

"You make me happy when times are grey," Betty continued with her smile beaming as brightly as the rainbow overhead.

Their sales pitch now redundant, Owen and Joe began to clear the Treasure Trove stand of anti-mozzie and fly products. "Thank Christ for that boyo, my strong Welsh legs were giving up the ghost," he said as he sat on the table with Joe.

"I don't know about you mate, but this payment we're supposed to be getting, better be bleedin' good, 'cause I don't see me doing that again."

"No, me neither."

"I wonder if Teach knows it's all over?" Joe reflected. "And what do you think's happened to her ladyship?" he said changing the subject.

"I'll be blowed if I know, but I am getting worried."

"Have you and her got something going?" Joe enquired.

"We 'ad a drink together all right, but no more than that. Besides, I didn't like the way she asked question after question, right enough."

"Teacher's been asking after Jet you know. I said the last I'd seen her was when she was off delivering fly packages near the lake."

Suddenly, there was a clang from the container behind in the car park. "Who was that?"

"It's him, Teacher, I wonder if she's with him?" Owen said as the rest of the market was beginning to stir.

Tubby and Linda were sat with Sandra and Susan at Johnny's café, crammed under a large table umbrella out of the rain, whilst Sebastian, not as welcome as some, was winding up his clocks and watches. They were discussing the Treasure Trove. "Well what's the point putting out our goods until we know what he's going to do next?" said Linda shrugging her shoulders.

"He's not allowed to sell anything the same or similar to us," Tubby reminded everyone.

"He was selling drinks, just the same as mine," said Johnny leaning over the van's counter above them.

"And then look what happened," Tubby added.

"Yeah, he destroyed every last bottle!"

"There vas no proof it was him," Sebastian shouted from his stall across the way.

"You mind your own business, Kraut!" Johnny shouted back instantly.

"Look, they're clearing their stall. Perhaps we'll find out what's next I wonder?" said Sandra standing to get a better view. "Whatever they do they've outstayed their welcome. In fact, I'm going to go over there to tell them exactly that!"

She marched across the now drenched market place, when Teacher, whether feeling compelled or having had some word from the gods, came out from the container to meet her.

"We're not happy!" she said looking directly at him.

"I can understand that. The Treasure Trove has been lucky enough to ride on the back of these recent ecological calamities, where you have not."

"Well yes, but we are worried that your next venture whether foreseen or not will have the same detrimental effect upon the rest of us, all over again!"

"I cannot change the course of life and our environment, or predict what will happen next," he said as he looked into her eyes.

"You cannot predict what will happen next," she replied.

"I can tell you that I intend to sell health foods next and as none of you sell a similar product, there should be no problem."

"It's no problem," she replied predictably.

"Well then, if it's no problem, then we're all happy," Teacher said as he turned and made his way back to the dry container. "And what do you two want?" he added to Joe and Owen who were standing like two daytime zombies absorbing nothing but the rain. "There's nothing to do and we're knackered," said Joe with more gusto than normal.

"Be back tomorrow morning with waterproofs and wellington boots," Teacher instructed. The two men looked quickly at each other and made a bolt for it before the instructions were amended on a second thought.

* * *

Just taken out of storage, Jake's mobile ice cream van came driving down the road like a scurrying hedgehog after a winter of hibernation. Its driver of the same name, had a grin on his face that may have indicated how pleased he was to be at work again but in reality, it was for another reason. Pulling into the council office car park, now full of vehicles as everyone made the effort to return to work, it stopped as near to the double entrance as it could. It didn't advertise its ice creams with a burst of 'Greensleeves' or 'Pop Goes the Weasel', but merely opened its passenger door and allowed the still half-naked Jet to slide out almost alluringly, before making a dash into the reception.

"Oh, good show!" said an office worker as the contents of his un-minded briefcase spilled out in front of him. "Much more effective than the boring old tunes you normally play…" The ice cream man smiled as he had been doing since picking Jet up from the roadside nearly three miles out of town. "They don't call me Mr Whippy for nothing!" he said.

* * *

Miss Fulton was sitting crossed-legged at the reception desk as Jet ran into the council offices, sheet pulled in around her as tight as possible. "Police, are the police team from Chillborough here?" she said looking around very conscious of how she might look to others.

"Oh my," Miss Fulton said as she threw her coat from off the peg around her, "What's happened here?"

"It's all a bit complicated, suffice to say I am a police officer and have got myself into a pretty serious situation. Are Sally Reid or Jock McCall here?" Jet buried herself further into the warm coat to cover both her modesty and embarrassment. But within minutes of the receptionist making some brief phone calls she looked up. "Are you a part of the police team too?"

"Yes, yes, are they here?

"Well, Sally hasn't been seen for some time, but someone called Jock is on his way up to see you," Miss Fulton smiled.

"Oh, thank you. You can't imagine the effect a half-naked woman has on people."

"Oh, I can, believe me I can!" Miss Fulton said as her perfunctory smile finally broke into one showing her true self.

As several members of the team arrived at the same time, they began fussing and consoling Jet, before even hearing her story, or spotting the fact that Teacher's old Ford Escort van had just drawn up outside. It stopped as a bus would, drawing in front of the entrance with its engines still running, until it was convinced that there were no passengers waiting or the driver had seen enough of what was going on inside.

* * *

Despite the rain, the market place was almost booming with its returning customers, all apart from the Treasure Trove which was desolate. Owen and Joe had left for the day as Teacher instructed, leaving nothing but a bare table, which despite the protestations of fellow stallholders concerning its recent domination over them, was in its naked state considered to be just as bad or even worse.

At 3 pm, under the cover of the significant re-population of the market, there came nobody other than Sally Reid. She was looking for Jet, who she believed had just stood her up again by not answering her phone. She had only ever been on the market once before when chasing Teacher, but couldn't give a damn this time as to whether she was spotted and recognised, or not. She was, however, surprised to find the Treasure Trove as quiet as an Egyptian burial ground. She looked around noticing that the other stallholders were all busy, selling or re-stocking their products, but there was no sight of Owen, Joe or more importantly Teacher. He had been in his container, but no longer as he had just nipped out to the newsagents across the way.

Sally then noticed the fact that the door to the container was open, and not one to dilly dally around an opportunity, she slipped between the stalls and crept inside, pulling the door shut behind herself as she did. It was dark, but rather than switch the lights on and risk being seen, she pulled a small mag-light from her rear pocket, but before she turned it on, she cried, 'Ouch', through clenched teeth as she bumped into Teacher's motorbike sat with keys in the ignition, only just catching it from falling.

This drew her attention to the racks of bulging shelving behind, full of empty plastic syringes. She pulled one down to examine it more clearly. It was large, almost 30mm in diameter, but had nothing else with it other than a small leaflet containing a code number of the chemical it had been manufactured for. She pulled her notebook out from a chest pocket and with the little pencil attached, noted them down before replacing the pack on the shelf.

Teacher was now turning away from the centre of town, back towards the market. Inside the container, on a little metal writing desk in the corner up against the door, Sally found several files containing receipts and letters, including one to be sent to Mayor Brian making demands for money to avoid the next calamity. She read it carefully having found something of importance and was scribbling in her note book again when Teacher began opening the door.

Sally dived for cover crouching down at the back of the container, but Teacher rather than entering, stood pondering and thinking to himself. "Owen and Joe were quite right. We all need some sleep," he finally said to himself. So, he put an arm in through the door, lifting down the vans keys from a peg as he yawned in submission. He was just about to lock the container when he stopped, remembering something more. Sally was perspiring, how would she explain this. Luckily however, he didn't switch on the lights, he knew what he needed, and thanks to Sally, who had replaced everything as she had left it, he quickly reached in and drew the file of letters for Mayor Brian. Then, before the rain soaked any further through his robes, he drew a padlock from his pocket and threw it around the two latches on the container, snapping it shut. He didn't want anyone going inside and finding the syringes!

* * *

Jet had been stressed before there was any stress to stress about. This undercover lark she understood to be undercover from Teacher, who had just tried to kill her, but nobody had mentioned being under threat from the local pervert! Jock was all for 'saddling up the herses and lancing the wee pervert up through his Jacksie', which wouldn't have helped the situation and probably be tantamount to police brutality.

Fortunately, Kylie came to the rescue and in a quiet room off from the emergency services, only just returning from the 'Plague of Flies, Part Two' as they called it, she dressed Jet, plied her with a warm coffee latte laced with a small rum and allowed her to cry her eyes out. Between the stop/start sobs and wiping of her eyes and nose, a brief statement was put together to work out exactly what had happened. Kylie then called Jock to make things official.

"And where is Sally Reid in all o' this?" Jock asked. "I'm beginning to lose ma coowl with that lassie!"

"It might have taken you a little while Sergeant, but my patience snapped some time ago," said Mayor Brian who upon hearing everything in graphic detail from Miss Fulton had also rushed down to the basement.

* * *

As the evening arrived and the light dwindled, Sally was still a captive in Teacher's container. She had tried everything to free herself, checked the validity of the steel doors to confirm that Teacher had indeed locked them, when she immediately pulled her radio from her pocket to place a call for help. Whether it was because the steel box was obstinately blocking her signal or that the radio was low on power, she wasn't sure and so repeated the process with her mobile phone, but very unprofessionally, she had allowed the battery to go flat. With her little pencil light, she then examined the shuttered window, the hinges on the door and every possible means of escape. She had now been incarcerated for nearly four hours and had concluded that she might be there until morning, when Teacher finally unlocked the door.

The only thing that was letting light into the container was a four-inch hole, jaggedly cut in the roof, designed to take a flue pipe from a wood burner, but she couldn't think of what good this might be. As her eyes acclimatised to the darkness, she focussed on keeping warm. There was an old towel hanging from the shelving, a sheet that had been used for some carefree painting and a motorcycle helmet sat on the back of Teachers Moto Guzzi. She wrapped them all around her and put the helmet on, sitting on top of one the packs of syringes to keep her bottom off the icy floor, looking very much like a garden gnome having been put away to protect it from the frost.

* * *

Jock had felt that the situation in Clearwater was getting the better of the police team, which was now fragmenting with no leadership other than his own unauthorised blundering. He knew they needed help and he knew it wasn't coming from Sally, so he went up to reception and called the Superintendent.

"What do you mean Jet's been assaulted; I've heard nothing of this."

"Aye, and that be the crux o' it Syr. We are leaderless and according to Mayor Brian, we are anticipating another attack from Teacher, imminently!" There was a considered silence. "Ok Jock, keep the team together at the council offices and I'll be there directly."

He was clearly fuming at the incompetence of Sally and Jet, both women, who had the effect of bringing on his nasal drip, which he could control in no other way than with sharp inhalations through his nose, and a grawl and spit of material into his waste paper bin. Only his daily cleaner would appreciate his intention to take over the investigation from the council offices in Clearwater. So, after changing from his shirt, tie and decorated tunic into field slacks and black top, the now Ninja warrior sped down the stairs into his waiting police Bentley.

* * *

Sally would probably be quite annoyed knowing that the Super was assuming command of the operation. However, being sat now in the container getting colder and colder, all she really wanted was to be rescued. She had envisaged forcing the locks and popping out the window of the container, but realised she had been nodding off to sleep and dreaming much of everything. The only thing she couldn't dismiss was an apparition of her with her hand up inside the flu pipe waving a flag over the roof, which probably wouldn't be seen at night but did give her another idea. Climbing up the racks of shelving she drew her radio and thrust it through the opening out into the dark. She clicked the button to transmit. "Five two to any call sign, come in, urgent message over," she shouted along the line of her outstretched arm desperately hoping that the radio was picking up her voice and not the harr of the passing wind. But there was no reply then or on the regular occasions thereafter as she persevered. Back at the council offices, Kylie was looking after Jet, Jock was in reception awaiting the arrival of the Super and Andy and Nev were asleep in the bunkroom, but the radio was in fact working, sat in the basement, just not being answered.

THE BREAKING OF CONTAINMENT

As the hands on the clock in the reception hall passed midnight and the witching hour began, the Superintendent had arrived at the council offices and called everyone, with the exception of Jet, into a team briefing. This had the effect of unshackling the guarded opinions of everyone and a unified complaint about Sally being presented very quickly. "Just so as I understand," the Super began, "Sally has been mistreating Jet, swearing and chastising her, was not visible at the sting that failed and has been constantly missing or unavailable. Like now…"

"That's correct Syr, aye," Jock said as everyone sitting about nodded their heads and made comments to support him.

"And that the sting that Sally arranged failed because of her mis-management?"

"She disappeared when most needed," Kylie commented still remembering her fall from the transit.

"Well, I'm taking command for now. Get Jet off to hospital for some R&R Jock, Kylie you assume comm-unications, man the radio, get a telephone set up in the basement and check to see all radios are charged and working. Andy and Nev get out there and see if you can find Sally, miscreant she may be but she could also be in trouble!"

As a brightly coloured ambulance, freshly washed by the rain, drew up outside of the council offices, it loaded a still sleeping Jet into its well-organised rear cabin. Kylie stood wanting to wave goodbye, but didn't really get the chance and so made her way to the basement office to service the radios. As she arrived, the micro LED lights on the receive portal had just gone out and all was quiet. She opened the drawer on a small upright unit and placed four hungry batteries for radios into the charger unit above, then lifting down the radio mike, she transmitted. "Five three from Five zero, radio check, over."

"Five three to Five zero, receiving over," came Nev's reply from the police car's integral radio.

"Five four from Five zero, radio check over," Kylie continued.

"Five four to Five zero receiv…." Jock's transmission was suddenly cut out.

"Say again Five four." There was a crackle on the line again, faintly at first, but from the voice of a woman who seemed to be in some sort of panic.

"Five four stay silent, second signal say again, over."

"Five zero this is Five two," came a very faint reply.

"Five two, is that you Sally?" said Kylie forgetting all protocol and using a name over the airwaves.

"Roger, roger, I need help! Teacher's container at the market, confirm over…"

"Roger Five two, roger. Stay cool, we're on our way."

As soon as Kylie passed the news to Jock and the Super, they ran out into the car park to grab the police Transit. Andy and Nev in the police car had activated their blues and two's and u-turned in the road with a screeching like a demented owl. Narrating their progress then on the radio to Kylie, they made their way through desolate streets, apart from the occasional drunk, switching off their emergencies as they got nearer to the market place so as not to surprise and scare off Teacher or his cronies, should they be there. There was no one in sight as they arrived, but with the silence and the rain still falling at a steady pace, they felt as if they were caught up in some sort of nuclear aftermath. Sally, after the flurry of radio calls, had fallen silent until the men pulled into the car park and with high powered torches began to comb the area. It was their whispering commentary to each other that alerted her. "Who's there?" she shouted nervously.

"Calm down Sally, it's the cavalry," Nev replied knocking on the steel door somewhat baffled after looking around the van for another way in.

"He used a padlock," Sally shouted not so helpfully.

"Yeah, I can see that, looks as if we're knackered then!" said Andy kicking the side of the container in frustration.

"Can't you use oxyacetylene or something and cut your way in?" she shouted.

"At this time of night?" Andy replied as Jock and the Super arrived together.

"Well, we can't leave it until morning, he'll be back by then," Sally said, acutely aware that the police investigation would be compromised if Teacher found her there.

"Quite right. We have to get her out and get away with the scene and our credibility intact," said the Super.

"Dina ye worry lassy, we'll 'ave ye oot be then!" Jock seemed to be the only reassuring voice, despite the fact that he wasn't directing things. The Super on the other hand, hadn't addressed Sally directly, since he had arrived, asked how she was or anything, so she made a point of not asking for him.

Then occupying herself whilst the quartet outside had a brief meeting and a tea from Nev's flask, Sally threw a plan into the black hole that had so far consumed any other suggestions, which sparked a quick con-flab and another cup of tea, whilst the Super adopted the idea as his own. He then made a few calls on the radio to have the resources required delivered to them quickly. It wasn't going to be easy and didn't take account of Teacher's propensity for quick thinking. But then it was the only feasible offering given the time available, that wouldn't require Teacher's arrest, there still being little evidence enough, to secure his imprisonment. "God help me if this doesn't work," Sally thought, "and God help me if it does!"

As the dawn arrived and the red in the morning gave its

warning, staining the shops and building frontages, everything was set and ready. Behind Guido's ice cream van a pavement access cover had been removed which was now surrounded by a small army of traffic cones and red tape, punctuated with some triangular signs that said 'Danger! Gas!' Within sight of this but out of sight of the Treasure Trove and container, Jock was sat with a complicated box of electrics and his police radio. Having removed the Transit and police car, the unmarked Sherpa was left sat, strategically, in the car park. It was used for surveillance and therefore had the most appreciated rear compartment containing heaters, seats and post box viewing ports in the side of it. It also had tea making facilities on a dedicated melamine shelf, which had been used frequently since its arrival and was now littered with empty cylinders of coffee, spilt milk and the crunch of wayward sugar. At around 7 am the rain stopped as abruptly as God's plumber turned the stop tap, leaving nothing but puddles on the ground and freshened air to breathe, offering a very good day for the market to catch up on its recent losses. As a few people began to materialise on their way to work and almost as soon as the police team was ready, a large lorry pulled itself onto the car park and reversed until it was sat alongside Teacher's container. It was clearly preparing to make a delivery when, as if aided by some sort of telekinesis, Teacher drove onto the plot to greet it. There was a mild panic in the Sherpa as cameras and binoculars were trained on pro-ceedings and notebooks made ready.

Upon hearing the sound of the lorry engine pulling up alongside, Sally quickly got ready to put her part of the plan into action. "Morning guv'nor," said a London lorry driver that had climbed down from his cab with a clipboard and pen to facilitate his delivery, only to look a little aghast at Teacher dressed in his robes and sandals.

"Have you got everything I asked for?" Teacher asked expecting as a reflection of modern retailing, some delay or exclusion.

"Oh, yes guv'nor, if you can't trust Trimbles, trust no one," the driver delivered his carefully rehearsed speech on the value of customer service. He lifted the lorry's rear concertina doors.

"What the hell does he want that lot for?" Nev asked the Super, as they watched the driver unloading crate after crate of disinfectant and packs of what looked like medicine.

"Keep your eyes on the container," the Super insisted, holding one hand above his head to ready the start, as Teacher began to search through his duffle bag for the keys.

"Wait, wait, wait," the Super continued until he saw the padlock being removed. "Now!" he yelled, pulling down his arm to start the race.

"Now!" Nev relayed down the radio to Jock.

"Ok!" Jock confirmed, as he flipped a switch on the panel mounted over his box of electrics.

Just as Teacher had begun to pull open the heavy steel doors, there came a flash from the pavement within the so-called gas company's hole in the ground, followed as fast as only a Concorde could ensure, with an almighty bang. It was louder than anything, a bit like the bird scaring machines at any modern airfield, but it had everyone arriving at the market with their hands in their mouths. Teacher, wheeling around to see what was happening, flinched as there was a second bang that seemed to echo from building frontage to frontage all the way up the high street and back. Being less surprising than the first, the second bang had people heading for cover or throwing themselves on the ground, especially after some anoraked army veteran shouted: 'incoming'! There was then a series of smaller bangs, still loud but close together, from which Sally took her prompt and having pulled on the motorbike helmet that was hanging off Teacher's Motor Guzzi, she had pulled it down off its stand and started it by virtue of the keys left in the ignition.

As a crack of light squeezed around the door, Teacher turned and shrieked, "What the bloody hell?" as the noise of the pyrotechnics faded and the bike's engine revved. He was now convinced that someone was inside. "Now, Sally, go now!" the Super shouted as with front wheel in the air she let off the brakes, battering the doors back on the hinges with a deep metal clang and charged out of the doorway. Teacher went flying if only to avoid being hit as the bike flew clean over the top of him, leaving him with his eyes flaring and irritable temper, of late, rising once again.

Everyone was now in the Sherpa. Jock had climbed quickly into the back, as Andy climbed into the driving seat and started the engine, taking off like an overweight greyhound, with all the intention of a quick getaway, but with all the problems of the additional tonnage. "Go on, accelerate!" the Super shouted as he grabbed onto something to stop him being thrown around and Andy and Nev finally managed to fasten their seat belts.

"Down't 'e be premature, it's noo over yet!" said Jock, who still had an eye to the observation port in the side of the van. "Teacher is a comin' after us!" he added seeing the battered old Ford Escort van charging across the car park.

"Call it in," shouted the Super, "white Ford Escort van exceeding the speed limit coming through town, up the pedestrian precinct." Nev followed instructions and called control on the radio as Andy turned left to head for the precinct realising what the Super had in mind. Every on-duty police car would now be heading there too. Teacher was none the wiser, but his trusty van was not as trusty as it once was, lurching forward at every junction and overshooting every give way sign as if on a lake of ice, due primarily to the antique brakes.

"Damn the very bowels of Belanos!" he yelled as even with only one driver and no passenger, he began losing ground on the Sherpa.

"Left onto Carnaby Street, turning down onto the high street," Nev continued to advise all the closing police cars of where they were and where therefore, Teacher would be in his pursuit. "Coming around past the Natwest bank to turn uphill at the junction into the precinct, now!" Hanging on tight as the Sherpa leaned into the corner turning on a dime, Andy could see two sleek police cars with their blues flashing and lights a-blazing, call signs six-one and six-two, coming downhill towards them. As they met, they parted one down one side of the Sherpa and one down the other, to pounce with great surprise on their prey to the rear. However, Teacher had fallen back such that he hadn't as yet, turned onto the precinct, so the two cars eased off the gas anticipating his late arrival. They sat for more than a minute when they had to conclude that there was no sign of him, so one car turned left in case he had simply driven straight on at the junction and one turned right back in the direction the Sherpa had come from.

Inside the Sherpa the men could still hear the chatter coming over the radio from the cars in all quarters in the town, including the car that had turned left at the bottom of the precinct. All had no sighting of Teacher. "What about six two?" Andy asked as he slowed the Sherpa and pulled into a parking bay in front of the local supermarket, where Nev sent a quick message using the Super's call sign to find out why.

"There's been no contact with six two, since he turned right at the bottom of the precinct, Sir," Nev explained as they sat listening to the repeated messages from control asking for a response from the lost car.

"Turn around," the Super said, "he won't catch up with us now, in fact he's probably in custody." The van three-pointed and drifted down the precinct turning right at the bottom when in only two hundred yards, they spotted six-two parked up at the side of the road.

"There's six-two, stop there," the Super instructed as he jumped down out of the back of the van before it had properly parked and ran across to the PC sat in the driving seat.

"Hello Sir, fancy seeing you here," PC Smith said.

"I'm a part of the surveillance team."

"I see, and what can I do for you?" he asked politely.

"The Ford Escort van you were chasing, where is it?"

"Ford Escort van?"

"Yes, yes! Have you lost him, did he go straight on at the precinct?"

"He didn't do that Sir," Nev interjected, "six-one says he's seen nothing going back that way."

"Then you must have seen him," the Super insisted of the blank faced PC, "white Ford Escort van, you came down the precinct after it!"

"Noo Sir, that wasn't me, I've been sat here the last fifteen or twenty minutes. It's all quiet here apart from some black clad motorcyclist going the other way."

"Sally!" the Super deduced.

"Don't know what her name was Sir, as I say, bin sat here for the last fifteen minutes."

"Have you really, PC Smith?" said the Super as he leant in through the window and snapped his fingers in front of the PC's face.

"Oh," Smith said as his glazed expression was suddenly replaced by one of shock and he looked up surprised to see the Super.

"Hello, Sir," he said. "What are you doing here?" The Super put his head in his hands.

"Did you catch him?" Smith added as some vague recollection of something slightly grazed his memory banks.

"So, you did see him then!"

"The bloke in the white robes, I did, pulled up right in front of me, I was going to book him for dangerous driving."

"So, why didn't you?" the irate Super was now trampolining up and down on the spot.

"Said he wasn't the Ford Escort I was looking for and that if I sat here long enough someone would come and explain."

"Bleedin' Hell Fire!" the Super finally exploded. "Hypnotised, he's been bloody hypnotised!" he said as he walked away despondently, leaving PC Smith looking like a school child that had just been told off for losing his ball over the school wall.

* * *

After Sally had all but exhausted the fuel in Teacher's Moto Guzzi, she found herself back at her flat in Chillborough. She could hardly keep her eyes open after surviving a night in the cold but put in a call to Control just to keep them in the know, really a dodge to avoid the inevitable call from the Super and more than likely, a grilling over how she managed to lock herself in Teacher's container in the first place. At least her credibility with Teacher would hold fast and her plans for him were still intact, only God above knew what she would have done if she had ostracised herself from both camps. She turned the radio off then and unplugged the landline from the wall, before pulling on her soft padded blindfold, as she always did after coming off a night shift.

Sure enough, from the minute the Sherpa had pulled into the Clearwater County Offices, the Super was on the radio trying to contact Sally. He was advised by Control at Chillborough that she had checked in and so was angrier now than he was concerned for her welfare. "What a bloody nerve! After all our efforts, police time, not to mention the expense, she should have called me, not me call her." His rantings and efforts over the radio had been overheard by Kylie.

"Sir, I think there's something you need to know," she said, "something Jet told me just before she was taken to hospital."

"Go on," he replied.

"She said she had followed the police team onto the airfield during the last operation to catch Teacher, despite being told not to by Sally, which is why I think she didn't tell us until now."

"Tell us what, stop babbling girl."

"Jet said she had seen Sally meet Teacher secretly in the bottom of one of the old bomb craters out there…"

"What did she mean, 'secretly'?"

"She said Sally even greeted him with a kiss, as if they were old friends and all."

"Oh no!" The Super was now more confused than before. Had he just rescued Sally from the clutches of her lover; was this a brilliant piece of police work or was she in league with Teacher in extorting the council?

A SETTLING OF SCORES

A perplexed Teacher, having turned chase to escape, had finally returned to the market place around ten o'clock, once he was sure there was no one else following him and the busy trading of the Tuesday morning provided a little cover. He sat still in the van to do some meditating, suppress his furious mood, bedazzled by recent events and analyse just what had happened. "What could be so bleeding valuable for a team of more than three, to break into my container?" he asked himself, "especially in such a byzantine fashion, using a getaway van and diversion of fireworks. And, how did anyone get inside in the first place. He parked, ratchetting up the hand brake, which had no effect whatsoever as in getting out the van rolled a good half meter down the meagre incline. He got out and arriving at the container, kicked the giant steel door, which he immediately regretted as his big toe, hanging out of his sandals, took the impact, like a tomato in the face of a lump hammer. Owen and Joe were inside, having arrived to find the open door on the container and a large delivery of disinfectant and medicine, which they had moved inside.

"Barbiturate 101, what's that then?" Joe had asked at the time, but there was no indication of what it might be. There was no certain clue now either, as to what Teacher wanted displayed on the stall, no retail tickets or price lists. "Hey, Teach, nice to see you here on time for once!" Joe said riding his advantage.

"Don't go there," was the response.

"Well, what are we supposed to think, you give us a day off, which was unusual enough and then we arrive ready to work our butts off and you're not here. We saw that you had left the container door open, but could only guess that it's the disinfectant that you're to be selling. And while we're on the subject, we're doing all this without being paid!"

"You'll get your cut when the job is done."

"Well er, I down't know 'bout Joe, Bach," interrupted Owen, "but we've been hanging around here all morning."

Teacher pointed as a four-ton lorry, with signage saying "Denzil's Free of Meat", hauled itself across the car park until with help from its farting braking system, it stopped. The driver dressed in a white boiler suit, with 'Denzil' emblazoned on it in bright pink, climbed daintily out from the cab and bounced as fresh as a daisy, to the ground below. He looked up, very campily at Teacher in his robes and sandals.

"Ooo, do you do bookings?" he asked in a very camp voice, throwing his head back in gay abandon.

"Take the delivery Joe, from this… Denzil, for want of a better word and place as much of the stock as you can out on the stall." Teacher turned, disappointing the driver and marched with his own white attire, still damp but not so much peppered with dead flies, into the container.

"Oh, I say chuck, what's his problem?" said Denzil.

"Don't worry about it Cariad, he's not grown up in these times and just doesn't understand the LGBT thing," Owen replied.

"Frankly my love, there are times when I don't! I just am what I am," Denzil said throwing his head back again as he began unloading boxes and boxes of products.

"Err, what exactly have we got here?" Joe asked peeling back some of the brown wrapping paper.

"All from my company 'Vegastronomy'. Millet purees, rosemary chilli spreads, fried bananas, almond pancakes, spicy muffins. Not to mention our starter kits, nibble boxes and gift hampers. It's becoming a big thing you know…" Denzil said, flexing his hand to a right angle.

"Let me get this right. All this stuff is meat-free, yes?" Owen quizzed.

"Yes. So healthy!"

"Well I s'pose Teacher will 'ave something up his sleeve to persuade people," Owen said, but he scratched his head nevertheless, as the two men began unloading and up-stalling.

Teacher was still biting his bottom lip as he took a pen and paper from the little desk in the container and began scratching out the next letter he intended to deliver to the Mayor. "To the very unwise Mayor of Clearwater on this, the cessation of your most recent testing. Faustitas, the white goddess of livestock, has formed an alliance with Belanos and left your fields and farmland. She has protected them from modern man but will now no longer do so; there will be no more protection for your horses, donkeys and camels, your cattle sheep and goats…she has withdrawn it! Only you can save them. You will have just twelve hours to pay my ransom, which has now risen to £100,000. May Belanos have mercy upon you." There were the usual banking details on the bottom of the letter and signature in hieroglyphics. The demand was then folded very precisely and placed in the usual silken envelope, with 'urgent' written upon it.

* * *

Sometime around lunch, after grabbing a McDonalds' quarter-pounder with cheese meal, Teacher pulled into the council office's car park and got out of the van with envelope in hand. He was ultra-nervous, not that he was showing it, given that the police cars standing around and the Sherpa van were all too familiar. But help was on the way as someone from behind him said, "Will you want me to take that?"

"Sally Reid! Seems you are becoming less and less a fish out of water," Teacher said not associating her in any way with the leather clad escapee from earlier in the day, as sensibly she had changed down and even done her hair.

"More and more a criminal?" she replied.

"I didn't say that, but your analogy is probably correct."

"I can't abide the force any more, you know that. The Superintendent is putting me down at every opportunity, never rewarding me with so much as a well done. That's why I'm here, to explain why I allowed you to get the better of the police team at the airfield."

"You didn't allow us to do that, merely helped that's all."

"Let's hope it's not for nothing," she insinuated looking at him for reassurance."

"I've cut you in for a share right enough, but don't climb above your station," Teacher warned whilst wagging a finger and attempting to stare at her, to top up what hypnotic control he had over her from past encounters.

"I take it, that's the next letter?" she asked, seeing what he was carrying.

"Yes, it is."

"Well then, give it to me, I'll take it to the Mayor myself. It will be less dangerous for you and I'll have more of an effect on him, convince him that this time he has to pay!"

"Show him a bit of leg?"

"I don't need to, his eyes are always all over me, like speedy Gonzales with a rash," she smiled pleased at least that she still had something to offer, even if all men were no more lecherous than him. Teacher handed the silken package over with only one comment, "No cash this time. He pays it into the account on the letter and quick if he wants to limit this next tasting; this one will be a vile affair. You tell him!" Teacher looked somewhat differently just for a moment, when Sally thought she could detect some flash of evil shoot across his face. He was very matter of fact and direct, without any cheeky grin or brilliance of light in his eyes and just as soon as he had told her what he wanted of her, he prompted her on, with a threatening inclination of his head towards the doorway.

Miss Fulton was delivering the mail to the Mayor as usual. She had an officious look this morning, peeking over the top of her crescent moon spectacles as her thrusting bosom entered the room before her like the nose of a winning racehorse. Mayor Brian was about to pop a cork as he eyed her up, including her in his fantasy of a weekend away in a woodland log cabin, with a steaming hot tub. Suddenly, his vision was dashed as Sally Reid followed her into the office with another of Teacher's silken envelopes tucked securely under one arm. "Oh, no, not you!" Brian said for many reasons, but his eyes were now at least focussed on the envelope. "What are you doing with that?" he said standing up from behind his desk.

"You're going to have to be much more careful this time Mayor Brian. Teacher had me deliver this in the hope that I might convince you to pay him what he wants. If you don't, I think he will do some irrevocable damage this time."

"Open it, open it," he urged her. She pulled the letter from out of its envelope but fell short of reading it, preferring to hand it to him still folded. He looked at her trying to read her thoughts, but unfolded it all the same and read it through to himself.

"One hundred thousand! Is he off his head!" Brian shrieked as he fell back into his chair.

"I already warned you Brian that he would jack the price up and on this occasion, you would do well to listen. He's only been playing with you so far and in my opinion, he is targeting your livestock this time, perhaps intending to kill them all!"

"Well you haven't helped have you, haven't pierced Teacher's armour plating from what I can see."

"Then 'ow is it that it's me that brings you his letter?" There was a brief silence.

"Ok, so you have a line to him that I don't have. You're either so far undercover that no one can see what it is you're doing or, God forsake us, you're working with him!"

"Don't talk so ridiculous, I'm merely tryin' to 'elp you work out what's best for the council and your towns-people and believe me Brian, your gonna 'ave to pay this time!"

"Well I'm going to call the Super, he's here in the building you know!"

"Good, you do that..." she said, making her way quickly out of his office, thinking that to meet the Super now, would be more difficult again. So she raced down the steps and out of the building, before inadvertently bumping into him coming the other way.

* * *

The day's trading at the market, provided a welcome return to counting profits with the banter expected of the stallholders. Betty and Guido had been engaged all afternoon in filling the air with the sound of music, all with a guiding theme; Goodbye – Goodbye, Goodbye stranger, Bye Bye Love, See You Later Alligator, whilst the stallholders forgot their preoccupation with Teacher. The Treasure Trove was all set out with its vegan foods and snacks, but there was no real interest from the public, apart from the odd hippy or personal trainer. This was of further amusement to the stall holders, as even Johnny had taken Sebastian a cup of tea in good faith; Lucy had taken to sitting on Tubby's knee behind the cover of a rail of kinky underwear and Susan and Sandra had been charitable enough to put on a two-for-one for all the chocolate-mad kids.

"Let's hope their luck has abandoned them finally," Johnny shouted as Sebastian's clocks all struck three o'clock together.

"We should evoke rule number twenty-two," Betty said to Guido as they stood together looking over the bristling market and the Treasure Trove stall, still devoid of custom.

"Reminda me, what is a rule twenty-two."

"We only have rules from one to twenty-one my dear, but I thought it about time we created rule twenty-two!"

"Bravissimo!" there was a pause. "For why, my love?"

"That's why..." Betty pointed at Joe and Owen behind the Treasure Trove store looking as if they had been stood in front of an empty fridge past breakfast, dinner and teatime.

* * *

Jet had finally discharged herself from the hospital in Chillborough and after going back to her home nick for an hour or two, she caught the first No7 bus to start running again since the flies had dissipated. She arrived at the market at five o'clock, as things were winding down. There was some audible chatter from some of the stallholders, who were quick to ask where she had been and if she was all right. She was well liked by them, always had the time to talk with them and share a joke, usually at Teacher's expense. But the concern and shock on people's faces was now more due to the fact that she was in police uniform. She walked boldly with the swagger that the role demanded, up the pedestrian zone, as the birds in the air and solitary dog dived for cover. She then stood, feet apart, in front of Guido's ice cream wagon, quickly drawing her telescopic police baton, which she open and closed, over and over again, in anticipation of a confrontation.

Teacher had been watching what was happening whilst nodding his head in justification; he knew he couldn't trust her, he knew that he was going have to deal with her. In newly washed robes and polished sandals, he walked then like a gunfighter, out into the market place to face her. This had the huddles of apprehensive stallholders whispering warily, keeping out of sight for fear of being looked or starred at. Many of the shoppers were oblivious to what was going on, so Jet stepped forward and twizzled her baton once again, which cleared them away like cactus balls rolling back onto the prairie. Jet was there as she felt it to be her god-damned duty, as one who would wear the Marshall's badge for all the chicken livered, and the 'I told you so' people. But, as Teacher made his way to stand right in front of her, waiting for her to make her move, he noted that she was looking a little unsteady on her feet, that she was either still concussed or, he thought, slightly inebriated. There was a silence that spread across the town, when Jet suddenly drew in a breath and cupped her hands around her mouth, set to give Teacher a verbal barrel of truths and slam him into handcuffs, when with no warning at all, Sally jumped out from behind a pyramid of Dog Gone meaty chunks and whacked Jet over the head with a five-kilo sack of Doggy Dental Do-Doos, laying her out cold.

Some minutes later as Jet opened her eyes, she found herself flat on her back, pulled under the apron of Guido's stall, reminiscent of her early days as a youth when visiting Glastonbury. Betty was knelt next to her, rubbing the back of her hand, in the misguided hope that it would bring down the bump on her head. The rest of the stallholders stood squabbling like seagulls outside a chip shop trying to scoop up the half empty wrappers, as most had seen what had happened and were now springing to Jet's defence. Sally was their obvious target, being the anonymous assailant with a fetish for dental snacks and so as they closed on her menacingly, to avoid being beaten up herself she had to pull out her warrant card, using it like some sort of Star Wars weaponry to fend off retailing freaks. Fortunately, as the clouds finally stopped spinning and Jet's vision returned, Sally's silhouette took on some clarity and Jet bailed her out at the last minute by identifying her with a "Hi Gov. What are you doing here?" Followed quickly as a half memory jogged itself free, "Oh yes, I seem to remember something now. Sorry Gov, sorry!"

* * *

"What was that all about?" Teacher said flippantly as he returned to the safety of the container.

"Oh, my God," said Owen, who had actually caught a glimpse of the dark-clothed woman assaulting what looked to be Jet. He paused by adding, "She's a copper?" He reminded himself of his developing relationship with Jet and how he had begun to treasure it as a possible return to normality, after so many grim times as a guest of Her Majesty in one of her prisons. Then again, he also considered the fact that her behaviour was always a little strange, as if she was trying to recruit him for some sort of Alpha course for perpetual criminals. Now it made sense.

"There's work to be done away from the stall," Teacher said

trying to drag them away from the scene. "Take a syringe from the stocks in the container and attach the needle from alongside. Then hold it in the liquid in the medicine packs and draw it up until full, remembering to replace the needle protector when finished. Be careful not to catch yourself as this stuff will kill you!"

"Kill you! Then what the hell is it for then?" Joe said with a look of panic in his eyes.

"Need to know and you don't need to know anything more than to be at the entrance of Fruit Tree farm, on the outskirts of town, with all the syringes, at 1am tonight."

"I hope we're getting overtime for this," said Joe trying to be as demanding as he hoped he was crucial to the success of Teacher's plan, but he was ignored all the same.

As Teacher left cranking and screeching once again in the van, Owen made an excuse and left the container to pay Jet some attention. She wasn't difficult to find as the melee of stall holders were still moaning and groaning to each other behind Guido's ice cream van, but the trick was to get near enough to her without getting boshed himself. "Excuse me, excuse me, Bach," he repeatedly said as Susan and Sandra bounced off his rugby frame and Tubby was swept aside with Owen's long right arm as he would have been capable of in the last twenty-five nearing the touchline. "Is that Jet there, Jet are you there!"

"Owen, is that you?" Jet answered having recognised his Welsh tones over all the others.

"Jet, what are you doing?" Sally said quickly, "You've blown your cover! Don't be talking to him."

"No wait, this is Owen," she said as the six-footer stood over the two of them. "He's not like the others, he's a man for turning."

"Never mind that Cariad, are you all right?" he asked compassionately whilst grabbing Sally by one arm with a grip like a tennis player upon his racket at match point.

"Yes, just been bashed by the boss is all."

"She be a police lady signor," Guido explained, which only caused Owen to tighten his grip whilst his face and eyes interrogated Jet.

"It's true and so I am," Jet explained as Sally fended Owen off with her all-powerful warrant card. "We should explain..."

Owen listened carefully to what was being said by Jet and Sally and began to realise that he was in enough trouble already and that should he continue to wander down this slippery road, he would probably end up back in prison playing patience till his dying day. Jet's pleas for him to turn and give evidence against Teacher however, were just too much, honour amongst thieves still being uppermost in his character, besides which, being built like a brick shit house or not, he was still very wary of the power and capabilities of his boss. The new road and direction that Jet was suggesting, her clear concern for him and his inkling that their relationship may be something more than just a damp squib, something precious, had him taking the plunge.

"If you are prepared to do what you can for me Cariad, keep me out of prison especially, then I might be able to 'elp ewe," he said shaking under the weight of his decision. Jet looked at Sally who looked to the sky, held her breath and said, "I'll speak to the Super. But what exactly you can do for us, I'm not sure?"

"Information, Cariad. I can tell ewe what be going down tonight, all about Teacher's latest testing!" Owen waited for a reaction, "Deal?"

"Deal!" said Sally, looking at Jet, but being careful not to reveal her crossed loyalty, "only if you give me *every* last detail."

"Right then, Fruit Tree Farm, 1am tonight, there'll be something going down. Teacher 'as asked Joe and I to be there with all the syringes 'e recently purchased, now primed with a medicine called Barbiturate 101. I down't know what the something is to be or whether you could catch him at it, but I suggest you plan to do so. I will carry on as normal, as Teacher directs me until you arrest me, in full view of him, but all peaceful like!"

"Sounds like a plan!" said Sally.

BEEFING THINGS UP

Armed now with a new development and a way forward, Sally radioed for a pick up from the market for herself and Jet. Concerned for the rookie and yet still incensed by Sally, the Super accompanied Jock in the unmarked Transit and approached Guido's ice cream van from the rear, like a hearse, so as not to alert Treasure Trove eyes. Owen had taken himself back across the precinct and was helping Joe clear away the stand, now knowing that the approaching night would be one of conflict and hopefully resolution. "Eh what are ye doin' here lassie," said Jock as he helped Jet into the van, glancing only with contempt at Sally as he did so.

"Sally bloody Reid," said the Super with both nasal cavities in flood, "you're suspended pending enquiries into your activity, or lack of it in this case."

"But Sir, I 'ave new info and a mole inside Teacher's gang."

"You better had and it better be corroborated by Jet, or it'll be the only thing that prevents the arse falling out of your career."

"Sir, that's wholly inappropriate."

"Get in the van Reid, just get in the van," the Super demanded through an uneasy silence that was just begging to be broken as the group arrived back at the council offices, whereupon Jock took Jet to be debriefed and the Super escorted Sally inside, where he confined her to barracks pending the enquiries he said he would make the following day. It wasn't long however, before Jock crashed into the Mayor's office, as if he was playing chicken on the canal again, where the Super was sharing a desk, as would two out of work comedians. "Sirs, I need to speak wi' ye, right noo," Jock said holding his burning notebook in his hands.

"What is it Jock?" the Super said eager to dismiss him and get back to flicking through copies of Mayor Brian's Scouting magazines. "It's Jet Sir, she claims she has information aboot Teacher's new testing and that it's set for tonight!"

"Tonight?" the Super exclaimed suddenly realising that what Sally was telling him was kosher, but without any timings or location. "What time and where?"

"She dinna know Sir, says she was still sufferin' from concussion at the time. She says for ye to ask Sally as she knows."

"Sally! Just what is that woman playing at." He stood thinking as Mayor Brian began fidgeting. "Fetch her, bring her here now!" the Super said decisively. "And put the rest of the team, including Jet, on standby!"

"Aye Sir," said Jock as the Mayor punched the sky.

* * *

Back at the market, Teacher was putting together the final details of his plan for the next calamity to befall Clearwater. He had some concerns and was chuntering away to himself as he would have if sat in an old age pensioner's home, having run out of tobacco. He was pleased that he would be in contact with Sally, who would advise just as soon as the Mayor conceded and made payment. He didn't want to target the whole farm, it would take nearly two hours to do that, but he would if the Mayor continued with his refusal to pay. He began loading the primed syringes now into three camouflage bags with leisurely, over-the-shoulder straps, placing them in the back of the van. He then changed his clothes from his white robes to battle-ready dress, number one pattern camouflage.

All was set.

* * *

Sally was now sat in front of the Super whilst they had cups of tea in one hand and pieces of cake in the other. "I want all the details Sally, every last thing, especially if you think you're going to get any sympathy from me!" the Super was adamant, which only had the resentment welling up like ink in Sally's eyes.

"They're gonna do sommat to the livestock on Field Farm. I 'ave it from my insider, that it's going to be tonight!"

"What time?" asked the Super pressing hard.

"The Mayor has been given a deadline, has to pay the demand by 1 am," she said, "or, presumably that's when whatever is going to 'appen, will 'appen."

"That's no bother," Mayor Brian said, "I'm going to pay all of it to the account specified in the letter, on the dot, then I'll radio Sally and your police team can move in and arrest everyone."

"It's a good plan, Sir. We have Jock, Andy and Nev, Kylie and Jet and possibly yourself from Clearwater."

"I'll see if I can get some reserves from Chillborough and possibly the police helicopter for extra support," the Super said.

"And what about me?" Sally asked.

"You can come along, but only as my advisor. I'll make sure you have a radio and a telephone. We better get him this time Reid or your police career will be over!"

* * *

Late that night in the pitch black, the three renegades with faces scarred with boot polish, arrived in their less inconspicuous van. They parked it in a small sunken road, largely unused and dragged a low hung branch from an ailing tree, over the top of its dirty but still shiny roof. Then, having donned one of the bags each and tested the small short wave radios, they slunk into the undergrowth to await their deadline of 1 am. Not far from them, the farm's scruffy dogs had heard their noisy approach and were now tearing at the shed door where they were kept. The police team as defined by the Super at the earlier meeting, were now training their ten by fifty binoculars across the fields, watching events from their various hideouts. They were expecting something more than the local fox to be on the prowl and were therefore, on the alert. Sally and the Super were sat inside the surveillance van, parked between the farm's tractors and weird-looking bailers, choppers and other machines, but it fitted in well. "What time is it?" asked the Super coughing as quietly as his nose would allow.

"Twelve-thirty," said Sally.

"No news from the Mayor yet?"

"I've told you a fousand times Sir, I'll let you know just as soon as I do!" The Super grumbled something about manners and women in the police force, as he opened the door of the van before getting out and stretching his legs, then choosing to go back and sit with Jock in the hay barn.

The control elements of the team had located themselves in the middle of the farm, strategically deploying the others from there. Andy and Nev, as ever partners, call sign Five three, were covering the slopes below the farm, where the clear majority of its prize heifers were stood still chewing the cud, or lying down in anticipation of a chilly night. Kylie and Jet, call sign Five four, were doing the same job but above the farm on hills that were more akin to sheep farming. This was of great preference as the two women could see the twinkling lights in the valley below, which gave them some reference point, when those below had none. To his credit, the Super had secured another eight, albeit irritable constables, having had to give up their off-duty time, who had been divided into quick response teams one and two. They were sat in the back of the hay barn, listening to developments over Jock's radio, ready to deploy at a moment's notice. Their call signs were Quebec Romeo One and Two. In addition, the police helicopter would swing by from its designated traffic patrol, every now and again, but apart from a distant thudding from its whirling blades, there was nothing to be seen of him overhead.

Teacher was carrying his bag and a radio, tuned in to receive Owen and Joe, both of whom had broken right and left below the farm and taken up their positions adjacent to the field with the cattle. He glanced at his watch again. "What! Still no word? Does this idiot think it wise to go playing games with the gods?" He was tempted to call Sally, but he knew she was sitting in the farmyard and suspected the entire police force to be within earshot.

The time was now 12:50 am as finally the little phone in Sally's pocket vibrated against her now cold thigh. She answered; it was an exhausted Mayor. "It's done Sally, the entire £100,000 has been deposited to the account at the foot of Teacher's letter. We'll just have to start our recycling programme next year, it's that or another rise in poll tax."

"Another rise, and you accuse Teacher of being criminally minded?" she replied being a police officer by trade but a tax payer also.

"Don't you start, I've just had three hours in a bleeding Tutelage committee meeting. Boy, could they learn from attending a Scouting training course on executive committees!"

"Ok," she said summarising, "I'll tell Teacher to stand down."

"Thank God for that," he replied, assuming it to be a done deal and that the plagues of hypnosis had come to an end.

As the hour came and went nonetheless, Teacher became more and more incensed, until finally he sent a small click on his radio to Owen and Joe, a pre-arranged signal to get ready.

As the Super also looked at his watch he tutted to himself and then breaking radio silence he sent a message to Andy and Nev, plus another to Kylie and Jet, to expect whatever Teacher was planning, to begin. Having received the message, they sat still silently, but shaking now, almost keen to stand up breaking their cover, merely for a better view. Finally, the QR teams were also put on alert and having dusted themselves down of hay and chicken feathers, they checked their weapons and kit in a final attempt to reveal a jammed gun carriage or twisted baton around their bristling utility belts. Despite an uneasy silence falling upon the farm and trepidations coming to the fore, very little was happening; even the two owls in the trees of the lower field had become so relaxed as to return to their conversation of twitting and twooing. Perhaps Teacher had been bluffing.

Then suddenly, from under the plastic oil tank at the side of the hay barn somebody lit what looked like a firework sparkler, which as it got brighter, got hotter, until the plastic above it began to wilt and melt. Had anybody dared move or at least used a bit of initiative, a bucket of water or even a half empty mug of tea, would have averted what happened next. With an almighty flash and explosion that sent a mushroom like fireball up into the sky, the oil in the tank ignited. It sent splashes through the air, that burst into flame and began showering the hay barn and the summer's stockpile that most of the quick reaction team members, had been ensconced upon only minutes earlier. The two pairs of officers in the fields stood up in shock, looking at the burning fireball that was still rising towards the now illuminated cloud base and heavens beyond. This was blinding to anyone, disguising the movement of the herd that was now heading towards the bottom of the field. Here, under the cover of the blinding light, from out of the bushes came Owen and Joe, both in dark sunglasses, with their bags full of pre-primed syringes. Pulling each out carefully, so as not to prick themselves, they then intercepted each of the terrified heifers and rammed an injection into their rears to a chorus of mooing and thudding of hooves. Like a massive shoal of fish the animals knew only to stay together until they were captured in the far corner at the bottom of the field. And so, in only minutes there were empty cartridges everywhere, most being trampled into the mud, snapped needles and the blood from the cattle awash in the puddles. But with the job done, Owen and Joe now headed like clumping elephants through the mud, towards the bottom gate. PCs Nev and Andy were stood expecting someone to exit through this gate and were too experienced to be taken in by the diversion of the oil tank. "Stand still, this is the police, stand still!"

The Superintendent had been fighting off the flames in the hay barn that had taken hold like a virus and spread rapidly, so much so that in making a command decision he ordered an evacuation. "Let it burn, get yourselves out!" he yelled at Jock and the QR teams. "Get after Teacher and his goons, this has to be them!" Making a last-minute check to see that everyone was out, he ran then to the surveillance van where Sally was sat in the driving seat, trying to start the engine.

"Did he not call, the Mayor, has he not paid the ransom?" the Super shouted over the roar of the fire.

"Not a dickie bird, Sir. Must have decided against it!" she replied with a very slight grin to the corner of her mouth as Jock came running up from behind.

"It be the lads Sir, they be at the fowt of the lower field, they are to be arresting two o' the blaggards," he said looking at the Super for further instructions.

"And Teacher?" Sally asked.

"Noo Lassie, we 'ave ne seen the sassenach!"

"Get down there, Jock," the Super replied," right now, whilst I send the quick reaction teams in, we've got to get a result here!" Without a second word Jock sprinted out of the farm yard and down the hill to find Andy and Nev, as Sally continued to try and start the now smoke-filled surveillance van. When it finally sparked into life, revving as its paintwork started to blister under the heat from the fire, the Super was nowhere to be seen. She quickly reversed it away from the hay loft, that was now glowing in the dark with a phosphorescence akin to a million clock hands.

The QR teams once assembled in the yard in two distinct bodies, received their instructions and were now charging down the hill towards, what they thought would be Teacher, two of his accomplices and the herd of cattle. But as Joe and

Owen stood with their hands over their heads in surrender, the cattle were keeling over, firstly onto their two front knees, then titanically onto their sides or onto their backs with their legs awkwardly in the air.

Looking up the hill, those at the bottom could see only the silhouettes of those approaching from the top, with the light from the oil tank still dominating the skyline. The heads of the QR teams were bobbing up and down like meerkats in a zoom lens, when without warning, down the middle of the field, came the bright headlights of what everyone thought was the surveillance van, sliding all over the shop on the cow shit and mud. But the noise coming from the engine didn't sound quite right, it was more gravelly and throaty than the van's usual diesel jangle and the headlights seemed wider ranging.

"That's no van!" exclaimed Nev, now even more blinded than before as one of the massive tractors that was parked in the farmyard, with wheels from off Arthur's Round Table guiding fifty thousand pounds of mechanical muscle, came growling towards them. Sat in the cab in all his camouflage gear, was Teacher laughing. It was becoming his trademark. He knew from the forest of cattle legs pointing to the sky, that things were going well. He was singing and praying to Belanos as he bounced up and down on the industrially sprung driver's seat as the police teams before him parted like waves before Moses. Incredibly, the tractor was not alone in its mission as it was towing a huge silage machine, from which huge clumps of crap were being thrown out of either side of it, some arcing through the air as a medieval battlefield would launch volley after volley of flaming tar balls, knocking the recipients flat to the ground. The Super was the first to go down with one huge hit right in the face, which put his nasal drip into perspective, followed by Jock cursing and swearing about the poor quality of English shit. Then, one by one the QR team members went down as if they were made of tin, to all intents and purposes. The fact that the silage had been sat solidifying for an eternity was bad enough, but the stench that accompanied it was truly debilitating. Neither Nev nor Andy could conceive of how they might avoid being shitted upon, certainly not with the raising of a well-directed hand or even a fully charged taser and what good would they be caked to the gills. "Run for it!" was Nev's conclusion.

"Too right!" was his partner's reply, smelling the oncoming barrage, as they dived over the hedgerow for cover.

As Teacher reached the bottom of the field, the dark carcasses of at least thirty of the cattle, met him quietly. He smiled as if knowing something they didn't before ditching the silage machine and gracefully uplifting Joe and Owen, who apart from mud to the knees, looked as fresh as daisies. "Oh, what a night!" Teacher said slapping his two compatriots on their backs as they bounced down the muddy lane that led away from the farm, it being only just wide enough for the tractor, let alone anything else.

* * *

At only forty miles an hour top speed, it wasn't long before Sally in the surveillance Transit was right up the tractor's backside, pipping its horn like the local mobile fishmonger. "Shit, there's a bloody copper behind us in a white van," yelled Joe over the noise of the engines.

"That's right Bach, and there be a marked police car behind that too!" Owen exclaimed. But Teacher was totally unperturbed and blocking the road with the giant tractor, he continued to tootle along whilst whistling away as if it were a glorious afternoon and he was gathering hay from the fields. Sally continued to flash her headlights whilst Andy and Nev zig-zagged behind her, trying to get a better view in the dark, of what was happening ahead. Suddenly without warning, the tractor pulled left into a passing place, just wide enough to allow Sally to slam the hammer down and overtake down the outside, as if she were expecting it. The wheels of the Transit spun violently as she pulled away, showering the windscreen of the police car with mud from the road, which by the time Andy had reacted with wipers and screen wash, was stuck behind the tractor again after it pulled out just as soon as Sally had passed it.

Summoned by the Superintendent on the radio, the brightly painted police helicopter, could now be seen above the little convoy. The chock-chocking noise from the rotors merely added to that of the other vehicles and until the brilliant spotlight was trained upon them, Teacher and his boys knew nothing of it. "Five zero, this is heli-police Three zero," said the pilot over his radio, "I have target in sight. One of your officers in white Sherpa van has pulled ahead of them and there is one marked car behind. All looking good for an arrest, over."

"Good work Three zero," said the Super whilst still spitting silage from his mouth and gagging from the smell. "Will send other local cars to intercept, over."

"Roger Five zero…Wow!" The pilot suddenly shouted as he noticed the black streaks of electricity power lines coming towards him, ready to slice him up like he was a block of cheese. He pulled back on the flight yoke as quickly as his brain could communicate with his arms, whilst gritting and grinding his teeth waiting for the bang and sizzling that he expected from being fried to death. He missed the uppermost cable by only inches and could hear it buzzing below him, as the engine screamed to accelerate as quickly as he needed it to. Calling on his training, he then flew straight and level for a short while, to try and recompose himself, but the spot from his searchlight had lost its way and was no longer focussed on the events below. He put the helicopter into the hover and looked down to reacquire the target. "There they are," he reported back, "still moving with the Transit at the front, tractor behind that and police car behind that."

"Five two, Five zero. Well done, Sally, even if it was without my permission, you can slow to a stop now to apprehend suspects." The Super thought he had things in the bag. "Five three is behind the target."

"That's a Roger, Five zero," Nev answered getting ready to jump from the car to make the arrest. But the convoy kept moving, frustrating the two men, irrespective of the fact that the tractor seemed to be slowing. Things now appeared a little odd to the helicopter pilot as he spotted the Transit seemingly pulling away at the front, the lasting legs of the probable race winner only telling as others faded. It still wasn't clear that there was a problem until the tractor slowly veered from the centre of the road and clattered into the high stone wall to its right, jolting it back again to veer to the left and clatter into the wall on the other side, still preventing Andy from getting in front of it. Pushing the yoke forward, after checking for any more power lines, the helicopter closed in on the tractor and with a piece a clever flying, he turned it until he was travelling backwards and could get a look straight into the tractor's cab. "Oh no!" he blurted out as he adjusted the spotlight and opened a channel on his radio. "There's no one there!"

AN ARRESTING PARADOX

The steaming Transit having pulled away, with Joe, Owen and Teacher now also on board, finally turned into a layby. It was no more than a rink of concrete with an in road and out, littered with the day's junk food wrappers and plastic bags full of used nappies. It served a purpose however, as it was disguised from the air by several overhanging trees and was convenient, being just off the main Chillborough Road. As rehearsed, Owen and Joe jumped down onto the slippery tarmac and unveiled a nearly-new Ford Escort van, from under a tarpaulin. It was batman black in colour and without any of the failing parts of the old van. Inside there was a bag of clothes and a packed lunch in transparent shrink-wrap, for Owen and Joe, as obviously, assuming the Mayor had paid up finally, they didn't intend to return. Teacher too had a duffle bag crammed full of his white robes and sandals, but little more. "Are you sure the transfer was made?" he said to Sally, "I am dependent upon the grace of the gods *and* the money, as are these men."

"You should 'ave no worries, Teacher. Mayor Brian rang me just as the fun started. 'E's paid the lot into the numbered account you gave 'im. I'm just sorry that 'e didn't do it sooner."

"Sooner?"

"If 'e'd bin sooner, you wouldn't have had to kill all those cows, would you!" Sally said looking a little distressed.

"Oh ye of little faith," Teacher smiled, "they're only

drugged. Should be up and on their feet within the hour."

"Did I hear you right? You are a bastard!" Owen said out loud having beaten himself up about it ever since the first of them fell after its injection. He did however, have a relieved grin on his face. Teacher didn't and he turned menacingly.

"You are so predictable. A Welshman with a conscience. A Welshman who thinks that he can grass on his compatriots, tell the police about our little stunt and expect me not to know?" A fright appeared in Owen's eyes as he realised that his fraternising with Jet and then his so-called 'deal' with Sally, had backfired as loudly as the old van in some of its recent episodes. He looked firstly at the fuming Teacher, then directly at Sally, who clearly had no loyalty or integrity and had just dropped him in the proverbial toilet.

"Get lost!" Teacher said succinctly as Owen's jaw hit the floor and he stood with pleading hands. "Go, get lost, now!" Teacher reiterated, but louder until, with his tail between his legs, Owen walked away down the road. From his point of view, it was obvious that Sally certainly was not a part of the police team as she had just helped Teacher to escape in the most impressive fashion, without the sting he expected.

From her point of view, all those years of contempt from a male orientated police force, all that lack of support, sexual discrimination and bigoted Superintendents, all evaporated away as Owen disappeared over a hill in the road and she gave Teacher a kiss on both cheeks.

"You'll have my money by lunchtime?" she asked.

"You have the word of Serapis and the thanks of Belanos; you have contributed to my quest. You will be worshiped."

Sally, having pulled on her shining biking leathers, kept in the back-seat locker of her Honda 750S, that had also been sat under the cover of the trees, started up the engine. She was very calm at this point, very unflustered as things seemed to be going well. "I'll meet you at the service station on the M6 then, one o'clock!" she said as she walked the bike out into the road. Then she was gone, the helicopter, not expecting a motorcycle, would have ignored her anyway, but it spotted neither her nor the sleek Escort van as it too cruised away, in all the darkness with its lights turned out.

* * *

Back at the farm as the herd of cattle began to revive themselves one after another, as whales would surfacing for air, Superintendent Daniels had ordered up several buckets of water for everyone to rid themselves of several layers of silage. Many of them had simply taken their clothes off, being more comfortable in nothing but their underwear than a coating of over-processed cow-shit. He was keen to know what was going on with the chase after Teacher, but guessed without much effort, as the car containing Andy and Nev, pulled up slowly into the farmyard. "What?" he questioned with his two hands outstretched as if pleading for good news.

"They dumped the tractor right in front of us!" Nev explained as the Super fell to his knees in despair.

"And what, were they then uplifted by aliens, beamed up to the Starship Enterprise?"

"We thought Sally had arrested them in the van."

"How?"

"Well she overtook the tractor right before it crashed."

"And where is she now?"

"Well, we're not entirely sure," Andy explained.

"What about her radio, can you get her on the radio?"

"No Guv, it's as quiet as them dead cows," said Andy whose eyes almost popped out of his head as the farmer led several of the beasts in through the gate from the field.

"Wait a minute, they were all in heifer heaven only minutes ago," said the Super whose bottom jaw seemed to hit the floor.

"Arr, but they weren't, see," said the farmer coming along behind them from out of the darkness. The Super grabbed Nev's radio.

"Helicopter Three zero, this is Five zero." The Super waited for a reply, which came back without asking what the question was.

"I've lost them. I saw three men leave the tractor and get into the back of the Transit. I assumed they'd given themselves up, been arrested by Five two."

"Oh, for Christ's sake Five zero, what have you been doing?"

"Dodging power lines if you must know. How did you get on there, over."

"Shite, if you must know, in more ways than one."

"We did catch this bloke, name of Owen. Found him wandering down the Chillborough Road and picked him up on a hunch. Turns out he is the chap Sally said she had 'turned' before the op," said Nev holding onto his catch by the scruff of the neck, like a wild salmon that given the chance would slip through his grip and be off down river.

"Wait!" Jet shouted as she came running down the field. "It was me that turned Owen, not Sally. She's double-crossed you, just as I said she would!" she growled, throwing her arms around the crumpled Welshman.

"So, what *has* actually happened?" the Super yelled, as he sniffled back a cascade of snot.

"You know what your trouble is?" said Jet, "You've been Teachered!"

The Super looked around him, despondent and now for the first time, appreciative of what Sally and now Jet, meant about Teacher, but he could only shrug his shoulders and with a carefree smile, take off his trousers and shirt tipping the remainder of the bucket of water over his head.

"Look out," Jet said as just then, the Mayor's car glided into the farmyard and an expectant Mayor Brian got out to see a crowd of half-naked men and women throwing buckets of water over themselves.

"I trust this is a celebration?" Mayor Brian asked with an expectant smile, "Did you get him, is my money safe?"

"Err, there might be a problem," the Super replied as he closed one eye. "We think we lost him!" Mayor Brian's face turned ash white.

"Notice how it's 'we', when there's bad news and only 'he'

when there's a success," Kylie countered, as she stood hard and fast with hands on hips.

"Bloody typical!" the Mayor stated. "I'm not surprised when half of the constabulary are cavorting across the countryside on some giant orgy," he said looking surprised initially but drooling over some of the women's more than flowery matching underwear. "And what about Sally, she has to be responsible for some of this?"

"Err, well there might be a problem there too," the Super admitted, "although she could have arrested them and be on her way back here right now."

"Well, I bloody well hope so. I don't know how I'm going to explain this to the Tutelage committee."

* * *

Much later that day, Teacher and Joe had made their way to the service station on the M6 for lunch and to meet Sally. The road wasn't so busy for the time of day but the car park was packed, including many a lorry that was still parked up with windscreen curtains tightly closed. As they arrived, Joe was first to jump out of the van and fetch two Costa coffees with froth and sprinkles, to compliment the success and mood of the pair. Nevertheless, they were encouraged by the occasional patrolling police car, to get back into the van, keeping the engine running, just in case there should be a problem. Teacher had arranged for a nice man from his bank to meet him there at exactly twelve thirty, with all the cash, neatly packaged in a metal security case.

However, after nearly an hour, as cups ran dry and Teacher began to ask himself why no one had showed, he broke his telephone silence and rang the bank. He did this whilst sitting on the bonnet of the new Ford Escort, leaving Joe guessing until he saw Teacher's shoulders droop and heard the volume in his voice increasing until eventually, without a word, he got back into the van, slamming the door behind him.

It was supposed to be a celebration, a sharing out of the

money and an 'au revoir', Joe thought, but knowing Teacher had checked his account and was now in deep depression, he assumed there to be a problem. "What's going on?" Joe asked, suspecting the worst.

"Take this," Teacher said as he took a small writing pad from the glove box and scribbled out a list on it. "We're going to need provisions to get across the channel; take this money and get as much as you can." Joe got reluctantly out of the van and walked slowly, but obediently across the quiet car park to the Marks and Spencer's store located in the glass overpass above the motorway. He knew there was something wrong and was brassed-off that it was him again, doing all the crappy jobs. "I know," he said to himself, "look to the positive. I'll get the stuff off the list and see if I can find some nice Welsh lamb burgers for tea."

"Sounds good to me Bach," he could hear Owen say in his head, as he began to climb the stairs to the overpass where he looked at the traffic zooming down the road beneath him.

* * *

As Joe was out of the way, Teacher admitted to himself that there wasn't as much as a dime from the Mayor, having been told by Sally that the money had been paid. He was as livid as an unearthed skull in a graveyard and would no doubt take it all out on her just as soon as he got his wiry hands around her throat. He grabbed the bag she had given him, for her share of the loot, and rifled through its interior, knowing as soon as he laid his hands on it, that she had left him a message. "To Teacher, for all the times you outwitted me, all the tricks and treats that left me in tears, all your fancy gods and pompous ceremonies. For all your treatment of your fellow man and all your disregard for people's feelings, I have now, finally, got the better of you! You should never have left details of that last letter to the Mayor in your container and certainly not have trusted me to deliver it for you, as it was so easy to change the bank details to my new account in Switzerland. Wishing you every success in any police authority now that I have left, Love Sally."

* * *

Joe had always found the traffic on the motorways fascinating, ever since being a child, when his father would take him with him on work trips. But he sighed, as he looked at the dirty state of overpass windows, there obviously being no one with pride in their work in this establishment. Suddenly, as he stood either tired or transfixed by the traffic, he looked down and saw, quite clearly, the new Ford Escort van with Teacher at the wheel, pull out of the service slip road and go hurtling off on the south-bound carriage way. "Bastard!" he shouted as with the list in one hand and cash in the other, he careered down the steps, out into the car park and at one point even looked for the exit to give chase. Being not so incognito, however, in fact looking as if he was just about to run blindly onto the motorway, Joe drew attention to himself like Usain Bolt in a children's playground. The two motorway cops that stopped him, were more convinced they had averted some bizarre suicide, until they got a whiff of his professional body odour, as described by Jet in the wanted description, circulated within half an hour of the recognised failure of the police operation.

"It's him you want officer, him." Joe yelled pointing towards the exit. But Teacher had gone, just as surely as Belanos himself had reached down from the sky and rescued him.

AN AGNOSTIC CONCLUSION

Two days later, Teacher was sat in a small room which was very bland, painted magnolia throughout. He was shaking as would a wet dog after a bath, but for no other reason than the failure of his campaign of plagues to satisfy his quest. He was an honest man he told himself, amongst fellow criminals at least and he never intended to leave Joe stranded, but what could he say to him. Owen on the other hand, deserved whatever the authority chose to bestow upon him, as Teacher would have no charity for a traitor. One thing was clear as day, given the chance, that he would have no hesitation in placing his wiry hands around Sally's smooth and perfumed neck, and strangling her to death. She had lied, merely to throw him off balance whilst she fleeced him into the bargain.

"Retribution is required," he kept saying to himself as he paced up and down the room. "I'm all out of ideas, out of assistants and way short of the money I need." As if this wasn't bad enough, he suddenly winced, as his mobile phone began ringing with the tone reserved for 'Cleo'.

"Paddy, is that you Paddy?" came Cleo's sharp and demonstrative voice, one that seemed to command an authority that had been invested in it for decades.

"Yes Mother, it is me. I am at your service, Mother."

"Have you had any success? Can I in my prayers to Serapis,

tell it that you have accomplished your quest?"

"By your mercy Mother, no. There were complications."

"Complications, what complications?" Cleo snapped.

"Mainly a police woman, name of Sally, she led me across the driest desert, Mother. She said the money had been paid." He stood looking at the small paper ticket he had requested from a cash machine, confirming a vacant, zero balance at its foot. "Please understand me, Mother."

"I understand that you are pitiable, that I and the gods at the very least will want to hear your explanation!"

"If it please my mother, I thought Sally had been converted, in support of our dilemma. I thought she had abandoned her police friends and was working against them, for the benefit of Serapis. But she led me astray as she always was working undercover, despite me knowing who she was, even after the debacle at the My Mind shop in Briars Brook, my last attempt to meet my obligation."

"I and all that is sacred are very disappointed in you Paddy. How can the dynasty be resurrected without its most loyal servants remaining true? How will we ever reclaim our legacy or heritage? How will Serapis ever forgive you?"

"I am at your mercy, Mother."

"That is correct, you are Paddy, and to that end you must redouble your efforts. Inherent you may be, but I feel I will call on Nekhbet to join you. Between the two of you with your talents combined, we will have no reason to fail. We must prevail!" There was a click as the call ended abruptly before the rivulets of sweat cascading down Teacher's face fell like tears, absorbed slowly by his robes. "I might have failed," he said to himself, "but is that any reason to send my sister?"

* * *

By the time the sunset had finally washed itself out beyond the horizon and the crying of the seagulls overhead had quietened, the 'City of Derby' cargo ship was well underway. Now at night, the duty rota was such that everyone aboard had a job to do, notwithstanding the appeal to be on deck, looking over the handrail at the glistening water and waves. This was reserved for passengers and Sally was the only one apparently, having had her tea alongside the captain in a galley as small as a prison cell. She had however, thoroughly enjoyed herself and probably eaten too much given the rolling horizon, but nothing was going to upset her now. She had ditched the police force with two fingers in the air, led them all astray and complicated the hell out of the Superintendent, whom she still regarded as misguided. The Mayor had seemingly been losing faith in her as the investigation continued and she worried that he had her sussed, but she had played him to the last minute. From out of her pocket she pulled a paper ticket entirely the same as Teacher's, but from her bank, which at its foot confirmed the fact that the exhausted Tutelage committee had paid her, one hundred thousand pounds exactly. What a cinch it had been. She giggled, partly in response to the wine she had been drinking, but mainly as she could see how easily she had duped her nemesis. Teacher was no match for her, he might have had a few skills in terms of hypnosis she told herself, but he was no more powerful than his decrepit and outdated gods!

In silhouette, against the stars in the sky, Sally leaned out over the side rail, letting the wind blow through her hair as the waves buffeted themselves against the side of the ship, sending a refreshing spray upwards to moisten her smiling face. She was so distant with thoughts of new clothes, a new car, a new home and a new life, that she didn't notice a movement from behind the life jacket locker. Neither did she realise how precariously she was holding herself and how easy it would be for her to slip overboard, never to be seen again. Neither did she realise and in this her trivialising was inaccurate, just how powerful the gods could be. As hiding, in the back of the shadows, contemplating his next move, was Teacher, with his hands stretched outwards and eyes praying to the sky, still muttering something about divine intervention and the power of retribution.

ACKNOWLEDGEMENTS

Once again, I must thank my wife Michelle, who puts up with all my moods and literary highs. All my friends and family who also support me with comments and encouragement, with a special mention for Bethan my Number One fan and critique.

I would also like to thank my editor Susan Miller at TeamAuthorUK, including Alan Jones for his fantastic artwork and Phil Burrows for maintaining the website.

ABOUT THE AUTHOR

Mark has been writing for years, despite his teachers at school saying he could do better. To be fair, it was an English teacher name of Mrs Bullock that extracted every drop of mental substance from him and fired up what turned out to be a mental bent and flare for story-telling.

Much of Mark's work comes from his experiences at work, in the air force, the building industry and third sector recruitment and development. As a sufferer from night-time epilepsy he has benefitted, in a strange way and been empowered to persevere in all that he does. In addition, his own sometimes riotous imagination fuels stories that are different, original and of cackling good humour.

In 2016, after much persuasion, he completed a quirky story entitled "At the Back of My Mind" and with the release of this book "A Plague of Hypnosis", he completes part two of an intended trilogy.

Go to Mark's official website www.mpwinson.co.uk and contact him for further news, freebies and invites.

Facebook @m.p.winson
Twitter: @winson_mark
Email: markpwinson@outlook.com

Email Mark and leave your email address with code "Teacher2" and he will send you his monthly Readers Bulletin, with news, articles and free short stories

Book 1 of the "Teacher" Series

'At the Back of My Mind'
Available *Now* on Amazon

http://bit.ly/BackofmyMind

The quirky and mysterious owner of a shop known as 'My Mind' further advertised it as: 'A treasure trove of mental observance. A cavern of psychic artefacts, scholarship and discipline challenging one's mind and interrogating its very humanity'. But things there are fantastically unbelievable; strange practices, weird behaviour and always an aura of disbelief that has led the police into taking an interest after raiding a similar shop the owner was involved in some months previously.

Book 3 of the
"Teacher" Series

'The Wrath of Serapis'

Is Coming Soon!

What follows is a sneak peek of Chapter 1…

CHAPTER 1

A GHOSTLY ENCOUNTER

As the English merchant ship 'City of Derby' glided across the channel, the dark of the night had enveloped her such that she appeared as a fairground carousel with all her lights blazing, whilst inadvertently blinding those on board to the details of the sea and the plethora of stars above. Sally, exhausted after being chased right across the midlands and south east of England by the police and her nemesis alike, had just finished a humongous meal of cod mornay, shrimps and mussels, at the captain's table. She was now on deck and hanging over the side rail, considering the dark water, transfixed by the twinkling reflections from port hole lights fragmenting on the wave tops. Not that she felt ill from the food, far from it, but seemingly this was where all the crew came for an after-dinner chat and a quick fag.

"And you be from where?" asked a solitary member of the bridge staff, with a more than portly belly.

"Well I 'ail from London, but bin livin' in Chillborough in the Midlands and workin' of late in Clearwater, d'ya know it?"

"Aye, I've heard about it. It be plastered all over the news not too many bells ago, some sort of plague of flies they had."

"Really? Sounds fascinating, I wish I'd bin there," Sally said, "I was workin' just outside of the town actually." She lied intentionally as she didn't want suspicion to fall upon her.

"So why the big secret?" the sailor asked.

"Secret?" Sally was shocked at first, thinking that he knew of her involvement as Detective Sergeant Reid, employed ironically, to investigate the series of plagues forced upon the town.

"To be truthful, the Captain said not to ask, but as you're travelling incognito making the crew complicit in whatever it is you have to hide, I thought it be only fair." Sally pursed her lips.

"I'm leaving my bleedin' 'usband, if you must know!" She lied again.

"I see," said the sailor, now satisfied enough at least for him to leave and get back to his duties.

* * *

"And what would this fictitious husband do now, if he knew that you had taken all his money?" came a different voice from behind Sally, a voice she thought she recognised.

She turned slowly, she was right, it was her nemesis, Teacher! This bizarre man, known by no other name, was dressed as always in white robes, although slightly grubby now, underneath his long white hair and beard that came down to his waist. He looked as if he had just walked off some grandiose film set. However, his reputation for practicing hypnotism and the ancient arts in extorting authorities and members of the general public, was terrifying. Sally swallowed hard and made a bolt for the door to get back inside the ship, but Teacher jumped forward like a mountain goat and slammed it shut with an almighty clang, nearly taking off her finger ends. By the look on his face and readiness in his gait, she knew he was ready for a confrontation and sure enough he stepped forward trying to look her straight in the eyes, which she avoided instantly. She knew of his gift of hypnotism, she still had problems getting up from the floor after a previous encounter with him and hadn't been able to get out of a bath since. "Thanks for the note you left in my van," he growled as he picked up a large deck spanner and swung it over his arms.

"It always pays to be polite," she replied, wearing a cynical smile as she dodged the flying lump of metal, which banged and sparked as it hit the deck's side rail.

"I still want the money you stole from me," he said, "please," he added returning the cynicism, as he pulled the heavy weight from off the deck, ready to swing it again, but more accurately this time. However, realising this, Sally quickly grabbed a bucket full of sand and fag ends, that had been sitting quietly on the deck awaiting an on-board fire or greasy pool of oil. Taking its considerable weight on one arm, she put all the force she could into launching it through the air, so accurately that it hit Teacher right in his face. He coughed and spluttered, wiping the grit from his eyes with a dangling cuff, only to see her making off down the starboard side of the ship across the lounge deck.

With little more visibility than that out to sea, Sally clattered into numerous plastic slatted chairs and tables, slowing her down and allowing Teacher to gain ground on her. She thought back, it was only in the weeks previous that the ball was on the other foot and she was chasing him, when he would throw obstacles behind himself to foil the chase. It occurred to her, now she was the chased, that this was very clever and so she began to do the same. Throwing table after chair, after lounger, all were dropped like mines across his path, some skating across the deck and bouncing clean over the side rail to fall into the waves below. However, it wasn't before she had run the entire length of the deck and reached the stern, tripping over the anchor chains laid out neatly in strong rows, that she dared turn to look for him. He however, was nowhere to be seen when he should have been so obvious, given his white beard and robes that reflected back the light, like the luminous ghost of some old sailor condemned to wandering the ship. So, confused, Sally took to walking backwards whilst scanning the dark corners and the rising and falling stairwells, remaining on her toes, ready to react. Teacher had of course outwitted her, not for the first time, by turning back inside the ship and running through the interior of the lounge itself, putting the wind up those off-duty crew members that always were convinced the ship was haunted. He could see her through the long line of portholes, stumbling and fighting her way past the over-abundant furniture, until he was ahead of her. Now, he emerged through the double doors at the stern and was standing without missing a breath, right behind her.

Fortunately, the second sense that Sally had acquired after years of policing, finally clicked in and feeling more assured, she turned as if on skates to face the oncoming threat. He stood, brandishing a large ice knife that he had grabbed from the sculpture in the lounge. "You wouldn't," she demanded of him.

"Yes, I would," he replied, as he feinted left, then right, then left again, finally tripping farcically over the anchor chains which gave Sally a get out, as she dived down the nearest stairwell to the lower decks. Teacher followed still unrecovered from his trip, hence falling on his backside, which with his speed of approach, caused him to bump down every last step with jarring clicks to his back until he sat somewhat dazed on the deck below. Sally suddenly jumped out on him from behind a canvas covered life boat and with a targeted strike, smacked him in the face with one of its wooden paddles. Toppling over with the force of the strike, the knife he had in his hand was sensationally catapulted through the air until it embedded itself in the deck beside her. Blood sprayed all around as Teacher's long nose broke instantaneously, leaving him looking like a post-fight boxer without a corner man. "Fluffing hell," he shouted with his newly bestowed impediment, "you'll fay for that, you fitch!"

"You're welcome," Sally shouted back as she legged it down the port side of the ship, dodging in and out of the other life boats still sleeping on the deck.

* * *

Hearing the almighty smack that resulted as Teacher was hit by the paddle, an anonymous member of the crew, trying to get some sleep in a nearby cabin, summoned the Master at Arms. Able Seaman Smethurst, known by the crew as 'Ape-man, had the stature of Hercules and was apparently as hard as nails. He arrived quickly, with a Colt revolver hanging by a leather lanyard from around his neck, a two-way radio in one hand and a hi-beam, brilliant torch in the other. As he slid proficiently down the stainless-steel stair ladder from the upper deck, Sally acknowledged him and pointed silently to where Teacher had disappeared behind a storage locker, to lick his wounds. He acknowledged her and the direction she was indicating, and with an apparently brave face he moved slowly towards his prey. What exactly he was expecting was contradicted however, as a white-robed, white-haired Teacher shot out in front of him as surprisingly as a jumping dolphin. "Well, spank me till I'm cross eyed," Ape-man yelled, "it be the Ghost of Captain Wainwright!" This was overheard by Teacher who ingeniously reciprocated by putting his arms in the air, waggling his hands and giving him a ghoulish "woooooo!" as he ran towards him. Shocked, the champion of the ship let out a high-pitched, almost childlike scream, not nearly as macho as his reputation demanded, and then in his panic, he jumped clean over the side rail, down into the dark murky waters below!

"Oh shit!" Sally cursed as Teacher without so much as a care for the man that had just been lost overboard, sprang forward knocking her down and pinning her to the deck by both wrists. His blood-soaked robes and crooked nose, rubbed and dripped a red stain across her white blouse, leaving her looking like some operative from a meat packing factory. Shuffling his bottom forward then, until his knees were over Sally's upper arms, Teacher grabbed her strangely, by both of her ears. "What ya gonna do now then Teach," she said taunting him, "we're in the middle of the English Channel. You can't get away from the navy boys, merchant or not, you can't 'urt me now without me shoutin' and alertin' 'arf the crew and you can't throw me overboard or kill me, 'cause you won't get your money back then, will ya?"

Teacher looked up to the sky and in prayer he said, "Dear Belanos, God of mine, please stop the stupid people from breeding so quickly!" However, taking his eyes momentarily off Sally was the excuse that she was looking for, as she employed her long-lost child ballerina skills, kneeing him firstly in the back and nutting him as his blood-covered face came within inches of her own. He fell from her then awkwardly, leaving himself spread-eagled across the deck as Sally, who had held onto him, was dragged conveniently, upright to her feet. She looked down at him briefly, even feeling a little sorry for him, despite the man that he had frightened overboard, before making off through the crew quarters' door to the interior of the ship. But this was not before her charity snapped and she stamped on him, quite viciously in his groin.

* * *

"What the hell is going on out there?" yelled the crew man that had reported the fight to the Master at Arms earlier, waking the other four off-shift operatives who began opening their cabin doors and standing in Navy fashion, naked when sleeping, out in the corridor.

"Ooaa, good evening gentlemen," said a very wide-eyed Sally with an admiring smile on her face as she ran and squeezed past each of them.

"Well, good evening yourself," replied a bleary-eyed man who had just realised that this crazy, blood-covered escapee, was a woman. "Have you not time for a coffee and a bit of what you fancy?" he laughed.

"Well, that might be a consideration," Sally said, figuring that even Teacher wouldn't take on this small flotilla of men, "but there's someone chasing me," she yelled. Had it not been for the fact that she was covered in blood, the reaction may well have been one of ridicule and no doubt, crass comment. However, macho faces keen to be regarded as such, turned to concern and the door in from the deck which Sally was now looking at in anticipation.

"Don't worry, love," said one very well-endowed man swinging around, oblivious of his untethered fire hose, "you're safe with us!"

'They may well be capable of dealing with Teacher,' Sally suddenly thought to herself, 'but they are also a danger of a different sort, a sex-fuelled foursome, which is just as frightening.' And so, without so much as a goodbye kiss, she exited the corridor at the far end and ran out onto the cargo deck. After only five minutes, the crew man that had reported to the Master at Arms, shouted for quiet once again, just before he wandered out into the corridor, with his tackle in his hand. "What's a man got to do to get some sleep around here?" he bellowed, but he was shocked. "May the saints preserve me," he said seeing his four ship mates on all fours, crawling up and down the corridor on the floor, barking and howling like dogs, pausing periodically to cock their legs against their cabin doors. "Is this some sort of sick hypnotic game?" he went on angrily, as three of the four canines totally ignored him and the third began licking his leg, with a noticeable faraway expression in his eyes.

* * *

The cargo deck consisted of a great expanse of wood underfoot and crane after crane parked besides canvas covered loading hatches. It was right out in the open and showers of sea and salt were blowing across it from one side to the other. Sally's make up was already smudged and heavily corrupted with the red from Teacher's nose, as she began to feel very exposed and tears ran down her face. The further she ran away from the inhabited quarter of the ship, the darker it became. She looked back; she was hoping that Teacher would be locked up in the bowls of the ship by now, but her police sensibility was working overtime, keeping her alert and open-minded. This was just as well as from the platform of the first crane on the deck, Teacher suddenly swung down with the skill of Tarzan on a zip wire and confronted her yet again. Before she could move, he hit her solidly, knocking her over onto her back, which ended her escape.

"Ith only Belanos cuth thee you now. How thilly you look," Teacher said still suffering from his broken nose and now partial hair lip, as he looked down at her facetiously.

"Silly, you're callin' *me* silly. It was you that lost one hundred farsand pouns by allowin' me to pay it into my account instead a yours. I 'ad you from the first day I apparently switched my allegiance, but you never suspected a fing, never delved deep enough to understand. You put too much bleedin' faif into Beleenyos, or whatever his name is!"

"You, are now on the thrun from Thelanos, from me *and* from the tholice force you also dethawded, I call that thilly!" Teacher then bent over her and as if driven on by some peculiar fetish and grabbed her by the ears once again.

"You're hurting me," she cried as Teacher once again looked into the sky for some divine assistance.

"Thigh the thower of Thelanos and the thwill of Serathis, thrant me thominion to inthluence the thoon and the thides, the thun and the thrain," he began as Sally recognised the fashion in which he cursed her previously, "help me such that Ged and Othithis enthure though the underthworld, that I comthleet my thwest!"

"Moon and tides, sun and rain, yes I think I got that, all to complete your quest!" Sally smiled pleased to be able to ridicule him again, but at that there was a searing pain to her ears that she thought was the prelude to some sort of bizarre death ritual, but as it subsided, Teacher then stood bolt upright and smiled.

"Au revoir," he said waving as he took his robes in hand, gathering them up beneath his bottom and jumped clean over the side of the ship, into the sea.

* * *

47810895R00125

Made in the USA
Middletown, DE
03 September 2017